TECHWITCH BOOK THREE

WICKED NIGHTS

M.J. SCOTT

FREE SHORT STORY

For Melissa who makes pretty yarn rather than pretty yarns

CHAPTER ONE

MY HEART HAD POUNDED for plenty of reasons in the last year or so. Grief. Happiness. Orgasms. Terror. Magic. The odd reluctant exercise session. Now, apparently, it was pounding for something that wasn't even real.

"Maggie, are you okay?" Damon asked.

I nodded slowly, not taking my eyes off the imp hanging in the air a few feet in front of me. The oily sheen of its dark skin, the glint of light on too many needlelike black teeth, and the lack of anything human in its eyes had every instinct I possessed screaming at me to step back. Or just flat-out run away.

No.

Not real. The imp existed only in bytes and magic of the strictly technological variety. Virtual reality terror. I'd played my share of games and faced my share of virtual monsters. But while my brain said "safe," my body was unconvinced. My heart pounded as I stared at the imp, mouth dry as a desert. "I'm good." I swallowed and licked my lips, watching the imp.

Chill.

"You don't sound good. I can hit the kill switch." Damon's voice was worried.

"No. Don't." I made myself turn away, toward the man standing beside me in the blank white virtual room. Damon Riley was far nicer to look at than a monster.

Sure, it was only his avatar next to me. Tall, brilliantly blue eyed, dark of hair, and chiseled of body. Dressed in a black T-shirt and cargo pants that displayed all that perfectly. Another virtual illusion. But unlike many people, Damon didn't really have to tweak his virtual self to look hot. In real life there were a few silver threads in the dark hair and maybe a few more lines crinkling beside the eyes. Which, in my somewhat biased opinion, only made him hotter. But he was stupidly handsome in person or in pixels. Even when he was frowning at me.

"Are you sure?" he asked.

I rolled my eyes and turned back to the imp. Against my better judgment, I took a couple of steps, stretched out a hand, and poked its belly. I didn't really know what an imp felt like in real life.

The only times I'd touched one, I'd been more focused on staying alive. The VR flesh yielded a little like any other creature I touched in a game. But unlike other creatures, the imp didn't react to the touch.

My breath whooshed out of me in relief. I trusted Damon, and he had promised me this was safe. And if the guy who owns the biggest virtual reality gaming company in the world and who also happens to be one of the smartest tech guys on the planet tells you his simulation is safe, it probably is.

Though he and I had learned the hard way that the darker elements of magic could wreak havoc even when you had the best protections money could buy.

I'd met Damon when he'd hired me to help him figure out a tech problem his army of in-house nerds hadn't been able to solve. Neither of us had expected magic and demons and chaos would follow.

Him because he generally avoided magic and witches. Me because, well, my mother—a witch who had dabbled on the edges of the darker part of magic herself—had told me I had no magic. After she died, thirteen-year-old me tried to forget all about magic and focus on the normal world with my grandparents, who'd taken me in.

But it turned out my mom had lied to me. I was a witch. One whose powers had been bound.

The fallout from that bond being broken had left me mourning the death of my best friend and Damon wrestling with a corporate scandal, his company, Riley Arts, having to recall games and game systems. One of the biggest recalls in VR history, in fact. Riley Arts had deep pockets due to their past success, but they'd hemorrhaged cash in the recall. The successful launch of *Archangel*, their latest game, was helping, but from the stories I read in the financial newslinks, it would take a while to completely recover.

And VR was a ruthless industry. Damon didn't talk about it much, but I knew the vultures must be circling, seeing if they could somehow trip him up while he got back on track.

Riley was about to hit back at the continued doubters. Doing something unprecedented and launching another flagship game and new game-tech only a few months after *Archangel*.

Not to mention a massive gaming tournament to springboard the whole thing. Damon had been working practically nonstop on the project.

Which left the question of just when he'd had time to build the imp.

"It looks amazing," I said, circling the creature. How had he done it? Running a corporation the size of Righteous—as the gamers called it—was more than a full-time job even when things were going smoothly. Damon had started off as a game designer, but he spent more time in boardrooms and video calls than coding these days. And I'd spent enough time hanging out on the Riley campus to learn just how time-consuming the sort of programming and design that went into producing VR creatures as realistic as this one was.

Damon hadn't entirely given up sleeping. I knew that because he spent most nights in bed with me. But his spare time was very limited. The fact that he was showing me the imp in a spare hour between meetings on a Sunday afternoon kind of proved that. Not to mention I'd decided to spend the day at the Riley campus to increase our chances of getting some time together.

"When did you even have time to do this?"

I tapped the imp again, more to reassure myself that it wasn't going to come to life and try to kill me —which was what every other imp I'd crossed paths with had attempted—than anything else.

"Here and there," he said. "And I had some help."

"Wait, what?" I swiveled on my heels. "Help? Who? Does Cassandra know about this?"

Cassandra Tallant was head of the Cestis in the USA. The big boss witch of the magical police. Magic wasn't a secret, but there were certain realities of magical life—like demons and the creatures they controlled, like imps and lesserkind—that were kept out of public knowledge as much as possible.

The normals knew that witches were good at healing and could do other useful things, but they didn't know there were demons trying to break into our world and feed on us.

Just as well.

"She knows," Damon said.

"Really?" Demons were terrifying. One of them had caused the Big One, the earthquake that had leveled much of San Francisco just over a decade ago. My grandfather had died in that quake. Really, my grandmother had, too. She'd never recovered from her injuries, fading away over a few months. And those were just my losses. So many people had died or lost their homes and businesses.

If a few demons ever managed to break through to our world together, they could quite possibly destroy it. Or enslave humanity. Given humanity didn't have a great record of handling grand scale threats to our existence well, I wasn't sure Cassandra would be that keen on Damon telling members of his team the truth about them.

I hadn't even known that demons were real, and my mom was a witch. Maybe she didn't tell me because I was just a kid. Or maybe it was because she intended to bind my powers to a demon the night I turned thirteen, wipe my memory of the rite, and let me grow up believing I had no magic.

She died not long after she sold my magic. After that, I lived with my grandparents, who had no magic and wanted to give me the normal childhood I'd missed living the itinerant magic grifter lifestyle with Mom. I was happy to leave that world behind.

No more magic for me.

I'd thought I'd had none, so no questions needed to be asked. Now that I knew what my mom had done to me, I had plenty of questions, but neither she nor my grandparents could provide answers from the grave. I never knew who my father was, so I was getting all my magical education from Cassandra and my roommate, Lizzie, the youngest member of the Cestis.

"Really," Damon said.

"And she's okay with it?"

He shrugged. "After what happened with Ajax, Cassandra thought it might be a good idea if we reviewed all our staff. She helped us identify who—outside the security team—has ties to the magical world and knows about this stuff. In case it was needed again."

Ajax. Even now, a couple of months after he'd kidnapped Damon and me, intending to hand us over to one of the lesserkind who'd served my demon, the name made my stomach clench. He'd died, killed by the creature he'd thought would reward him, but the harm he'd caused didn't end with his death.

For the second time, Damon had to do a major reexamination of his companies as a result of my magic and my past. The fact that his own security team, the people he trusted with his life and his business, had been compromised had shaken him more than facing a demon.

"Are you sure this is what she meant by 'needed'?"

"We were talking about my ideas for the Archives, and I told her I wanted to try a couple of things to show her."

"I'm guessing she was imagining a database, not a VR imp," I said. Damon and I had only learned about the Cestis's archives of magical information a few months ago.

Damon's technology-loving soul had been horrified by the fact that the Archives were analog. Here in the US and in every country where there was a Cestis. He'd been trying to convince Cassandra to let him start digitizing it for safety ever since.

I didn't know when Cassandra had agreed to a trial. But even if she had, I doubted this what she had in mind. But Damon wasn't the kind of guy who let an idea go once he'd decided on a course of action. And ever since Ajax, he'd been determined to keep me safe. If he thought dragging the Cestis kicking and screaming into this century was going to help him do that, then it was going to be interesting to see who won if he and Cassandra butted heads.

As long as I could watch from a safe distance.

Damon shrugged again. "This is better. At least when it comes to the various creatures. A picture isn't the same as seeing something like that." He flicked his hand at the imp, and it rotated slowly.

I stepped back. I couldn't disagree with his logic. The Archives had volumes with detailed pictures of the various imps encountered by the Cestis or other witches over the centuries. They'd been drawn by the best artists witchkind could provide, and they were good. But they weren't the same as seeing an imp brought to life in hideous detail in VR. "You're thinking this could be some sort of training tool, beyond identification?"

The first time I'd used my magic had been to fry an imp sent to hunt down Damon and me. A purely instinctual burst of power that, luckily, had killed the imp and not fried both of us in the process.

"It would help, wouldn't it? If people knew what to expect? Knew how these things move, what they can throw at you. How you should respond."

So maybe I shouldn't have been surprised that my tech god boyfriend had built me a virtual imp and wasn't going to stop there. Pixels and programs were one of his love languages, after all.

"I'm not sure Cassandra will think practicing magic virtually is a good idea." Magic was all about manipulating energy. Going through the motions of a spell or using an incantation without working the energy as well wouldn't work. And it might not be a great habit to develop. Though maybe there might be some parts of magic—like mixing potions or something—where a safe way to practice proportions or whatever might come in useful. And he was right about the identification part. Seeing an imp in the flesh for the first time might be less terrifying if you had faced one down in VR.

The imp was still revolving slowly, oil-slick skin glistening. As a feat of design, it was a masterpiece. I didn't want Damon to think I didn't appreciate all his hard work. But I didn't want him to waste his efforts if Cassandra was going to kill this idea.

He wasn't superhuman or even magical. But he'd push himself to his limits if left to his own devices.

He wanted to take care of me, but I was also going to take care of him. "This is amazing work. But you need to tell Cassandra about it now." I turned and reached out to take his virtual hand. "If you're going to do this right, you need her blessing and her help."

For a moment it seemed as though he was going to argue, but he nodded. "You're right. I'll call her." He pulled me in closer, and I hugged him back. He felt warm and solid, but I missed the smell of him. We were using game chairs and headsets, not a chip interface. You needed a chip to get scent and the really fine details in VR. Complete immersion. Though if I'd been able to smell Damon, I'd probably also be smelling the rotten meat stink of the imp.

My lack of a chip spared me that. Though maybe for the last time. I'd finally decided to get a new interface chip. My surgery was slated for two days from now, which would give me three days to recover before the big charity gala that would kick off Damon's tournament.

I'd had chip surgery before. It hadn't taken me long to bounce back from the procedure, but the chip had malfunctioned and had to be removed. But as far as anyone could tell, that had been because of my bond with the demon. I had no bond now, and there were other witches who had chips.

Damon swore I'd be safe. The technology was evolving, the neurosurgeons who worked with the chip company had consulted with healers, and everyone seemed convinced it wouldn't cause me a problem.

He already had one of the new chips. During the kidnapping, his old one had been damaged, and the replacement was the new generation. The silver-and-gold shimmer of the chip in his right wrist was smaller than before, less obvious. One day they'd probably just look like skin.

The new chips were supposed to give the most real experience in VR yet. I wasn't sure how much more realistic they could get than the experiences I'd had playing Riley Arts prototypes in the brief time I'd had mine, but Damon assured me it was amazing.

These new chips were cheaper, too. So far it was mostly hardcore gamers—the kinds who competed in the leagues—or people who worked in industries that used VR who forked out money for chips. There were plenty of gamers who, like me, still happily used headsets. Though, unlike me, most of them would probably jump at the chance at a chip if they could afford one.

The launch of the next-gen chips was expected to be huge. So huge that Riley Arts and InX9, who made the new chips, were rolling the dice with the tournament to launch it. Big bucks. Big prestige. The finalists would be the first to get the new chips and then play the full version of the new Righteous game.

I'd stopped paying much attention to what was going on in the gamer world after my best friend, Nat, died and Damon had broken up with me. Now that we were back together, I was back in the thick of it. It was Damon's world, after all, and I wanted to know what was happening.

And chip tech was spreading beyond gaming now. I couldn't troubleshoot tech if I couldn't use it. I rubbed my hand over my left wrist reflexively. The faint scar left behind when my first chip had been yanked was barely visible now. And of course, my avatar didn't have the scar at all.

Damon glanced down. "You can reschedule if you really want to."

Tempting. But I couldn't put it off forever. And I wanted it done before the tournament.

I wanted to be there for Damon. All the signs were good so far. The spectator passes had sold out in less than fifteen minutes. Competition for the game team slots had been fierce.

I was happy for Damon but nervous that something would go wrong.

That was on top of a whole other set of nerves. The gala the night before the tournament began would be the first time I appeared publicly as Damon's girlfriend/partner/significant other. When we'd first dated, we'd been too caught up in magical events to worry about that side of his life. Then we'd broken up, so it hadn't been an issue. The last few months, he'd been too busy to squeeze in social events even if he'd wanted to, so we hadn't had to deal with it.

But the tournament was going to change that. Two weeks of practice runs and then heats, all recorded and vidstreamed. Every media outlet, game vlogger, and entertainment vidblog would be there, recording and streaming and re-streaming. Damon would be putting in appearances every day.

I'd had to choose whether or not I was going to be with him. Whether we were making our relationship public. Dating one of the richest guys on the planet came with issues I hadn't initially considered.

I'd grown used to the level of security he lived with. But now I was about to get a taste of the other side of his life. The side where his private life made headlines. I'd spent my first thirteen years with my mom deliberately flying under the radar. As an adult, I was well known in the parts of the tech world that might need my services, but otherwise, I was a nobody.

That would change as soon as I stepped into the spotlight as Damon's partner. We'd been talking about it for weeks, and I'd had some quality time with Mitch Angelico, the head of his security team, as well as Ayesha Leonard, who oversaw Damon's public relations. She was part of the broader Righteous comms team, but the fact that she spent most of her time just on Damon had been a wake-up call that this was going to be a big deal. At least initially. Damon had done his share of dating, but he hadn't been seen publicly with anyone for over a year now.

I was going to be the subject of online gossip and newslink stories whether I liked it or not. I didn't want to hand them another thread to pull in researching me by making them wonder why someone dating Damon didn't have a chip.

I wanted the least interest possible. To be unremarkable. But I didn't want people crawling through my past. The Cestis weren't that keen on the idea either. Cassandra had flat-out warned me that raising my profile might bring ghosts of my past into the light.

"Are you going to tell me what you're thinking so hard about?" Damon asked, and I started. I'd completely forgotten where we were.

"Nothing important." I made myself smile. "Day-dreaming."

He made a slightly disbelieving sound but didn't push. "Maybe that's a good sign."

"Me daydreaming is a good sign?"

"You being relaxed enough in VR with an imp—even a fake one—right in front of you to daydream. It seems like progress."

We'd spent a lot of time in VR since we'd gotten back together. Damon was determined to get me comfortable with it, and I knew I needed to get over the aversion I'd developed since Nat's death.

I worked as a troubleshooter for misbehaving computer systems. I'd called my company Tech Witch because it seemed like a good marketing ploy, and, well, because I was damned good at what I did, even though I didn't think magic had played any role.

I still had plenty of work if I wanted it, but like the chips, VR was starting to be embraced by all kinds of industries. I had to embrace it, too.

Damon had been taking me on a virtual world tour, conjuring one gorgeous and relaxing VR destination after another where we could just hang out and talk. Given he wasn't likely to have time for a real vacation soon, and he had his own issues to deal with, I suspected the moments he stole for our trips were helping him as much as me.

About a month ago, we'd added some very basic gaming.

Croquet and table tennis and other silly sports. A few very low-key games involving nothing even resembling danger. The sorts of virtual worlds that were more about wandering around looking at cool stuff and completing quests by solving puzzles. The first time we'd tried one of those, I'd lasted about five minutes before I'd tapped out. But I'd managed an hour a few days ago, and Damon was right. Now that I'd accepted the imp wasn't real, I'd relaxed.

"I guess it is. How much time do we have?"

He smiled back. "Am I boring you?"

"Never. But you said you had a meeting." Being a billionaire had many perks, but the relentless schedule wasn't one of them. He kept telling me it would ease off after the tournament. I hoped he was right.

"Crap." He lifted his head. "Time check."

"Time is 3:27 p.m.," the system voice said. "Session end time planned for 4:00 p.m."

Normally it would have been the voice of Madge, Riley's in-house computer system, or Cat, Damon's real-life assistant reminding him of the time, but we were in a clean room, a VR setup walled off from the rest of the world.

I'd thought maybe he was going to give me a look at *Serenity Falls* when he'd brought us to a clean room, but apparently virtual imps rated the same security as game releases. That, at least, should please Cassandra when Damon finally told her.

"Thirty-three minutes." Damon sounded smug. "We can have fun for thirty minutes." He wriggled his eyebrows, laser blue eyes turning devilish.

While we might have occasionally made out in VR at his house, I drew the line at doing it at Righteous. I wouldn't put it past Mitch to find a way to monitor Damon even in a clean room. "Unless you're planning on taking your meeting from here, you need to get back to your office. And I need to go meet Lizzie at Cassandra's."

"Store or Archives?" Damon asked.

"Archives. More exciting magical theory for me." I wrinkled my nose. I was determined to come to grips with my magic now that I had it back. It would keep me safe. Keep *us* safe. But it turned out I couldn't just snap my fingers and make up for all the time I'd lost. Now that Cassandra was happy that I had basic control over the fire I seemed to call easily, she had gone back to square one, giving me the building blocks that would let me do more.

Eventually.

Not soon enough for my liking. I had some practical lessons with Cassandra, but lately I spent more time stuffing my head with magical history and lore than using my power. Some of it was interesting, but a lot was as dry and dusty as the volumes containing it.

I was trying my best to make it all stick. It didn't help that I'd been working ridiculous hours, too, clearing my work schedule so I could spend two weeks at the tournament.

Damon worked, hung out with me, slept. I worked, studied, hung out with him, slept, and tried not to fret that I wasn't learning fast enough. If worse came to worst and we faced another magical threat at the tournament, I wanted to be able to help. Cassandra was focusing my practical lessons on shields and fire. There was a lot of "but really, if something happens, call for help fast" worked in there.

Between that and the self-defense and security briefings from Mitch and the how-to-be-a-billionaire's-girlfriend-and-not-embarrass-him-in-public lectures from Riley's PR team, it was like being given the world's most-likely-to-make-you-paranoid homework assignments all at once.

I'd get used to it all eventually, but honestly, I was starting to feel like the few days it would take me to get over the surgery would be a nice break. Maybe I could wheedle Doc Barnard, my surgeon, into giving me the good painkillers. Usually I didn't like drugs, but something that eased the worry for a little while kind of sounded good. Not that I could admit that to anyone else.

"I'm getting the intricacies of currency exchange movements and pricing our component supplies for our next viddeck," Damon said, pulling a face. "Wanna swap?"

"Nope." I grinned up at him. "I'll leave the boring business magnate biz to you. You love that stuff." I could talk code for hours, but finance on the scale that Damon dealt with was worse than the dullest magical volume Lizzie unearthed.

"Get Boyd to drive you, and then I'll come and get you later. That way I can talk to Cassandra as well."

"Okay." We'd driven to Riley together earlier, so I didn't have my car.

Damon had been not so subtly pushing me to use his drivers more and more rather than drive myself. We were going to have to talk about it at some point because, sure, being driven was nice, but I also wanted to be independent. Not to mention it was going to be hard to explain to my clients if I started rocking up to their premises in chauffeur-driven vehicles. They might start thinking I was overcharging. But today, there was no reason to fight him on it, and an hour with Boyd was a more fun proposition than navigating the BART or rideshares.

"Good," Damon said. He gestured with his left hand, and the room's menu came up. "Now, if you're not going to let me kiss you for the next thirty minutes, we need to find something else fun to do."

CHAPTER TWO

LIZZIE WAS SITTING on Cassandra's front steps, typing madly away on her datapad, when Boyd pulled the car up to the curb. Her hair, which had been canary yellow when I'd left for Righteous that morning, was now a far more sedate shade of pale pink. It didn't go with the rest of her outfit—yellow skirt, black-and-lime-striped tee, and orange boots —but it did go with the silver dress she'd bought for the gala. She'd tried to convince me to change my hair, too, but no. That was staying my usual boring brown.

The dress I'd chosen was a green several shades darker than my eyes, and that was as far as I was willing to go in the name of color coordination.

Lizzie looked up as I opened the car door,

waved, yelled, "Hi, Boyd," and then climbed to her feet, shoving her datapad into her backpack.

"Thank you, Boyd," I said, grabbing my purse from the back seat. "Hope the traffic isn't too bad getting back."

"It's no problem, Ms. Lachlan," Boyd said. "You have a good night."

"I will. You, too." I stopped myself from reminding him to call me Maggie. Since Damon and I had gotten back together and it had become clear that I was more than a fling, Boyd had grown more formal with me. He called Damon "boss" or "Mr. Riley" depending on who else was around. But I was now "Ms. Lachlan" all the time.

Boyd had been Damon's driver for a decade. And Damon paid well enough that he now owned a small flotilla of cars and had drivers working for other clients. But Boyd still liked to be the one to drive Damon whenever possible. And I liked knowing he cared about his boss. After Ajax's betrayal, it was good to be sure of some of Damon's closest circle.

Lizzie waved again as I joined her by the steps, and Boyd lifted a couple of fingers from the wheel in acknowledgment before the big gray car purred away.

"Good day?" she asked as she turned and put her palm on the reader by the front door. The entrance to the Archives was inside Cassandra's house, and Lizzie, as a member of the Cestis, had permanent access privileges. Me, I knocked if I arrived on my own. The security system knew me now, but it felt odd to just walk into Cassandra's house.

"Good enough," I said. I didn't feel like mentioning the virtual imps just yet. Better to wait for Damon. After all, he could explain exactly what he'd done. "How about you?"

"Busy," Lizzie said. She worked part-time fundraising for Spark, a charity that helped homeless and at-risk teenagers. She often spent time at one of their drop-in centers on the weekends as well, hanging out with the kids. I was surrounded by workaholics, it seemed. Not that I wasn't just as bad in my way.

Most of the other members of the Cestis had jobs. I didn't quite understand why, when there must have been enough magical trouble in a country the size of the US to keep them all busy, but maybe it helped to keep the knowledge that the Cestis existed mostly on the down-low if they all had other things going on.

No point giving the more stupid and extreme ends of humanity reason to get any more up in arms about witches and magic than they sometimes did anyway by revealing there was more to the world of magic than they knew. I guessed having their own income also kept the government from trying to gain more influence over them by offering funding.

Whatever the reason, Lizzie still worked, Cassandra had her store, Radha was a healer, and Ian, well, Ian did whatever retired wealthy guys did. Philanthropy, art collecting, and socializing, as far as I could tell. Fine by me. He helped people by means other than just his magic *and* spread his money around. He deserved things that made him happy as well. All the Cestis did.

Another reason I wanted to keep any scrutiny I received as Damon's partner to the bare minimum if I possibly could. I didn't want to draw attention to my connection to the Cestis. They'd helped me—saved me, really—and I was determined not to cause more trouble for them.

"I like the hair. Are you sure you won't get bored with it before the gala?" Lizzie changed her hair color like other people changed clothes.

"I'm not changing my dress, so no," Lizzie said with a grin. "Most charity galas aren't that interesting, but I'm sure Damon will make this one fun." Damon had chosen Spark as one of the charities the gala was supporting, so Lizzie would've been invited even if she hadn't been my roomie and a mad-keen gamer. He'd invited all the Cestis, but as far as I knew, Ian was the only other member who'd taken him up on the offer.

"Entertain the rich people and they'll give more money?"

"Definitely. Offering a sneak peek of the game at the gala is genius. All the more cash for my kids." She rubbed her fingers together in a "gimme gimme" gesture. "This kind of fundraising is easy."

Lizzie was close-lipped about her past. I knew she'd left home young, and that was what had drawn her to Spark and her work, but she hadn't offered details, and I hadn't asked. She'd tell me if and when she wanted me to know.

I understood. My early years had been no picnic, and the less I talked about them the better. Lizzie knew a little bit about my mom—well, the part where Sara had bound me to a demon—and the fact that I'd lived with my grandparents from thirteen until the quake, but she didn't ask for more either.

It was possible that Lizzie knew more about Sara than I did, given her access to the Cestis's records, but if she did, she'd never mentioned it. Our mutual reluctance to relive the past kind of confirmed her childhood had been as crappy as mine.

"Absolutely. Take their money and make those kids happy." Lizzie loved the kids she worked with. She'd met Yoshi Liebfield, my intern, through Spark. He'd been semi-homeless, hustling his tech skills on the streets and game clubs to pay his way and help support his little sister.

He was going to college now, having just finished up an early admittance summer subject. Thanks to the salary I paid him and a scholarship he didn't know came from one of the programs Riley Arts funded, he'd graduate debt free. At that point, I was pretty sure I'd lose him to one of the big tech companies who could pay him way more than me.

With his scholarship, he probably didn't need the salary I offered. But he was determined to work and take care of his little sister. She was about to start her final year of high school. She lived with a foster family, and now that he had his own apartment, I knew he was trying to figure out a way for her to come live with him and put money aside for college for her.

Lizzie and I chatted as we worked our way through the security to get into the Archives. Normal roommate stuff about what needed to go on our grocery order and plans for the final phase of the remodeling work at the house. Lizzie was finalizing her plans for the garden, preparing for when the main construction would be done and the backyard would no longer be crammed with junk left behind by contractors and constantly trampled over by men in work boots.

I was giving her free rein as long as she kept my

gran's roses, which so far had been tough enough to survive a decade of neglect and the chaos of remodeling. She knew far more about plants than me, though she involved me in all the choices. It was, after all, my house.

Getting into the Archives took some time. They'd always been locked down tight with wards and other magical protections, along with normal security systems. Finding out there was a magical library in Cassandra's basement had been a little bit like discovering there was a secret weapons lab under your favorite aunt's house. From the outside, Cassandra's house blended in with all her neighbors'. Not a hint of what lurked below ground.

These days the non-magical part of the security system was the best money could buy. Maybe better. Damon had helped Cassandra upgrade it, and it was entirely possible he'd added some custom touches that weren't available to your average consumer.

No doubt it would get tighter still if Damon got Cassandra to agree to digitizing the contents. There were witches who worked in museums who advised on how to best preserve the books and scrolls and other artifacts in the collection, and the Cestis had their own magical methods, but Damon was right—even with magic, paper and vellum wouldn't last forever.

Though if Cassandra ever agreed, I had the

feeling that I'd be spending even more time under-ground. The collection was sizeable, and the Cestis weren't going to let just anyone assist with the process. Scanning in old books about magic didn't exactly require my level of knowledge, but I was more tech savvy than most of the Cestis. Lizzie could handle her tech and was a reasonable gamer, but she didn't work with computers and touchy systems for a living.

But that was a problem for another day. Today, I had to focus on magic, not tech. Lizzie and Cassandra seemed intent on making sure I was intimately familiar with at least some sections of the archives. I had to look up each book they wanted me to read in the old-fashioned card catalogs, then go find it on the shelves. Or drag Lizzie with me to find it if the codes in the catalog indicated that there was something about the item that required magic to handle safely.

I didn't want "eaten by a magical book" on my headstone, so I was more than happy to let someone else who knew what they were doing take over at that point. Not that there'd been many of those so far. Lizzie and Cassandra being cautious, maybe. A couple of the herbaries had protection spells. The ones that were full of deadly plants and the kinds of potions that would be one of the last things that whoever drank or ate or sniffed or breathed them ever encountered.

I'd objected the first time Cassandra has as-signed me one of those. It seemed unlikely I'd ever want to kill someone. But, if I did, it would be in a situation where I needed to do it fast. Going away and brewing up a poison wasn't going to be the an-swer. But Cassandra had told me in no uncertain times that most of the plants in question could be used for more than one thing, and I needed to know what to watch out for.

That had sold me. Damon had been tricked into marriage when he'd been barely twenty-one using a love potion. It had left him with a bone-deep wari-ness of magic that had been the reason we'd broken up after Nat's death. My mom had peddled in that kind of gross magic, too. I wasn't going to let either of us get hurt by something like that again.

Not that all witches used such things for dark purposes. Most witches who loved plant lore were healers who worked alongside non-magical hu-mans in healthcare or private practices.

Healing was the part of magic that, other than witches who specialized in wards and protections or even glamours for rich clients, was most common in the normal world. Good press, so to speak, though there weren't enough healers to go around and even magic couldn't save everyone.

To give me a break from memorizing plants, Lizzie snuck in some warding lessons at home as well. Though, so far, I didn't know if anything I'd tried had really made much difference to the wards she constructed. Other than the one time I'd managed to ward myself into my own bedroom and it had taken about thirty minutes before she stopped laughing long enough to let me out. Though she'd studied the ward for a few minutes, trying to work out exactly what I'd done before she dissolved it. So far, even though she'd explained to me what she thought had happened, I hadn't been able to do it again.

The more complicated magics, like glamours and illusions, would come later. Along with all the ways witches could manipulate things in the real world.

Maybe by the time I graduated to those, I'd lose some of my own fears about my powers. I'd called lightning, and it had been terrifying. And not only because I'd been fighting a demon. That much magic...it could do real damage.

There was a reason witches hid some of the truths about magic from the normal human world. Some of it was hard to accept.

Like the mental tricks some witches could play. My own mother had wiped the memory of her binding me to a demon from my mind. Or maybe the demon had done that. Either way, it was frightening to think someone could just make you forget a chunk of your life.

Maybe that was the reason Cassandra insisted

on doing things slowly, so my confidence could grow in step with my power.

In the meantime, it was me and the Archives and the darn card catalogs. Even digitizing those would save us all a heck of a lot of time finding what we wanted. Damon was right about that much.

Cassandra claimed it would take some time to figure out if it was safe to digitize whole spells. Given that the first time I'd met a demon, it had been in a video game, I couldn't argue. That was for her and Damon to wrangle over. But surely starting with the indexes should be easy enough? Index cards could be scanned, then cleaned up, and then the text could go into a database. Once we'd figured out a proper taxonomy and tagging system.

It would be slow going but worth it. One day I might need some of the information in here in a hurry.

The last heavy steel door into the Archives swung open slowly. Not far inside, Cassandra stood talking with a tall skinny white guy with a shaved head who I'd never seen before. I stopped, startled to see a stranger in the Archives.

"Trick!" Lizzie squealed, then bolted forward to hug him.

Apparently she *had* seen him before.

"Hey, Lizzie," Trick said once she let go. "How's things?"

They grinned at each other in mutual delight. The cool strip lights in the ceiling glinted on the ring in his eyebrow and the multiple earrings in each ear. He looked more like an aging rock star than someone I would have pegged as a witch.

"Fine. You didn't tell me you were going to be in town," she said, sounding indignant.

"Last minute," Trick said. He exchanged a look with Cassandra over Lizzie's head.

Cassandra shook her head slightly, watching them both with a smile playing around her lips. As usual, she wore jewel tones, today's choice a linen shirt in the bright red that seemed to be her favorite over charcoal linen pants and flat tan sandals. The red made her silver hair appear brighter. Sometimes I thought she deliberately played up the fact that she looked like everyone's idea of the perfect grandmother to lull people into ignoring her. But anyone who underestimated Cassandra Tallant was in for an unpleasant surprise.

Before I had time to join them and introduce myself, a younger man walked out from the nearest row of bookshelves, stopping just a few steps past the end of the row. He wasn't quite as tall as Trick, but he was solid muscle, not wiry, so he somehow seemed bigger. Handsome, with close-cropped dark hair and skin and a slightly wary expression. His blue eyes locked on to Lizzie like she was the only one in the room.

She didn't see him at first, but when she did, she froze, the happy grin disappearing as though someone had hit a reset button. She swung around to face Cassandra. "What's *he* doing here?"

He? Interesting. Who was this guy?

"Trick finished the job he was doing on the East Coast and came back to help out," Cassandra said. "We're shorthanded. You know that."

"Not *Trick*," Lizzie said.

Cassandra's golden eyes narrowed. "If you want to know why Zachariah is home, then you should ask him," In other words, put on your big girl pants and deal with it. Cassandra might look like Mrs. Claus, but she was tough.

Lizzie's hands clenched, and she turned her glare from Cassandra to Zachariah. She was too well trained to use magic carelessly, and, as far as I knew, witches couldn't actually turn people into toads. Judging by Lizzie's scowl, it was just as well.

Zachariah met her eyes for a few seconds, then dropped his gaze, mouth twisting.

Yep. There was a story there somewhere.

Lizzie's expression didn't change. I walked over to join them, hoping an interruption might ease the tension.

Trick stuck out a hand heavily bedecked in silver rings, and I shook it before turning to Zachariah, who still stood a few feet away.

"Hi, I'm Maggie," I said, trying to give Lizzie a

minute to catch her breath. I knew all about being blindsided by some guy you didn't want to see turning up unexpectedly. I didn't know if that was exactly what was happening, but obviously Lizzie wasn't thrilled to see Zachariah, whoever he was.

"Maggie Lachlan," I continued. "I'm new here, too."

"Zee Anderson," he replied. "I'm not so new. But also not so here, it seems." He looked past me to Cassandra. "You said this was chill." There was a hint of something other than straight California to his accent. It sounded almost...English? But not quite.

"It is," Cassandra said. "You and Lizzie are both adults. I expect you to remember how to behave accordingly." She turned her gaze to Lizzie. "Elizabeth?"

I didn't think I'd ever heard her call Lizzie that. And Lizzie, who was twenty-four but looked younger, suddenly seemed like a kid faced with a principal she didn't want to deal with.

"Fine." She tipped her chin at Zee, mouth flat. "Welcome back." Then she turned to me. "C'mon, Maggie. Let's work."

CHAPTER THREE

I LET AT LEAST ten minutes of silent reading—or pretending to read, in Lizzie's case—pass before I asked, "Do you want to talk about it?" Strange accent or not, clearly Zee knew everybody here, and they knew him.

Lizzie had dragged me way down to the other end of the Archives, past the long rows of wooden bookshelves. The room was big, and we were about as far away from the others as we could get without leaving, but their voices were still just within hearing. Though Lizzie had steadfastly refused to look back in that direction. I knew avoidance when I saw it. And given she tended toward the "let's just get it out in the open" school of dealing with things when it came to my problems, maybe it was time for the same approach.

At first, I thought she wasn't going to answer, but eventually she sighed and put down the book she was holding. "Do I look like I want to talk about it?"

The words were nearly a whisper, and she glanced over her shoulder before picking up the book again, staring at the pages. Clearly she didn't want the others to hear.

"No. But you usually bug me into talking when I don't want to, so I'm just offering the chance to vent if you need to." I tilted my head. "You kind of seem like you need to."

"I'm fine."

"Fine the way I was fine when Damon turned up again?" Whoever Zee was, I didn't think he and Lizzie had just been friends. In my experience, ex-friends didn't cause the kind of reaction where you went and hid at the other end of the room to avoid talking to them.

Her mouth went flat, and she looked back over her shoulder again. The aisle between the shelves gave us an easy view of Trick and Zee and Cassandra still talking. None of them were looking at us, though something in the line of Zee's shoulders told me he was *not* looking with an effort.

"I don't want to talk about it," Lizzie said.

"Now or ever?"

She shrugged and picked up her book. "Definitely not now."

"Okay. I take it Cassandra didn't tell you those two were going to be here today?" The thought made me uneasy.

"No." She bit out the word. "The four of us have talked about bringing in some more experienced witches to help out. We're still down one member, and it takes time to fill that gap, so extra hands are useful. But we hadn't gotten down to any names. I thought Trick was still in New York."

Trick, not Zee. Did that mean she didn't know where Zee had been? Or just didn't want to talk about it?

"Well, Cassandra is right. You are shorthanded." They'd been busy enough doing cleanup after my demon had been destroyed. Then there'd been the lesserkind and his army of imps. None of the Cestis were telling me much about the cleanup from that, but the fact that they hadn't told me everything was taken care of meant they weren't done.

And they still hadn't appointed someone to fill the vacancy left by Antony's death.

"You need a fifth. Could that be it?"

"Trick doesn't like to stay put for very long. He's powerful, but I'm not sure he'd want to do it."

I'd never asked how the Cestis chose their members. The first few weeks I'd known them had been chaos and trauma. Then I'd ignored them as much as possible for nearly nine months. Then there'd been more chaos and trauma.

I wasn't a candidate. I hadn't been a witch long enough to have the sort of skills required. And I wasn't sure I would want to join the Cestis even if I did. They lived their lives fighting magical fires, so to speak. They did hard things and made hard choices, and there didn't seem to be a lot in it for them. Other than keeping the world safe.

I couldn't argue with that goal. I just didn't know if I was the kind of person who could dedicate her life to it. Maybe Trick wasn't either. But it had been over a year since Antony died. They had to fill the vacancy sooner or later.

"What about Zee?" I asked.

"No. He has magic, but he's not Cestis strong." She cast another quick glance over her shoulder as though she couldn't help looking for him. "He does other things."

I looked back, too. If neither of them was a candidate to take Antony's place, why were they here?

Trick was gesturing as he talked, the movements fluid but rapid. Maybe he was one of those people who never really stayed still. That would explain the wiry build.

Zee, on the other hand, struck me as the solid, silent type. One of those big guys who knew he could seem intimidating and didn't say much because of it. Though maybe the quiet approach was more about not wanting to deal with Lizzie in this case. Still, my gut feel was he was a stay-in-the-background-but-get-shit-done kind of guy. So what, exactly, did he do for the Cestis?

Lizzie's mouth turned down as she focused on her book again. I could keep asking, or I could give her some space to process. She'd done that for me when Damon had unexpectedly turned back up on my doorstep nearly a year ago. Though there'd been some gentle teasing and some pushing me in the right direction. But she'd known the history between us. And I had no idea what the deal was with her and Zee other than clearly something had happened that was making the whole situation awkward.

In my experience, that usually meant a relationship gone wrong, but it could be something else.

I should wait until Lizzie told me the whole story. I owed her. She'd looked after me after Nat died and Damon left. Sure, she'd done it by mostly moving herself in and refusing to take any of my not-so-subtle hints that I wanted to be left alone, but that didn't change the facts.

She'd dug her heels in and stayed for no other reason than she was worried about me. I mean, sure, the Cestis might have set her the task of keeping an eye on me, but keeping an eye on me was different to becoming my roommate and living in a house currently more construction zone than home. Especially when commuting from Berkeley into the city for her job and for Cestis business was hardly convenient. She'd lived in Inner Richmond before, but none of that seemed to factor into her considerations. I needed help, and she could help. So she did.

She was only twenty-four, but she was going to make a very good mom one day if she wanted kids. Sure, she was goofy and obsessed with pop culture, and her fashion choices sometimes hurt my eyes, but she had a very good heart. Driven by a deep need to care for others.

I'd had a crappy childhood with my mom, and even the years I'd had with my grandparents after that, surrounded with nothing but love and caring and support, hadn't entirely rid me of the basic wariness I'd developed in thirteen years of growing up with a witch whose main purpose in life was getting whatever the hell she wanted or thought she deserved.

Usually what she wanted was to extract as much money as she could out of the residents of whatever out-of-the-way, dead-end town we were in, or whatever guy she'd zeroed in on, and then get the hell out of there. We'd moved a lot, living in a series of crappy apartments and trailers. Sara had been very good at conning people but less good at holding on to the money she made. She'd also been very good at putting a solid dent in my basic faith in humanity.

Lizzie, whatever it was that had happened to

her, seemed to have had nearly the opposite reaction. She wanted to help everyone. And she just got on and did it, giving most people—as far as I could tell—the benefit of the doubt. Which made me wonder what Zee could have done that was bad enough to make her cast him out of her very wide circle of friends and acquaintances.

I mean, I'd been awful to live with in the beginning, but she'd ignored that and pitched in, helping me remodel my house, making sure there was food in the refrigerator, and that I was eating and sleeping and all those basic things in the first few months when I'd been fogged with grief and guilt and barely managing to put one foot in front of the other.

By the time I started to emerge from the worst of it, we were friends. And I liked having her around.

So no. I wasn't going to push her about Zee. Not yet. Time to change the subject.

"If Trick doesn't want the job, are there other candidates?" I asked.

Lizzie shrugged. "We've been thinking about it. Sometimes it's easy to fill a gap, and sometimes we have to wait for the right person to come along. It's not just about strong magic. It's about...the fit. Synergy. We need to be able to work together seamlessly. That's not so easy to find."

That I understood. I'd seen the power the Cestis could wield together when they really wanted to.

Their magic seemed effortless, though I knew it wasn't. It was complicated enough learning to use my own magic. I didn't know how I'd go about working with others the way the Cestis had when they'd rescued Damon and me from a lesserkind.

"If you were a business, the experts would be saying you need some succession planning in place," I said with a grin. "But I guess it's not that simple."

"No. It's not a short-term gig. People don't leave once they're appointed. Well, most retire eventually, but other than that, it's not like there's a lot of turnover. We identify other strong witches, of course, but it's hardly fair to dangle a chance at joining us if we're not going to have a spot for years and years. Ideally, we'd want someone older than me but younger than Radha. It's easier if there's a bit of a spread of ages. Minimizes the chance of having to fill two spots at once. Not that anything is a guarantee," she said, then bit her lip.

I ignored the lingering pang of guilt that shimmered through me. Antony had died trying to help me face down my demon and save Nat. He'd given his life to save ours, and then I'd still failed at saving Nat in the end.

Logically I knew it was the demon who was to blame, but honestly, even with all the time and therapy I'd done, part of me still thought I should have saved her. That if I'd just been better somehow, or worked out what had been going on faster, Nat might still be the one sharing my house with me. But wishing for things to be different was pointless. I couldn't change what had happened. Not to Nat. Not to my mom. Not to me. Not with Lizzie either. The only way was forward.

"Yeah, telling someone they might have a shot seems like a recipe for trouble."

Lizzie nodded. "Yeah. There have been times in the past where it got ugly." She grimaced but then brightened. "Who knows? Maybe the fact that Damon is hiring witches will bring some new blood to town. That's the other part of the problem. Not everyone wants to uproot their lives and move here to do what we do."

"What about the tournament? Teams are coming from all over the world. Some of them will be witches, too, yeah?"

"A few," she said. "The rules make it harder in the paid leagues. But that leaves the same problem. Even harder to get someone to leave their own country. And anyone powerful enough is probably in contact with their own Cestis. It's not exactly polite to poach."

"If they're gamers, then moving to San Francisco to be closer to Righteous is a good cherry to dangle. I'm sure Damon would play along if there was someone you wanted. Real gameheads would find an offer from Righteous hard to refuse."

"Not everyone who games is a tech nerd though."

"Riley Arts is a big company," I said. "Plenty of non-nerd jobs going."

"I guess we'll see. The witches on his security team will be on the lookout for magic being used anyway. And they'll know all the competitors with magic. They have to declare their magic, after all."

I'd never met a witch who gamed. Or maybe I had, and I'd never known. Back when Nat had been playing, I'd been intent on ignoring magic. But there were a few. Enough that leagues required witches to declare their magic, and it was definitely against the rules to use it during a game. Not that I knew how exactly someone might use magic to influence virtual reality. But they could influence the gamers themselves.

Righteous had had enough trouble with the demon causing issues for the beta testers it had managed to get through to. Damon wouldn't want any further hints of magical scandal. The rules to the tournament made it crystal clear that no magic would be tolerated.

"Well, you can keep an eye out, too."

Lizzie was supposed to be coming with me to most of the tournament heats. Damon would be in business mode, and I wanted company. I'd hardly had to twist her arm to get her to agree.

"I will be," she said. She glanced back again,

just briefly. So fast I wasn't sure she even realized she was doing it. But that was none of my business.

I straightened my shoulders and turned my attention back to the table. "Okay, time to get to work, I guess. What's next?"

Lizzie looked grateful for the change in subject and reached for another book. One with a familiar cover. It seemed to be her favorite book on herb lore. "Let's look at some calmative herbs. It will give you some reading for the next couple of days while you're resting after surgery." She flipped through the pages quickly, marking her place with a finger, and then focusing on me. "You are still getting the chip, right?"

I nodded, ignoring the roll of my stomach. "Yes."

She smiled approvingly. Damon had offered to pay for a chip for her, too. Guess he was keen to expand his initial sample of magical chip testers beyond just me. Yoshi's scholarship would pay for one for him if he met the grade requirements at the end of his first year. He was already talking about it, but Lizzie hadn't made up her mind. Maybe she was waiting to see if I did okay this time. "Then you'll need some distractions while you recover."

"Homework isn't resting. I was thinking more binge-watching *Strange Adventures* and lots of naps. I only get a few days' recovery time before the gala."

"You can do that and do some of this," Lizzie said. "You'll be too busy to study much during the tournament."

"I don't think I could cram a few weeks of study into a few days even if I wasn't recovering." As much as I wanted to.

She stuck out her tongue. "No, but you can make the most of your free time while you have some."

I wasn't going to win the argument. At least not the part about making the most of it tonight. I wasn't going to make any promises about what I'd feel up to after surgery. "Potions it is," I said and laughed as Lizzie rolled her eyes.

Lizzie and I worked for an hour or so. She kept her attention firmly on the book and me. Not even the occasional soft male laugh floating down from the other end of the room made her move, though I noticed her shoulders stiffening every time that laugh was particularly low.

Guess that was Zee. But if Lizzie was determined to play "nothing to see here," then I was going to play along. At least until my eyes began to protest. Too much time deciphering old, faded copperplate writing. I needed a bathroom break and a caffeine fix.

"Coffee?" I asked, pushing my chair back.

"Can you bring me some tea? That lemon ginger one if Cassandra has it. I need to make a call," Lizzie said. She handed her travel mug to me and then grabbed her datapad.

I didn't know if she really did need to call anyone, but that too fell under the "play along with the friend in denial" rule.

I made my way back through the rows of shelves, skirting around Cassandra, Trick, and Zee with only a nod in their direction, and let myself out into the foyer outside the main room. There was a small kitchen through a door in the right-hand side of the hall. Cassandra kept it stocked with basic snacks and drinks and, occasionally, cookies.

I hardly dared eat or drink inside the Archives themselves, too scared I'd ruin some centuries-old manuscript and doom humanity to a horrible fate. Lizzie was more relaxed—as the travel mug indicated—but she was a member of the Cestis. I was not.

I fiddled with the coffee machine, wondering when Damon was going to arrive. Virtual imps might be just what the doctor ordered to give everybody something to focus on rather than whatever the hell was making it so awkward between Zee and Lizzie. I was wondering how long I could believably put off going back inside when the door opened, and Zee walked in.

"Hey," he said, doing one of those manly chin-tip things that passed for a nod.

"Hey, yourself," I said. I reached for a pod and slipped it into the machine. "Sorry, I was daydreaming. This won't take long."

He shrugged. "I was after water. Trying not to do much syncaf today. Still jet-lagged."

Jet-lagged? Where had he come from? The time difference between the East and West Coast was an adjustment but not bad enough, I suspected, to make him call it jet lag.

"Are you sure? This is the real stuff." I pointed at the container of pods. One of the benefits of dating Damon. He could afford real coffee. And kept my house and the Archives supplied. I still drank syncaf if I was out and about without him, but even though the science proved syncaf had exactly the same effect as the real stuff, coffee was just better.

Zee's eyes widened briefly. "Can't remember the last time I had real coffee. But today's not the day to start."

I did my own chin tip at the cabinet over the sink. "There's tea. Herbal stuff. Some of Cassandra's blends."

He made a face that suggested he'd experienced some of Cassandra's less pleasant potions in his time. The woman was a master when it came to herbs, but she didn't worry much about making it taste good if she thought a mix would do the job without any frills. "Water's good, thanks."

I pointed at the next cabinet. "Glasses in that one. There's bottled water in the fridge, or the tap has a filter on it, so it's good to drink." As soon as I said the words, I realized this probably wasn't Zee's first time here. But if it wasn't, he was too polite to point that out.

Instead, he nodded and flipped the cabinet open. I caught a glimpse of gold and silver on his wrist as he reached for a glass. A chip.

I stared at it a bit too long. He was the first witch I'd met with one. Not that I'd met many witches yet.

"Something wrong?" Zee asked.

I started and looked away. "No, sorry. Just checking out your chip."

"Right," he said. "Not many of us have them yet."

I rubbed the barely there scar on my left wrist. "No." My failed chip wasn't something I wanted to discuss with a complete stranger. "So is this welcome home?" I asked. "Are you from San Francisco originally?"

He slanted me a glance as he turned on the tap, filled his glass, drained it, and then filled it again. "Not originally, but it was home for a stretch."

"You've been away? Somewhere interesting? Or

does that fall under secret Cestis business thou shalt not speak of?"

One side of his mouth quirked, amusement lurking in his brown eyes. "You're here. You must know some secret Cestis business yourself."

"Some," I said. "But I'm hardly inner circle."

"You're the one with the demon, yeah?"

Ugh. It seemed my reputation preceded me. Which meant he probably did know about my first chip. I didn't like talking about the demon, but if I was going to try and find out a bit more about Zee, maybe it wouldn't hurt to offer up a tidbit or two of my own. "Not exactly with. But yes, there was a demon. Until I fried it." My lightning had been enough to destroy its physical form here on Earth. But based on the fact that it had sent a lesserkind after me, it seemed it wasn't dead, just back in its own realm. I just hoped like hell it would stay there. "But you didn't answer my question."

His mouth quirked again. "Noticed that, huh?"

"Yep. Fair's fair. I answered yours."

"England. But the rest does fall under secret Cestis business. You'd have to ask Cassandra. Or—"

He stopped, but I could almost feel the "Lizzie" he'd bitten off.

"Is the demon how you got mixed up with these guys?" he asked.

I nodded. "I didn't know I had magic before that."

His eyes widened. "How does that happen?"

"Long story."

"It would have to be." His dark eyes were calm, waiting to see what I said next. Whatever he was thinking, he was very good at not letting it show on his face.

"Lizzie and Cassandra have been teaching me," I said, throwing him a bone.

"Might as well learn from the best."

"That's what Lizzie says whenever I complain about doing my homework."

He smiled properly then. "She always was bossy."

"Better her than Cassandra," I said. "Sometimes I think we should just let her run the whole damn country."

Zee laughed then, and yep, it was the low rolling rumble of a laugh that had had Lizzie flinching.

My datapad beeped, and I pulled it out of my back pocket. I smiled when I saw a message from Damon telling me he was about five minutes away.

"Good news?" Zee asked as I put the datapad back and picked up my coffee.

"Just Damon," I said. "My...boyfriend," I added, realizing he probably had no idea who I was talking about. The term "boyfriend" felt weird at my age, but I didn't have a better word for our relationship yet.

Zee nodded. "I heard about that. You're dating Righteous, huh?"

"Well, I'm dating the guy who owns Righteous," I said, hoping he'd heard about that through Cestis gossip, not real-world gossip. "I take it you're a gamer?" I pointed at his wrist. "Or do you do something work-wise that you need that for?"

He scrubbed a hand over the stubble starting to show on his chin. If he'd flown from the UK, he had to have been traveling nearly a day at this point if he and Trick had come here from the airport rather than been here for a day or so already. His clothes had that wrinkled, travel-worn look that suggested the former. "Yeah, I dabble. I used to be more serious," he said. "Haven't had a lot of time for it the last year or so. But I pay some attention. Big tournament coming up, yeah?"

He did more than pay attention if he had a chip. Especially if he'd had his a few years. Chips were starting to come down in price, but the first few generations had cost a lot.

"Yep. Good time to come back if you're into it."

"That's not—" He bit off the words. Did the chin-tip thing again. "You'd better go let him in."

CHAPTER FOUR

DAMON WAS TAKING a call when I opened the front door. He held up a finger, so I stepped onto the porch to wait for him. The car parked outside the house was his dark blue Ventra. He had flashier and more expensive cars, but the Ventra, while not exactly cheap, was a brand that had gained a lot of market share in the last decade or so. They'd made a breakthrough in electric engines that had given them much more range, and the rumor was they were close to cracking hydrogen.

Whether or not that was true, Damon had picked the Ventra for his "nothing to see here" car. The one he chose when he drove himself and wanted to avoid attention. Which was most of the time. Cassandra's neighborhood was a nice one, but some of Damon's cars would have stood out.

Boyd's big gray sedan wasn't unusual. It was the sort of town car that any number of car services used. Granted, most of them probably weren't bulletproof and armed with the sorts of defenses Damon's was, but neither of those things was apparent from its appearance.

Thanks to Damon, the tech companies had been some of the first to come back to San Francisco post-quake. He'd convinced quite a few of them—even those who'd been headquartered in Silicon Valley for decades—to open at least a head office back downtown to help rebuild and revitalize. Most of them hadn't built entire campuses like he had, but it had helped.

Drawing companies back to the city had brought the people back, too. Both to San Francisco and the surrounding cities like Berkeley and Oakland.

Damon ended his call and bent to drop a quick "hello" kiss on my cheek. The dark stubble starting to shade his jaw tickled and I smiled as he straightened. He still wore the jeans and pale blue T-shirt he'd had on at the office. Not as slick as his avatar, but to me, the real thing was better.

"Hey," he said, stepping back. "How goes magic school?"

"Awkward," I said, then slurped some of my coffee. The mug was full, and I'd nearly spilled it on Cassandra's pristine, polished floorboards before

I'd opened the door. Safer if I drank some out here. I wanted Cassandra to be in a good mood when Damon told her about the imp.

"Awkward? Did you set something on fire?" he asked, closing the door.

"You're funny." I turned and headed back toward the basement. "No. But Cassandra brought a couple of new witches along. Two guys."

"Why is that awkward?" Damon asked as we started down the stairs. He sounded confused.

"There's some tension between Lizzie and the younger guy."

"Well, Cassandra wouldn't let anyone who was bad news down here, would she?"

"Not that kind of tension. More like 'we have a past' tension."

He snorted. "That sounds like the kind of thing the two of them need to figure out."

"Probably. But like I said, don't be surprised if it feels weird. But pretend you don't notice. Lizzie's not talking."

"Got it," Damon said. "I just want to talk to Cassandra and then get home. You need rest before your surgery."

My shoulders tensed. I sped up my pace, heading for the first scanner, not wanting him to notice my nerves. The chip was my choice. The anxiety was my problem.

Nothing bad is going to happen.

My inner voice wasn't exactly full of confidence, but I repeated the phrase as we worked our way through the various security checks and reached the Archive foyer.

Damon pulled me close before I reached for the final door and pressed his lips to mine. All thoughts of chips and Lizzie and what Cassandra was going to say about virtual imps melted from my mind as I sank into the kiss, twining my free arm around his neck to pull him closer.

Somehow, I managed not to spill my coffee, and Damon was smiling when he let me go.

"What was that for?" I asked.

"You wouldn't let me kiss you properly at the office," he said.

"And you thought here was a good place to make up for lost time?"

"Fooling around in the stacks is a time-honored tradition," he said with a grin.

"Not these stacks," I said, grinning back. "If the books didn't get us, Cassandra probably would. And so far, I haven't found anything in there that proves she can't turn us into frogs."

"What a way to go," he said.

"I'd prefer surviving long enough that we get to be alone somewhere private. You're just going to have to park your library fantasies for another time."

"Are you saying you're willing to put on glasses and a tweed suit for me?"

I laughed. "Am I a librarian from the twentieth century in this scenario?"

His eyes darkened. "Would you like to be? I mean, I do have plenty of bookshelves."

It was true. He had quite an impressive collection of old paper books in the library in his house. Paperbacks and hardbacks, not the kind of fake leather-bound books you saw in the few bookcases that still appeared in the background in vid shows or movies. Even more impressive, he read them, even though almost any book in the world could land on his datapad in seconds.

I suspected the paper books with their lack of tech offered him a rare break from technology. Maybe the kind he didn't even know he wanted.

The thought of him kissing me—or doing other things—among all those tall wooden shelves was distracting, and he laughed again as he reached past me for the door handle. "Let's shelve this conversation for now." He wiggled his eyebrows at me.

"Bad jokes aren't sexy," I said.

"You like my bad jokes just fine," he said smugly.

I had no argument to that. I liked almost everything about the man. And I was suddenly as eager as he was to get this discussion with Cassandra over with so we could go home.

Trick and Cassandra were seated at one of the long tables by the card catalog when we walked back into the room. It took me a moment to spot Zee. He'd tucked himself away, sitting on the floor by the farthest row of shelves, a datapad in his lap. Pretty much as far away from Lizzie as he could get without joining the other two. He didn't look up as I led Damon over to the table.

The round of introductions didn't take long. We sat down at the table. Lizzie didn't join us. I could just see the back of her pink head at the table where we'd been working earlier. Zee stayed where he was, too.

"Are you here to just take Maggie home, or did you want to talk to me about something?" Cassandra asked. "I still don't have an answer about the books and what we can do with those."

Damon slanted a glance at Trick, one brow lifting.

"Trick is aware of your ideas," Cassandra said. "He works for us. And he's going to be in town for a while. He's safe. Your Mr. Angelico even cleared him."

Ah. Mitch. Of course Cassandra had given him a heads-up if she was going to introduce Damon to new witches. Ever since Ajax kidnapped us, Mitch had been doing his best to make sure Damon didn't go anywhere or meet anyone who Mitch didn't know about in advance. The fact that Damon arrived here alone should have tipped me off that Mitch knew about this meeting. Otherwise, there'd be someone from Riley security with Damon. There probably *was* someone keeping track of him from a distance.

Damon nodded. "Okay, then." He didn't ask about Zee. But if Mitch had given Cassandra the okay about Trick, it was unlikely she'd have forgotten to ask him to do the same for Zee. She understood the need for security. You didn't get to be in the Cestis—not to mention its oldest member—by being an idiot.

"Good," Cassandra said. "What did you want to talk about?"

"I had another idea," Damon said. "Something that might be helpful for you. For the Cestis. Or others who help you." He glanced at Trick.

"Something involving technology, I assume?"

"Yes."

Cassandra's eyes flicked toward me. "Something Maggie knows about, too?"

"Not until just earlier today," I said. "We haven't been hiding anything." Well, maybe Damon had. A little. Though he'd probably argue he was just getting ready to tell Cassandra. "And Damon is the one who knows how to explain it." I nudged him gently. "Go on."

"It might be easier if I show you," he said,

reaching for his backpack and sliding out a viddeck.

"Isn't that one of your game things?" Cassandra asked.

"This one is more a projector," Damon said. "It lets you view the game as it would look in VR—or at least give you a sense of that—without you actually having to be hooked up." He glanced around. "Maybe Lizzie should see this."

Cassandra shrugged. "She's down the other end of the room. She knows you're here. If she wants to come join us, she will."

There was a distinct edge to the words. Definitely not happy with Lizzie. I hoped she wasn't going to turn that bad mood onto Damon once he showed her his imp.

He hit a button on the side of the deck and then picked up his datapad, typing something onto the screen. A glowing sphere of light appeared above the tiny deck, only about a foot in diameter.

Small was good. A tiny imp would be less of a shock than full-sized.

"I was thinking about how hard Maggie has been working, learning magic," Damon said. He shot me a sideways smile, and I smiled back automatically.

Cassandra's expression softened, but she didn't say anything.

"I know she's come to this late, and I'm sure it's

easier if you start learning young, but I was thinking about if there were ways technology might help. And then I was wondering how the people who do what you do"—he gestured between Cassandra and Trick—"learn what you need to know as well. I mean, how do you know how to fight off an imp if you don't know what it looks like?"

"That's what the books are for," Cassandra said, sweeping her hand back toward the rows of shelves. "Anyone likely to come into contact with imps on the regular can access those."

"But it's not always regular, is it?" Damon said. "Maggie had to deal with imps before she even knew she had magic."

"Maggie is somewhat of an unusual case," Cassandra said.

"Agreed. But speaking from personal experience, if I was someone who was going to have to deal with these things, someone who was wading into the magical...problems side of being a witch, then a book isn't enough preparation. You need something more lifelike." He hit a button on his datapad, and the foot-high version of the imp sprang to life over the table.

Cassandra didn't so much as flinch.

Trick made a humming sort of noise, then leaned in closer to study the holo. "That's pretty good."

"Thanks," Damon said drily.

"It's even more impressive at full size," I said. "In VR, it's almost like seeing the real thing."

"And once you've seen it, then what?" Cassandra asked.

"We can program it to move and respond in as real a way as possible," Damon said. "Even fight. Someone who was learning could interact safely."

Cassandra's lips pursed. "You can't use magic in one of those machines though."

"No. Though we can program something close," Damon said.

She shook her head. "That wouldn't be a good idea. If someone practicing in VR needed to stifle their actual magical responses, then what's to say they wouldn't stifle them in real life?"

Damn. I'd hoped I'd be wrong about that.

Damon sat back in his chair. He didn't immediately respond, then said, "Go on."

"I know people train in your virtual worlds for many things now. Driving and such. Medical procedures. Even fighting. I can see it would be helpful for that. Easier to learn how to change gears or operate a machine or practice a punch before you try it in the real world. But magic is different. People like Trick, who put themselves at risk facing down magical threats, they need to summon their magic instinctively. Like Maggie did when she fought that first imp. With some of the things we deal with, even a second's hesitation, the tiniest pause while their brain switched to 'this is real, I can use my magic' could be fatal."

Damn. I'd suspected that might be her answer.

"I—" Damon began, but Cassandra held up a hand, cutting him off.

"I know your instinct is to protect Maggie. That's understandable. Commendable, in fact. But she can't learn magic in a make-believe world. She has to learn it here." She tapped the table, the sound echoing sharply.

"Though," Trick said before Damon could reply, "I think you may be on to something with the identification part." He tugged at an earring, expression thoughtful.

Cassandra turned to look at him, one brow lifted.

He shrugged and waved a hand at the holo. "Face it, that is a lot better than trawling through fifty books trying to figure out what you might come across if you're on an assignment. And even for identification of plants and other things. More helpful to see something in real life than look at a black-and-white drawing."

For a moment I thought Cassandra was going to tell him he was wrong, but she nodded after a beat.

"You may have a point." She turned back to Damon. "We can talk about this more, but right now shouldn't you be focused on your tournament, not the Archives?"

"I can do both."

She rolled her eyes. "The Archives have survived for a very long time without you. They'll survive a few more weeks. If you're concerned about keeping Maggie safe, then the tournament should have your focus."

"We're taking security very seriously. You know that."

"I know," Cassandra said. "But part of security is not to let your attention be drawn away from what's truly important." She pointed at the imp. "That can wait. You both need to keep your wits about you."

Damon and I had been receiving various versions of this speech from both Mitch and Cassandra since we'd told them I'd be attending the tournament with Damon in an official capacity.

"We know," I said. "Trust me, we've been preparing. Mitch has this under control."

"Unless you have reason to believe there's some new threat we haven't considered?" Damon added.

"Nothing concrete," Cassandra.

What? "Care to elaborate?" I asked, stomach sinking.

Cassandra and Trick exchanged another look.

"We can't deal with a threat we don't know about," I said. "What's happening?"

"Nothing definite. And nothing terribly reliable. Just a few witches with premonitions. Bad dreams, that sort of thing. They were starting to settle after the lesserkind, but I've been hearing about them again. Trick told me that some of the witches in New York felt it, too."

"Premonitions?" Damon asked. "What exactly do you mean?"

"Some witches have a talent for seeing the future. It's rare, and it's usually not strong. They're wrong as often as they're right. But not always."

"And what exactly have they been dreaming about?"

"Nothing precise. Just...feelings of threat. Here in San Francisco."

"Couldn't that just be the fallout from the lesserkind?" I asked.

"Maybe. I wasn't that worried until Trick told me it was happening elsewhere." She shrugged. "But you're right, it's nothing concrete. You just have to be focused. This tournament is drawing all sorts of people here. It provides good cover for someone dangerous to slip in."

"We are focused," I said, hoping my voice sounded steadier than I felt.

"I know," Cassandra said. "So then you'll listen to me and leave this until the tournament is over."

She looked at Damon. "You're drawing attention to yourselves, and I understand why. But you're used to it, Damon, and Mitch understands the threats you'd usually face. But Maggie...well, we can't predict what might come of a lot of people suddenly knowing who she is. And where she is."

"Because of the demon?" Damon asked. "Is that what you're worried about?"

"Not just that. I told you before that there were risks to going public with your relationship. We've done our best to protect Maggie's identity in dealing with the demon and everything else, but...."

"But what?" I asked flatly.

"People talk," Trick said. "Maybe most of the magic world doesn't know, but a demon, and even a lesserkind, makes the kind of noise that's hard not to notice. For people with the right kind of knowledge and the right kind of power. And people talk. There are whispers. Rumors. They don't all have the story straight, but a lot are close enough. I heard them over on the East Coast, and Zee said there was even some talk across the pond."

Damon put a hand over mine. "We can't jump at every rumor."

I agreed. He'd never leave the house if his team locked him down at every threat. That had been the hardest part of being brought more into the center of his world. I'd gotten a clearer picture of its dark side.

I'd known some of it. That he got threats, etc., but Mitch had told me some scary truths about the percentages of those threats that were actually dangerous. And it wasn't just physical threats. Riley Arts was a tempting target too. It had money. It had cutting edge tech. It had research that could make people a lot of money. But Damon didn't let it stop him.

I wasn't going to let it stop me either, even though I'd had far less time to get used to the idea. After having a demon hunt me, the kinds of threats the mundane world could throw at me seemed less dangerous, but I still needed to take them seriously.

"No, but the facts haven't changed. You're a target because of who you are. Maggie might be a target. Or at least of interest, with her potential. Or because of her mother."

"What's my mother got to do with this?" I asked.

"She had enemies, dear. And she clearly dabbled in some dark things. Maybe she hid you well when she was alive and your grandparents kept you out of sight, but you bear her name, and as much as you deny it, you look something like her. After Friday, your face is going to be everywhere. Not so hidden anymore."

Which was nothing I didn't know. Nothing she hadn't told me before. So just how worried was she that she was telling me again?

"You think I should stay home?"

Cassandra sighed. "No. The two of you have to deal with this sooner or later. It might as well be now while Damon has the perfect excuse to ramp up his security. I just need you to be smart. Leave the imp for now. I'll think about it, and we'll talk again after all the fuss is over. And in the meantime, we have an idea for an addition to your security that we hadn't considered."

"Which is?" I asked.

"Both Trick and Zee are good at undercover work," she said. "Trick is probably a bit too well known here to use for this, though he can maybe be Lizzie's plus-one at your gala and not raise too many eyebrows for anyone with magic. But Zee, well, he's been away for a few years. And he was young when he left. He hadn't worked for us much back then. Not enough to be well known, anyway. It could be a good idea to maybe see if he can join the tournament as a player somehow. Be on the inside."

It wasn't a terrible idea. Mitch would have both uniformed and undercover members of his team in the crowds, but there was no way for a Righteous employee or contractor to be slipped into one of the teams. Not without causing a big scandal if the truth got out. But Zee wasn't connected to Righteous.

"Can he play?" Damon asked.

"He used to be good," Cassandra said. "Or so I understand. He and his friends played in a league."

There were many kinds of leagues.

"He needs to be more than good to be part of one of the teams that stand a chance of making it through to the finals. Even in the lower leagues, the best players are coming from all over the world," Damon said.

"He doesn't need to win though, does he? Most teams will hang around after being eliminated, won't they?" I asked. "There must be a team who'll need someone last minute. Even as a tech guy or strategy."

The elite teams had support crews. Depending on the game, not all the members of any given squad could always play at once. The ones with the best reflexes and decision-making in-game tended to get the deck time, but for the big, complicated games, they went in with plans. And people who were good at strategy—the ones who might have been running the gameplay back in the day when people played tabletop games and real-life role-playing—could get a seat.

Damon frowned. "It's risky. It would be bad if he was discovered to be a plant."

"Zee's good," Trick said. "He's been dealing with some heavy stuff in the last few years. Big assignments. He's pulled all of them off."

"Why is he home, then?" Damon asked.

"Even the best need time off. And it's not a good idea to stay too long in one place if you're undercover, even when you're good. The magical world is smaller than the human world. People talk. Information gets out."

"In other words, he's burned," Damon said.

"No, he's getting out before he gets burned," Trick said. "He's too good to let something go wrong."

"Lizzie said he didn't have strong magic," I cut in.

Cassandra nodded. "Not as strong as hers. But not many people do. He's very good at illusions. From what I've been told, he's learned a lot."

"And it's not just magic that makes him good," Trick said. "He's good at getting along and blending in."

"He is?" I focused on Zee for a moment. Difficult to imagine a big, handsome guy like him slipping under the radar.

"He knows how to handle himself," Trick said. "It's not always about how a person looks. Zee learned how to get along and survive young. Just like Lizzie did." He looked at me. "I'm guessing you did, too."

What did that mean? "You knew my mom?" How old was he? Mom would have been in her early fifties if she was still alive. Trick didn't seem that old.

"Not personally," he said. "But I've heard about her. She kind of vanished, didn't she? Not many people with her abilities manage to fall off the Cestis's radar completely. I'm guessing that involved a lot of moving around and...other things."

It sounded like he had some familiarity with some of those other things himself. Things like fake identities and skipping out of town. But I'd only just met him, and it didn't matter how much Cassandra vouched for him, I wasn't going to discuss my childhood. For one thing, I didn't want to remember.

"I mostly grew up with my grandparents," I said. "Right here in Berkeley. But I understand what you're saying. Damon, what do you think?"

"I'd need to talk to Mitch. Cassandra said he's done the checks, but if we're going to run something alongside what he already has planned, he needs to know about it."

"The more people who know about it, the less undercover it will be," Trick said.

Damon shook his head. "Mitch is my head of security. I literally trust him with my life. And he's proven worthy of that trust many times. Telling him is nonnegotiable. Besides, his team has been vetting all the entrants. He'll have some idea about which teams might be open to this."

"Oh, we have that covered," Trick said. "Trueno Diablo."

My jaw dropped, and Damon grunted in surprise. Trueno Diablo were one of the best US game teams around. They'd dominated the world championships the last few years. Nat had been a fangirl.

"You know Alicia?" Damon asked.

The tiny and fierce Alicia Chan captained Trueno Diablo and had propelled them to the top. I knew her play style well thanks to Nat making me watch endless replays of championship bouts. Smart, tough, and competitive. Not the kind of woman who'd randomly allow someone to join her team as a favor. Not with so much at stake.

Trick shook his head. "No. But Zee knows Carlo. He used to run with him when they were younger. Him and Lizzie. And Jaali Heng."

Lizzie knew Carlo Winters? She'd never mentioned him, and she was a gamer. My curiosity about exactly what had happened between her and Zee ratcheted up a few notches, but I pushed it away. I needed to focus.

Carlo had joined Trueno Diablo a couple years ago. But even before that, he'd been a name in the San Francisco game clubs. Both for his skills but also because he had a reputation as being a bit of a tech whisperer, known for his deck jacks and mods that pushed the boundaries of what any deck was supposed to be able to handle. He was one of Yoshi's heroes. Trueno Diablo didn't need a tech guy. They had Carlo. Which meant Zee would need another story.

"That's a very high-profile team to choose if you think Zee should be under the radar. Or are you trying to hide him in plain sight?" Damon asked. "If you want him to do undercover work here in the US, then that isn't the greatest idea. His face will be seen by a lot of people if he gets any screen time during the tournament. It's not just the game play that's streamed. There will be crews out shooting B-roll of all the teams, interviews, that kind of thing."

"Zee's up for one last ride," Trick said. "After that, we'll see. No one does deep undercover forever. It's tough. Especially if you want any sort of normal life."

Was that why Zee had come back? Looking for something normal? Understandable. The reason I was pushing through with chip surgery and getting my face plastered all over the place at the tournament was for that, too. With Damon.

Sure, given who he was, it would be an unusual kind of normal. Hardly one I'd ever imagined for myself. But then, I'd never even been sure I'd settle down. Sara wasn't the kind of mother who provided a vision of home and domestic bliss to fill a young girl's head with dreams of love and family. My grandparents had done their best to make up for that, shown me what love looked like, but the scars my mom left behind had made me skeptical that they weren't just a rare outlier.

Then I'd met Damon. And lost him, which for nearly a year had only confirmed my worst fears.

But we'd found a way back. And now, no matter how weird our normal was going to be, I knew I wanted it. Wanted him at my side. Crazy virtual imps or otherwise.

I looked across to Zee. He'd leaned his head back against the wall, earbuds in his ears, eyes closed. If it hadn't been for the fact that one of his fingers was tapping a rhythm on his right thigh, I would have thought that jet lag had gotten the better of him and he'd fallen asleep. "Shouldn't he be part of this conversation?"

"He knows what I'm suggesting," Trick said. "Said to tell him if it was a yes or no."

"And what about Lizzie?" I asked. "It seems like the two of them have a past."

"That isn't a factor," Cassandra said. "This is about safety at this tournament. For you and Damon and for everyone else who'll be there. That's Cestis business. I'm sure Radha and Ian would agree with me that what Trick is proposing makes sense. If the details can be worked out."

In other words, Lizzie would be outvoted if she objected to Zee.

I hid my wince of sympathy. Lizzie could handle herself, and I was sure she'd be professional about this, but as her friend, I wanted to object. But when it came to the Cestis, I didn't have anything approaching a vote. I was their current object of interest, and they liked me well enough, but I wasn't one of them. Particularly if my only real argument was "I don't think Lizzie and Zee like each other much."

Or, at least, I didn't think Lizzie liked Zee much. How he felt remained to be seen.

"Damon, what do you think?"

He wasn't Cestis either, but it was his tournament. He definitely had the power to say no. But Cassandra had played a card that I didn't think he would be able to ignore: my safety.

"If Mitch says okay, and Zee can embed himself into a team, I think it's a good idea," he said. "The final roster of teams and the schedule for the heats will be announced at the gala, so we can make it work. It shouldn't be a big deal. Well, not any more of a big deal than the Diablos making a crew change would usually be. That will bring some attention, so you all better be sure this is the play you want to make."

"He understands," Cassandra said. "How about you organize a meeting with Mitch, and we'll go from there."

"It will need to be tomorrow," Damon said. "Maggie has her surgery Tuesday."

Cassandra nodded. "Tomorrow, then. Let us know when."

CHAPTER FIVE

I STILL FOUND it odd to see Cassandra at the Riley Arts office. She seemed out of place in such a glass-and-steel temple to technology. Lizzie fit right in with her wild hair and clunky boots, but Cassandra never looked entirely at ease.

It wasn't her age. Not all Damon's employees were young. He valued talent, and while there were plenty of bright young things in the programming and design teams, there was a balance of thirties and forties and older staff, too.

Mitch, with his sandy gray hair and bright blue eyes, looked closer in age to Cassandra than the rest of us. When I'd first met him, just a few short months ago, there'd been more sand and less silver in his hair. But the last few months had taken a toll.

The knowledge that someone he had trusted to be his second in charge had been the one to try and take out Damon had carved extra lines into his craggy face. Throw in something the size of the tournament for him to manage, and I guessed he wasn't getting much sleep.

Next to him sat Maia Lin, one of the new members of his team, her "don't notice me" gray suit and white shirt hugging her curves. Recruited for both her magic and her security skills. Her black hair was braided back into a ponytail off her face, her only real concessions to vanity the killer flick of perfect eyeliner setting off her brown eyes and the darker red gloss slicked over her lips.

She didn't look like a martial arts guru, but she'd kicked my butt without breaking a sweat the first time she'd given me a self-defense lesson and had proceeded to run rings around me in every session since. Anyone who looked at her, saw her body and her sunny smile, and dismissed her as a curvy girl who couldn't possibly be a threat would be in for a nasty surprise. She could shoot, fight, and, if she had to, take them out with magic.

I was more than happy to have her on the team. On *my* team specifically, given she was the one who'd be taking my detail during the tournament. That told me she was probably even more of a badass than I realized. Damon wouldn't settle for anything less when it came to keeping me safe. His own team, usually several of them now, tended to look more like your stereotypical security guys, but those were the ones who were supposed to stand out. There were others who, like Zee, were supposed to go unnoticed. I was never entirely sure how many people were guarding him at any moment. Which was how it was supposed to be.

Zee and Trick seemed unfazed to be surrounded by the security team in a meeting room several levels underground.

Trick had raised an eyebrow the first time Madge, the Riley Arts computer system, had spoken when we'd been scanned into the building, but Zee had smiled. He looked more awake this morning, taking in the surroundings with interest. He had on a variation of the denim and hoodie outfit he'd worn before, in various shades of gray and black, but he had a leather messenger bag slung over his shoulder rather than the backpack.

Lizzie carefully selected a seat as far away from him as possible while staying on the same side of the table so she wouldn't have to look across at him.

I'd probed a little more to see if she wanted to talk when we'd gotten home from the Archives. Damon had worked upstairs while we waited for takeout. She'd shut me down fast and hard, so I'd backed off.

Mitch made the introductions, then settled back

in his seat. "Ms. Tallant, you asked for the meeting. Do you want to start things off?"

Cassandra nodded and then outlined the plan for Zee to join one of the teams.

"And Trueno Diablo are okay with this?" Mitch asked, sounding skeptical. "We got their final team roster a few days ago."

"You'll get an email soon," Zee said softly. "I spoke to Carlo last night. It will be chill."

Mitch sipped his coffee, studying Zee's face. "You work fast."

Zee leaned back in his chair, seemingly unbothered by the remark. "Carlo's a friend. He's happy to help. It's in the team's interests if everything is icy at the tournament."

"The Diablo have never declared a team member with magic before," Mitch said. "That could pull some attention."

"Actually, they had one back in the day," Zee said. "Not me, but there's a precedent."

"If he has to be declared, how does that help with undercover?" I asked.

"We don't disclose the names of the players with magic. That would be a breach of privacy," Damon said. "We know who they are, so we can monitor those teams if needed. That's enough."

I hadn't thought about that. But I'd had a bit of a crash course in the legalities surrounding witches in the last few months alongside everything else. There were certain limited situations, like this one, where a witch could be asked to declare their abilities. Otherwise, it was illegal to ask. And illegal to disclose their names without permission if you knew, other than in, again, limited circumstances.

It hadn't always been that way, but the Cestis had had those laws passed a few decades ago.

"He won't be the only one," Damon said. "Several of the top teams have members with magic. The usual rules apply. Which won't be a problem for Zee. He's going in to keep an eye out for interference, not to play."

The usual rules being that any players with magic weren't supposed to use their abilities in the game. It was a condition of every game club I'd ever been in. It had been one of the reasons I'd felt comfortable in the clubs back in the day. Even though I'd mostly watched Nat play rather than competed, game clubs were places that were free from magic, and I'd been all about avoiding magic where I could.

In reality, that rule wasn't well policed at the lower levels because those clubs didn't necessarily have the means to hire witches to monitor for magic use. Besides which, the money involved at that level wasn't worth the effort of cheating. But the top leagues involved big money, and they, and the big tournaments like this one, could afford to enforce the rules. Using magic in-game would get a team disqualified. Possibly barred for life.

I didn't know whether it had ever happened—though I was going to look it up.

"We've never had an incident with magic in any of our tournaments," Mitch said. "Our reputation is solid."

An understatement. The top gamers in every country had been moving heaven and earth to get a slot in the tournament even with the short time frame to qualify.

"Won't it be kind of obvious, if they lodge a notification that they now have a magic user on their team and Zee is the only new member?"

"He's not the only new member," Damon said. "They've changed up their tech team slightly, and two of their subs were in a car accident a few months ago. Bad concussions and a few broken bones. Neither of them is gaming again yet, and the Diablos have been recruiting. There's been a lot of buzz around who they might announce. They have a history of making some out-of-the-box choices. That will pull more attention than them adding an-other tech guy." He looked at Zee. "Was that part of the reason for choosing them? You knew they were short on their roster?"

Zee shook his head. "I've been out of touch

with Carlo for a bit. I was out of the country. So, no. It came down to us being friends." He nodded at Damon. "I don't want to mess that up. If there's any blowback about this at any point, it falls on me, yeah? They shouldn't be punished for helping out."

"Unless they break the rules, they won't be," Damon said. "This is all just an extra precaution. There's no reason to think there'll be any trouble."

Mitch half snorted.

"No more reason than usual," Damon amended.

The gamer leagues were big business, and big money came with temptations to try and manipulate things. The prize on offer was large, sure, but the real draw was the reveal of the new game and access to the new technology that went along with it. But Righteous was used to handling game tournaments and security. And managing the release of new tech.

Though I was a wild card factor. Me and the magic that kept drawing the wrong kind of attention.

But the demon was gone, and its lesserkind had been burned to ash. The last few months had been uneventful. There was no reason to think anyone was trying for me again.

Cassandra had said premonitions were unreliable. We were prepared. It was all going to be fine.

It had to be.

"Okay, so Zee slots into the Diablos and keeps an eye out for anything weird," I said. "Trick hangs with Lizzie and is another pair of eyes on the ground, even if some people might know they both have magic. The rest of the team does their thing. Nothing to worry about. Unless I spill champagne on the wrong person at the gala."

It was a lame joke, but it broke the tension, and Damon wrapped up the meeting fast.

Once we were back outside, I hung back with Lizzie, leaving the others to walk ahead. "Are you sure you're okay with this?"

"I'm fine," she said. "I like Trick. He's good company."

"And Zee?"

"Zee is going to have plenty to keep him busy," she said. "The Diablos will work him hard."

"You hadn't mentioned you knew Carlo before." I figured she'd probably change the subject again, but hey, it was an opening if she wanted to take it.

She hunched her shoulders. "It's not as though we've spent a lot of time talking about the game leagues. And it was a long time ago."

Apparently that was "No." But I wanted to be sure she was okay. "You're twenty-four. It can't have been that long."

"It was a whole other life. None of us are who we were back then." She straightened, snapping her chin up. "I'm fine, Maggie. Don't worry about me. You have plenty to think about as well. Like surgery."

I wasn't sure if she was just changing the subject or telling me to back off by bringing up something she knew I wasn't keen to talk about.

I shrugged. "You all keep telling me there's nothing to worry about with surgery. So I'm not worrying."

"You're staying at Damon's tonight?"

"Yes. My admission at the clinic is early. Yoshi and I got through the admin for that last job I did, so my schedule is officially free. So is his."

Gaming was popular across the board, but the core audience was still college kids and teenagers. High schoolers had their own leagues, and there was a category for them in the tournament, but the pro leagues required you to be over eighteen. A lot of the large tournaments were held over the summer. Righteous had just squeaked in starting mid-August. It was late for some schools, but any college kids who were pros had to be used to missing classes. Hell, some colleges had leagues as well.

"He's revved about the tournament. And the hackathon," Lizzie said. "It's all he talks about."

"Tell me about it." I smiled, thinking of Yoshi's chatter. "He works hard. He deserves it," I said. Besides, I'd have to be a bitch to deny my gamehead intern tickets to my boyfriend's tournament. Yoshi had only been working with me a few months, but he was worth his weight in gold. Lizzie and I had finally told him that we both had magic after the first few weeks, and he'd simply said "Yep, worked that much out," and gone back to work.

He'd said nothing about having magic of his own and hadn't shown any interest in finding out. He had the same kind of intuitive feel for tech that I did. He'd won his place at the hackathon Righteous was running at their offices during the tournament with his skills, nothing to do with me or Damon.

When I'd lost my connection to my power, my ability to figure out the kind of obscure tech problems that people paid me big bucks to solve had vanished as well. I hadn't lost any of my knowledge, but the sparks of connection that helped me hunt down the tiny section of code causing unexpected consequences had died. Luckily, I'd gotten my power back before it became a problem.

In Yoshi's case, his feel for tech might just be sheer brainpower. Damon had no magic, and he was a tech genius. If Yoshi didn't want to know anything about magic, then I wasn't going to push him. He had enough on his plate between work and school and trying to negotiate for at least partial custody of his sister. He deserved some fun.

And he was smart. He wouldn't do anything to

jeopardize the life he was building for himself and Aoki. I'd only met her a few times, but she seemed as clever as her big brother. I was already planning for there to be another convenient scholarship for her college if that's where she was headed. But she had high school to get through first.

"He deserves to blow off some steam," I said to Lizzie. "So do you. You're not going to spend all your time working the crowd for Spark, are you?"

She smiled. "I can have fun and get donations. But no. The gala is work, but the tournament will be different." She blew her pale pink bangs out of her eyes. "You sure you're ready for this?"

"Everyone needs to stop asking me that," I said. "It's not like I'm marrying the King of England. I can handle being in the newsfeeds now and then."

"Damon *is* kind of the king of the tech world."

"Parts of it. There's a lot more to tech than entertainment and VR." Though VR was spreading its tentacles. "Anyway, I'm not marrying the man."

"Yet," Lizzie said with a grin.

"We're a long way from anything near that," I said, but I couldn't stop myself looking ahead to where Damon was walking with Cassandra. He glanced over his shoulder as though he felt my attention and grinned. I smiled goofily, then focused back on Lizzie.

She rolled her eyes. "He should just buy a ring already. You two are gone."

"Don't get too cocky. You know what happens to people who are in love. I might start trying to fix your love life." Lizzie dated off and on, but she hadn't been serious with anyone in the time I'd known her.

"Like you said, I'm twenty-four. I have plenty of time."

"Maybe you'll fall for a hot gamer," I said.

She shook her head, expression suddenly fierce. "Nope. No gamers."

"People change," I said softly.

"Sometimes," she said. "But not everyone deserves a second chance."

The chip surgery went smoothly. Well, smoothly apart from the fact that I'd spent most of the night fighting not to throw up from nerves.

I had smiled at Dr. Barnard and said all the right things, but he'd maybe seen through me and taken extra time to reassure me that they'd done everything possible to ensure I wouldn't have a reaction to the chip this time. And then he'd given me something to take away the anxiety on top of the usual nerve block.

I'd spent the surgery with Damon holding my other hand, just like the first time I'd had a chip installed. Only this time I didn't have to act like I didn't care whether he did. Last time he'd made shadow puppets on the wall of the operating room to distract me. This time he just talked softly about nothing in particular, and I floated in a haze.

Toward the end of the surgery, Meredith Dempsey, one of the healers who worked at St. Isidore's, the hospital Dr. Barnard's clinic was attached to, came into the room. She'd said something to me, and I nodded but didn't really take it in.

She peered closer, then shrugged and rested her fingertips on my forehead for a time. Her magic had glowed around her, a soothing pale blue, but in my half-stoned state, I just stared at the light, then eventually closed my eyes. When I opened them again, she'd gone, and Dr. Barnard was removing the screen he'd put up to block my view of my left arm while he worked.

"All done," he said. "How are you feeling?"

"Good," I smiled, still mostly floating. "You have the good stuff."

He laughed. "Apparently so." He looked at Damon. "I can give her something to reverse the antianxiety med, but she seems happy. Take her home and let her sleep it off. I've sent the aftercare instructions to both your datapads, but you know the drill."

"Of course. Thank you." Damon leaned across and shook the doctor's hand, and his own chip glinted gold across my line of sight.

I turned my head to study my wrist. There was a clear surgical shield over the small wound, but it didn't hide the metallic gleam of the chip. "Look, we match now," I said to Damon, lifting my wrist to show him.

He grinned and gently caught my forearm, lowering it back down to rest across my chest. "We do," he agreed. "But then, we always did." He bent and kissed the tip of my nose. "Now, how about we get the doc to give you a sling so you don't keep waving that around, and I'll take you home?"

The next morning, I woke up alone in Damon's bed with very little memory of how I'd gotten there. Until I rolled over and my wrist protested.

"Ow," I said as the events of the day before came rushing back.

As if on cue, the door to the bedroom opened, and Damon came through, carrying a tray. "Hey, you're awake."

He set the tray down on the nightstand. Coffee, toast, bacon. A vase with a single yellow daisy. And a glass of iced water. It all looked and smelled wonderful. "How are you feeling?"

"Good," I said. I tried to lever myself up in bed, and my wrist pinged again. "But ow."

"Gotta use that other arm," he said. He reached

into his pocket and pulled out an orange tube of pills. "You're due for one of these."

I pulled a face. "It's not that bad."

"The gala is in three days. You are going to rest and follow doctor's orders. A day or two of these and you'll be good as new."

I knew he was right. But now that I wasn't dreading the surgery, my usual dislike of drugs resurfaced. Anything that left me foggy-headed and feeling out of control made me nervous. Nothing that had happened in the last year had changed that. Control was more important to me than ever. I needed to see what was coming at me. But Damon was right. I also needed to recover. And if there was anywhere I was safe, it was here. In a big expensive house on a gated block with the best security money could buy monitoring the situation.

I wasn't going to let fear rule my life. I couldn't. Not if I was going to be with Damon.

I held out my good hand. "Give me the damn pill."

By Thursday I felt mostly normal. My wrist ached on and off, but I wasn't going to be doing anything overly strenuous at the gala. At my follow-up appointment, Dr. Barnard had me connect briefly to a VR deck, and everything worked perfectly.

When I'd disconnected, he studied my wrist again. "Nothing odd happening since the procedure?"

I shook my head. "No, it's been fine." The weekend after my first surgery had been strange. Lights dying and screens turning on and off and a few other weird things. Those had been the first signs that that chip had interfered with my magic. Or rather interfered with the magical bond that had bound me to a demon and made my magic mine to control again. But nothing like that had happened at Damon's house. I'd napped and rested while he worked.

"You let me know if anything feels different," Dr. Barnard continued. "I'd tell you to take it easy, but I'm guessing that might be pointless."

"Damon's the one who'll be working," I said. "I get to enjoy the tournament."

Dr. Barnard raised an eyebrow, and I added, "I'm not playing, don't worry."

I wanted to heal more before I attempted a full VR environment. A simple short session like the doctor had tried didn't put any strain on the chip or the nerves it connected to, but full VR was different. The chip sent data into the nervous system at a rate that fooled the brain into believing it was real. I didn't want to blow it out by rushing things.

"Good," Dr. Barnard said. "And you're going to see Meredith?"

"I'm meeting her at Cassandra's store," I said. "They'll do their thing."

Lizzie had already checked me several times. She hadn't seen anything different with my magic, but I'd feel better with a second and third opinion. If Cassandra and Meredith said my magic hadn't changed, I'd believe them.

"Well, then, perhaps I'll see you at the gala to-morrow night," Dr. Barnard said.

I smiled. "That would be lovely. Nice to have some friendly faces in the crowd." It didn't surprise me that he was on the guest list. As one of the top chip surgeons in the country, he earned enough to be invited to charity galas. Though there would be other guests who had the kind of money that made even someone like Barnard seem working class.

Wealth that vast was difficult to understand. When I'd been with my mother, we'd usually been either flush with enough cash to make life fun for a week or just getting by. I'd lived in dodgy places and gone hungry plenty of times. My grandparents had been comfortable, but they'd been careful, too, and they hadn't just given me everything I wanted.

I respected money. I appreciated that I'd done well in my career and could support myself. But being around people who could snap their fingers and, well, probably buy one of the small towns Sara had dragged me around to—or all of them—was daunting.

Damon was one of them, of course, but I knew him now. Knew he was a person separate to what the rest of his life was. I was doing my best to try and keep that in mind for the gala. Everyone there was just another person who put their pants on one leg at a time. I had to give them a chance if I was going to live in their world.

CHAPTER SIX

THE SMELL of Cassandra's store as I opened the door settled over me like a comfortable old cardigan. The mix of oils and spices and the polish she used on the wooden shelves was as familiar as my own house. Apparently it had become the smell of safety.

My shoulders relaxed as I closed the door, the tinkle of the bell fading away. Maia had driven me but had stayed in the car, leaving me to talk with Meredith and Cassandra in private.

I wasn't worried. Few things were strong enough to take Cassandra out on her own turf, let alone her *and* Meredith.

And that was a thought that was slightly paranoid. There was no reason to think that anything would be coming after me here. I took another breath, letting the smell chase away the idea.

Cassandra was behind the counter, wrapping up some purchases for a customer. She smiled at me and pointed at the stairs. The blond woman she was serving glanced over her shoulder, curiosity lighting her eyes. I didn't recognize her, but many of the people who shopped at Cassandra's were actual witches rather than just humans with an interest in herbs and aromatherapy.

After all, if you were after magical supplies, then buying from a store run by one of the Cestis guaranteed quality. The store did good business, despite the fact that it wasn't in the best part of town.

The woman at the counter looked like she might have been out for a run, her teal T-shirt showing off suntanned arms and a heavy-looking smart watch that no doubt fed all her stats back to her datapad. I peeked at her energy field and was rewarded with a glow of sunny yellow. Not that it told me much. A witch who wasn't using magic and a normal human looked pretty similar.

I just smiled and headed for the stairs, ascending cautiously, trying to avoid the worst of the squeaky spots on the old treads. Upstairs was the small room that Cassandra used to do the odd private consultation or take her breaks. Beyond it was an even smaller kitchen where Meredith stood at the sink, filling the kettle. Her long brown hair was caught up in a messy bun, and the faded jeans and pale green sweater she wore were a change from the hospital scrubs or lab coat that I usually saw her wearing.

"Maggie, hi," she said, looking up as a floorboard squeaked beneath my feet. "Tea?"

"Real tea?" I asked. Cassandra had a taste for herbal concoctions that were sometimes ghastly. She said they were good for me, but that was no real consolation when you were drinking something that tasted vaguely like compost. Or worse.

Meredith smiled. "Sure. No reason why you shouldn't have caffeine." She moved the kettle to the counter and plugged it in. "How are you feeling?"

"Good," I said, taking a seat at the tiny table. As usual, one of Cassandra's cookie jars sat on it, and I reached for it. A sugar fix sounded like just what the doctor ordered. Even more than the tea. "Doc Barnard says everything looks good."

"I know. He messaged me," Meredith said. "And you haven't noticed anything unusual?"

"No, nothing." I opened the cookie jar, hoping for chocolate chip. But the scent of cinnamon wafted up to me. Snickerdoodles. Almost as good. I grabbed a couple. Cassandra was a baking goddess, and I'd yet to try one of her cookies I didn't like.

Meredith slid a plate onto the table in front of me. "Here. Don't drop crumbs."

"Do you want one?" I offered the jar.

"No, I'm good, thanks."

She looked past me, and I heard footsteps on the stairs as the kettle began to beep. Meredith turned back to it as Cassandra came through the doorway.

"Sorry," she said. "I've put the Closed sign up now. We won't get interrupted." She stretched her neck and rolled her shoulders.

"Are your hands bothering you?" Meredith asked.

Cassandra shook her head, smiling. "Just a busy morning, dear. I'm fine. But thank you." Today she wore emerald, the color extra bright in the sunshine. "How was your appointment, Maggie?"

"Doc Barnard says the chip is working fine."

"Good," Cassandra said. She pulled out the chair next to mine and sat. Meredith put a cup of tea in front of her, then passed me a spotted blue mug. She joined us with her own cup cradled between her hands a few seconds later.

I blew on my tea and then sipped. Meredith had added just the right amount of sugar, and the hot sweet tea washed the last of the stale taste of my nerves out of my mouth. I'd been bracing myself for Dr. Barnard to tell me something had gone wrong with the surgery and the chip wasn't working.

Apparently I'd worried for nothing. That was one hurdle cleared.

Meredith and Cassandra's tests would be the next one. The one I really should have been more nervous about. But I'd take tea and cookies over doctor's offices and surgery any day.

"Are you sure this is a good time?" I asked.

Cassandra shrugged. "We'll be fine for an hour or so. I don't want to miss the lunch rush."

It was close to 11:00 a.m., so hopefully that meant whatever Cassandra and Meredith had planned to test the chip and my magic wasn't going to take too long.

"We should get started, then. I don't want to keep you away from the customers."

I had the final fitting of my gala dress at three. Which was something I'd never expected to have to slot into my calendar. I was pretty much an off-the-shelf or online shopper. With body scans and other tricks, it was easy to find clothes that fit. But a charity gala hosted by Riley Arts required a gown, not just a dress. And not the kind that came from any store I usually shopped at.

Damon had suggested a few designers, and Lizzie had narrowed down his list. It had been a strange experience, to have an actual human measuring me for clothes and to choose fabric and discuss the nuances of color and style with someone who understood them the way I understood code.

Strange, but also more enjoyable than I'd expected.

The final quote had been eye-watering, but I'd paid happily. I had the money, and while it seemed inevitable that Damon would try to start funding my wardrobe if this kind of thing became a regular occurrence, for now I'd keep paying my own way. No doubt there'd be gossip about me being a gold digger once we went public. I wasn't going to give them any ammunition.

But in order for me to go public, I had to make it to the final fitting. Serissa, the designer, had offered to come to see me at Damon's house, but I didn't want to take time out of her day when I was in the city anyway. Even though I might need something more than tea and cookies to get me through the afternoon.

I was only taking ibuprofen for the last edge of the ache from the surgery now but still felt tired and slightly foggy as the heavier medications worked their way out of my system. Being out and about would do me good, but so would a hefty dose of caffeine.

I fought the urge to yawn. "We can get started whenever you're ready."

"Have you been sleeping?" Meredith asked, frowning. She knew my history of nightmares. Sleep and I weren't always the best of friends, though I slept better with Damon next to me.

"I've done little *but* sleep the last few days. It's just the tail end of the meds. You know how it is."

"I do. I can also do something about that," she said. "But that will have to come after the testing. If I give you a boost now, it might mess with your energy flows. We need to be able to see what the chip is doing with no interference."

That made sense. Magic, as witches saw it, was just the manipulation of energy. If the chip had changed my magic again, there'd be a difference in my energy field. Or at least that was the theory we'd come up with.

"What do you want me to do?" I asked.

"Nothing hard," Cassandra said. "We'll give you some tasks, and we'll see how you do at them." She rose and went over to one of the cabinets, then came back to the table with a familiar-looking candle in a silver candlestick. "Let's start with something basic."

I bit back a sigh. Lighting a candle had been one of the first things I'd learned to do with magic. It had also been the task that had nearly driven me crazy when I'd lost my magic. Trying to light one over and over and failing repeatedly meant it wasn't one of my favorite things to practice now. Even though Cassandra and Lizzie both still insisted I did. I was pretty sure I could light a candle with both eyes closed if I had to.

Still, I hadn't tried to use my magic since the

surgery, and my stomach twisted nervously. What if something *had* gone wrong?

Just get it over with.

I stared at the candle. Let my vision shift to the place where I saw the glow of energy around all the objects in the room.

See the energy. Change the energy.

I snapped my fingers, and the wick ignited into a perfectly sized flame. A smile of satisfaction crept across my face. "Next?"

Cassandra nodded at me and then looked at Meredith. "I didn't feel anything different. You?"

Meredith shook her head. "That looked normal to me. Maggie, how did it feel to you?"

"Like it always does." As far as I could tell. Lighting it didn't exactly take much effort.

"Well, that's promising," Cassandra said. "Let's try a few other things." She pointed at the candle. "Set a ward around it so I can't blow it out."

"Really?" Warding wasn't an area I felt confident in. I didn't even know Lizzie had told Cassandra we'd been practicing.

Wards could be used for all kinds of things. Warnings. Protection. But one that would block a physical action was more complicated than one that would just provide an alert. And I hadn't tried doing it to something as small as a candle. And there was the flame, dancing around on the wick. Moving. How would I even shield that?

"I'm not sure—" I started to say.

"It doesn't have to be perfect," Meredith said. "But we need you to try a more complicated working. Gives us more time to see what's happening with your magic. Just do what you can."

"Think of the exercises from the Justinian grimoire," Cassandra said. "Start simple."

She'd definitely been talking to Lizzie. The Justinian grimoire was not my favorite book. And the copy I was using was a translation from Latin, not the original. Lizzie had not yet bullied me into learning Latin, though she and most of the Cestis seemed to know it and several other ancient languages. Translated into English, Justinian, whoever he had been, had the personality of a dead log, and his dry descriptions of how energy should be arranged to construct wards sucked all the fun out of it. But his methods were the simplest, according to Lizzie, and so far, I wasn't being given the choice to learn any others.

So boring dead Roman magician it was. I studied the candlestick. A ward that wouldn't let a breath of air through. That meant convincing the air around the flame that it was more solid. But the flame itself still needed oxygen. It was an interesting puzzle, and I forgot about Cassandra and Meredith watching me as I worked my way through it in my head.

By the time I started to try and work the magic,

picturing the air becoming tiny clear boards to form a wall around the flame, the room around me might as well not have been there. I actually jumped when Cassandra touched my arm and said, "Not bad."

"Did it work?" I asked.

She leaned toward the candle. Blew out a breath. The flame flickered, but it didn't extinguish. "You were on the right path," she said, "but there were gaps. Still, as I said, not bad. We'll have to see if we can get you some time with Trick after the tournament. He's a master at warding."

I nodded. "If he has time."

"He'll make time. He likes teaching, too. It's why he's good with the younger witches, like Zee and Lizzie."

"Lizzie doesn't seem like she has much to learn," I said.

"There's always more to learn," Cassandra said reprovingly. "Lizzie didn't know much when I first met her."

"And Zee?" I asked. She'd said he was good at illusions back in the Archives, but if the Cestis trusted him with undercover work, that couldn't be his only talent.

"He's a bit of a generalist other than his illusions. He doesn't have the raw power of some, but his control is excellent. Which comes in handy doing what he's been doing." She and Meredith exchanged a look.

"I'd ask what he's been doing, but I'm guessing you wouldn't tell me."

"Not yet," Cassandra agreed.

"He didn't get hurt, did he?" I asked.

Meredith tilted her head. "What makes you ask that?"

I frowned, trying to figure out the answer. "He felt...tired. More than just jet-lag tired."

Meredith raised an eyebrow. "Did you get any other feelings about him?"

"No. And he looks healthy enough. Maybe it's just me being fanciful."

"Or maybe not," Meredith said. "I'll make sure someone talks to him. Even if he's physically fine, the kind of thing he was doing can take a different sort of toll." She smiled approvingly. "But we were talking about you, not Zee."

Cassandra nodded. "Did the ward feel unusual in any way?"

I shook my head. "I don't know if I've done enough of them to be able to tell. But no. Did you see anything different?"

Both of them shook their heads in unison.

"Well, that's two out of two, then," I said. "Anything else?"

The clock hung above the door to the stairs told me we'd spent thirty minutes on this already. Which meant I'd been so focused on the ward that I'd lost track of time somewhere along the line.

"Do you think you can try an illusion?" Cassandra said. "Something simple. Make the candle look like it's not lit?"

"I have no idea." I hadn't tried any illusions yet.

"It's just bending the light, at the simplest. In this case, removing the image of the flame. Think of what the candle looked like before you lit it. Then build that image to replace what we see."

"That doesn't entirely make sense."

"Think of it like virtual reality," Meredith suggested. "How does that fool the brain?"

"Honestly, I'm not 100 percent on how that works either. Damon might be better at illusions than me," I said. "I mean, I get how you design a virtual environment, but the neurological part is above my pay grade." The kinds of systems I dealt with were complicated, but not in the same way as a VR network. I stared down at the chip on my wrist.

"Maybe we should try something else," Meredith said. "If Maggie hasn't done much illusion work, then she might not even be able to tell if something felt off. She's still recovering from the surgery. She can't push too hard."

I smiled gratefully at her.

"Maybe you need some lessons with Zee, too," Cassandra said.

"Not sure Lizzie would appreciate that. I'm sure she can teach me illusions when I'm ready."

"You need to learn from more than one person."

"I already have you and Lizzie and Radha," I pointed out. "Ian, too. That seems like plenty. Besides, you told me to focus on the tournament."

"Recognizing a glamour might be a useful skill for that," Cassandra said. "I'd imagine some of the people at the gala might utilize one."

Some people used beauty illusions. To me, it seemed like a hassle. I had agreed to a hair and makeup artist for tomorrow night because Lizzie had threatened to do my hair herself if I didn't. And I didn't trust her not to turn it green. I wasn't bad at makeup when I wanted to wear it, but as Lizzie had pointed out, I needed to make a good impression, and I was going to be filmed and photographed. Better to leave it to a professional.

"Well, it's a bit late for me to add that to the repertoire now. Zee's going to be busy. We'll have to make do. Now, is there anything else you want me to try?"

Cassandra considered for a moment. "No. Meredith's right. We shouldn't push. There's no sign of anything being wrong. You go do whatever you need to do, and we'll talk after the gala."

CHAPTER SEVEN

"LAST CHANCE TO BACK OUT," Damon said as he tied his bow tie with practiced motions. I stood in the middle of the lounge room, trying to not succumb to temptation and sit down. I didn't want to wrinkle my dress, even though Serissa had assured me I couldn't crush nano silk.

Besides, it felt wrong to lounge about in a gown that was close to a work of art. The first time I'd tried it on and seen it in the mirror, I'd been tempted to have it framed. Serissa was worth every penny.

Boyd would be arriving in a few minutes to take us to the gala, so I'd find out whether or not she was right.

Damon's tone was light, but his expression in the mirror was serious. He finished his tie with one final tug and turned back to me.

He'd give me the out, if I wanted it. Though where that would leave us, I wasn't sure. We couldn't hide away forever.

"What, and waste all this effort?" I asked, keeping my voice light. "I had three fittings for this dress. And I'm wearing heels. Expensive heels." I did a slow twirl, smiling even though there was a whole swarm of butterflies doing more than just fluttering in my stomach. The skirt swished around me, then settled again, the silk gleaming.

"I can appreciate all that effort by myself," Damon said, moving closer. "You look beautiful." He leaned in and kissed me lightly, not messing with the deep red lipstick the makeup artist who'd just left had spent way too much time applying. "I'm happy not to share."

"Oh no, this was all your idea. We're going to go get this show on the road."

He straightened with a smile. "In that case, I think you need these." He pulled a dark green velvet-covered case from his pocket. The kind expensive jewelry came in.

I eyed it suspiciously. "What's that?"

"Just a little something to say thank you for going along with the dog and pony show."

He held the case out, and I took it warily.

"Open it," he prompted gently.

I stroked the velvet with a finger. "You don't need to buy me gifts."

"I know. But I want to. Open it."

The lid lifted as smoothly as the velvet slid under my skin. Nestled inside was a pair of earrings. Not huge but large enough to be noticed. The stones sparkled in the light. Emeralds and diamonds and a paler green stone falling in short fringes from a teardrop filigree base. Beautiful. And probably worth more than most of my wardrobe put together. Including my gown.

I wanted to protest that it was too much, but I doubted it would do any good. And would probably only hurt Damon's feelings. "They're glorious. How did you know to get green?"

He smiled. "I wanted something that matched your eyes."

"Smooth," I said, but the butterflies changed for a moment into a warm pleased glow. "Lucky for you I didn't go with blue or bright yellow."

"Green will always look good on you," he said. "Green like those eyes, Maggie mine. The pale ones are peridots. Good for protection."

I blinked. "You looked that up?" Or had he perhaps gotten some hints from Lizzie? Either way, the thought of him taking the time to make sure the stones were perfect made me smile.

"Just covering the bases." He lifted the box from my hands and detached one of the earrings, holding it out to me. "Put them on."

I eased the wire into my ear, repeating the action with the second when he handed it to me. The weight of the stones was less than I'd expected. "How do they look?"

"Perfect," Damon said. He leaned in and pressed a kiss to the side of my neck, and I shivered in pleasure. He pulled back and nodded at the mirror. "Take a look."

I hardly recognized the woman reflected there. Between the silk draped around my body, Damon's stones sparking green light at my ears, and the immaculate hair and makeup, I could've been an avatar. Though I'd never bothered to make my avatars look this perfect. I tilted my head, watching the emeralds and peridots shimmer.

I wasn't perfect, and maybe Damon wasn't either. But he was perfect for me. I needed to get used to the version of me reflected in the glass, because I had the feeling I was going to be seeing more of her.

The camera flashes and viddrone lights surrounded us even before Boyd pulled the limousine to the curb. Damon reached for my hand. "They can't see through the windows, don't worry."

"I'm not worried," I said. "I look great." I stuck my tongue out, trying to make him laugh. It might have been more bravado than truth—at least the part about not being worried—but it worked.

"You want me to go round back instead, boss?" Boyd's voice came through the intercom.

"No," Damon said. "The detail will be waiting for us here. We'll be fine." He squeezed my hand. "Just wait until you get the ping from Maia before you open the door."

"Sure thing." The limo came to a stop, but the engine kept humming.

The car had some sort of shielding on it, deadening the noise from both ways. I leaned closer to the window, peering out. A pack of media and photographers waited at the end of the red carpet, yelling at us and waving their cameras and vidcorders. Tiny drones whirred overhead as well. The expressions of the pack, ranging from curiosity to a sort of avid hunger, set the butterflies whirling again.

I sucked in a breath. Let it out. Took another.

"Maia and the guys are almost at the door, boss." Boyd's voice came through, and the screen that separated the driver's compartment from the passengers slid down. "You ready?"

Damon looked at me. I pasted on a smile and nodded.

"We're good," Damon said. His grip tightened on my hand. "I'm out first. Then I'll help you. Maia will be on your left side once we're out, Mitch out front, and the other guys behind us. It might be crowded for the first few steps, but the press can't follow us onto the red carpet, so you'll only have to deal with them for a minute max."

"I know, I remember the drill," I said. We'd practiced this part, getting out of the car, letting a security team get into place around us. It was weird but not difficult. The difficult part would come as soon as everyone out there started to file their stories and post on their socials. When I officially became Damon's girlfriend—or whatever they were going to call me—in the eyes of the world.

I took another breath and straightened my shoulders as the limo door eased open and Maia's smiling face appeared.

I could take whatever they were going to throw at me.

The next minute or so was a bit of a blur, but not too bad. Loud as hell and bright and too many people crowded too close, but the team hustled us through the crowd of press and onto the carpet outside the Phenix faster than I'd expected. Maia inspected me as we caught our breath and gave me a discreet thumbs-up, which I took to mean Serissa had told the truth, the dress had survived the limo ride unwrinkled, and nothing else had been too rumpled in the process.

I smiled back as Damon's assistant, Cat, glided up to us, looking elegant in a steel-gray satin gown and simple silver jewelry. She wore a tiny earpiece that I probably wouldn't have noticed if I hadn't known to look. Damon and I wore them, too. His had a live feed, Cat or Mitch able to give him information. Mine would only turn on in an emergency. I had to concentrate on remembering names and faces and what I was supposed to be doing, and I'd decided the chatter of Mitch's team would only distract me.

"Everything is ready inside," she said. "Maggie, you look lovely."

"Thank you," I said. Cat still wasn't my biggest fan, but she seemed to have accepted that I wasn't going anywhere, and her attitude had thawed. Fractionally. My presence in Damon's life had caused a lot of chaos, so I didn't blame her for resenting me. And I knew I could trust her. She might not like me, but she had too much pride in her work to do anything less than a stellar job for Damon. Even if that meant she had to do a stellar job for me.

"You only have to talk to News 256. They're the official media outlet," Cat said. "The rest is just photographs unless you want to answer any questions. News 256's correspondent is Ellie Luna. Dark hair, violet gown." She tipped her head in the direction of the hotel, where a young woman who fit that description was talking to a guy in a tuxedo about halfway down the red carpet.

"Got it," Damon said. "Maggie, you okay?"

"Ready as I'll ever be."

Cat nodded. "Okay, I'll meet you back inside." She disappeared off to one side.

Damon offered me his arm, and I took it, smiling. Just him and me. That was all that mattered. "Let's go."

I let him do the talking and smiled and stood still for photographs as we made our way down the red carpet and into the relative safety of the foyer, where Cat joined us again.

"Okay?" Damon asked as heads immediately turned in our direction. The Phenix's foyer seemed huge, all honey-colored marble and gilt and tinted mirrors that made it hard to get a sense of how big the room really was. Which didn't really matter. Whatever the size, it was full of people dressed in expensive evening clothes who apparently found the sight of the two of us fascinating.

Looking at their curious faces, I wasn't sure that maybe the press wasn't the easy part. They had to follow rules. These people didn't. I tried not to feel like a bunny about to try and survive dinner with a pack of curious and not necessarily friendly wolves.

"Everything went well outside?" Cat asked. Damon nodded, and she smiled briefly. "Okay. The Arctos datapads that are guest gifts are on the tables," she said. "Yours have both been activated, and, Maggie, I've sent a copy of the guest files to yours if you need any refreshers."

"Thanks. That might come in handy," I said. Along with Mitch's security training, I'd had briefings from Cat on who all the important guests were at the gala, and she'd done her best to make sure I wouldn't make a fool of myself. My own datapad was back at Damon's house. Anyone likely to call me was already attending tonight, and Mitch had been worried that someone might try and steal it to dive into my background.

Arctos, one of the other sponsors of the gala tonight, made tiny expensive datapads that were too small to be useful for me at work, so I'd never felt the need for one. I used a stock standard Legacy. The latest Arctos models had holo projections and virtual keyboards, cost a bomb, and it was crazy to think that everyone who bought a ticket for the gala was just going to get one for free.

Surely it was better to give the equivalent to the charities running the events? But apparently this was how things were done. Lizzie had just shrugged and nodded when I'd told her about all the freebies.

"Anything I need to know?" Damon asked.

Cat shook her head. "So far, so good. You can head into the atrium for cocktails. The event staff will move everyone through for dinner. Your speech is at eight thirty, before dessert, and then Aries will take over as MC for the auction. After that, dancing and the demonstration booths."

Aries Vea. One of Nat's favorite actors.

Damn, she would have loved this.

I blinked away the sting of longing for my best friend and focused back on Cat. Behind her, a waiter was offering cocktails in various shades of green and yellow. I didn't know what they were, but I suddenly wanted one badly. But I had to keep a clear head, so for now, I was going to have to do this stone-cold sober.

"Time to go to work," Damon said, offering his arm again.

I took it, resting my hand on the smooth wool of his tuxedo, the solid muscle beneath my palm comforting. This was no different to any other networking event I'd ever been to. More dollars at stake, perhaps, but people were people. Even rich people. I'd never loved corporate schmoozing, but I'd done my share. These days I tended to get client referrals via word of mouth, but in the early days, I'd had to work for each job.

We made our way around the room. I smiled and said, "Hello," politely when introduced and made small talk with whichever partner wasn't the one intent on talking to Damon if it was a couple we were talking to. Occasionally I let my gaze slip and looked for any signs of magic. But there was nothing to see, and I was wary of giving myself away to anyone who might be watching, too.

It wasn't all bad. Some of the people we talked

to were even fun, like the short woman whose gown looked like sleek dragon scales, shades of green and blue that complemented her bright green eyes —so bright they had to be enhanced. Tattoos filled almost every inch of her arms and shoulders, apart from the square on her wrist which framed her chip, and her hair was a blazing shade of hot pink that shouldn't have worked with the dragon dress but somehow did.

Clearly someone more interested in the game than the man.

She half rolled her eyes as her partner, a tall blonde in a slinky navy number, started talking about some odd point of international trade law and then said, "So, Maggie, what do you do?"

"I'm a tech troubleshooter, mostly," I said. "I have my own business."

Pinky—that was how she'd introduced herself— gave me a more genuine smile after that. "Oh thank God. I thought you might be one of the boring ones who think arm candy is a career. Not that Damon usually seems to go for that sort." She studied me a moment. "Though to be fair, dating a guy like him is enough to keep someone busy."

"So I've heard," I said drily. "But no, I love my job. And how about you? I take it from the conversation that Ivy is some sort of lawyer?"

"Yep, boring corporate all the way. But she's interesting the rest of the time, so I forgive her weird fascinations with contracts. Especially when she vets mine."

"Yours?" She didn't look like someone who should be buried in contracts.

"Freelance composer," she said. "Films, games, that kind of thing."

"Sounds fun."

"It is. I like the variety. If I settled down and worked for just one place, I think I'd get tired of it. But freelancing makes for a lot of paperwork. Which Ivy loves dealing with. Just as well, as I couldn't afford her firm otherwise," she said with a grin.

In other words, she wasn't angling for a job at Righteous. Which let me relax about this particular conversation. "You have a chip. Are you going to try one of the demos tonight?"

She traced the square of skin around her chip with one finger. "I need it for work. But yes, I'd like to get a sneak peek. If the lines aren't too long. Is it worth the wait?"

"I don't know," I said. "He hasn't shown me yet."

That got me a raised eyebrow. "In all this time? They must have been working on this forever."

True. But development had started in the time Damon and I had been broken up. Before they'd launched *Archangel* even. Damon had decided the best way to restore faith in his company was to come back out swinging. Two games so close to-

gether was unusual for Righteous, but it was definitely working as a PR exercise if the crowd here
was any indication.

"He likes surprises. And honestly, with all this
going on, he's been so busy at work that I don't
want to make him think about it more when we're
together."

"I get that. Though people like him never really
stop thinking about it." She grinned again. "I'm the
same way."

"Composing must take a lot of time."

We chatted about her work for a few more minutes before Damon broke things up. Pinky waved
as she walked off with Ivy.

"She's nice," I said as we started walking again.

"Pinky? Yes. She's also very good. I offered her
a job once. She turned me down."

"She mentioned that she thought working for
one company would be boring." I grinned. "Immune
to your master of the universe charms, is she?"

"Plenty of people are immune to my charms,"
he said. "I'll try again in a few years, maybe. She
did the soundtrack for *Citizen Time*. It was great."

Not a game I'd ever played. But if Damon was
impressed, that meant Pinky's work was solid. I'd
have to look some of it up.

We finally made it into the atrium after we were
stopped by five or six more people who wanted to
say hello or just "take a moment" with Damon.

"Is it like that every time you're out?" I asked as a waiter offered drinks again. I took a soda.

"Big social things like this, yes," Damon said. "But it's part of the job. This is work, not play. But don't worry, it's not like this if I'm doing private stuff. You've seen that."

Maybe. We hadn't actually spent a lot of time just doing ordinary couple things. Date nights or wandering around the city or even going to a movie or a club. Damon's security had been cranked up to eleven since the kidnapping, and it was honestly easier to stay home most of the time.

His house had all the toys a girl could want, including a chef if we wanted one and a home theater room that was bigger than some actual movie theaters I'd been in. He'd turned out to be reasonably competent with power tools when we spent time at my place, so there we worked on the house or just vegged out.

Add in Damon's workload and my schedule and there hadn't been much time for even trying for normal couple things. A couple late dinners in his favorite restaurants, where I suspected the chefs were doing him favors and keeping the kitchen open for us.

"Anyway," Damon added, "we can split up in here, if you want. In half an hour or so, once most people have seen us together. You can go find

Lizzie, take a break from this part of it." He lifted a glass of champagne off the tray.

Around us, the buzz of conversation in the room was getting louder, and faces were once again turning our way. If we'd been in a game, there'd be little thought bubbles of "Damon is here with somebody?" and "Who the heck is that?" popping up over their heads. Only likely far less polite language than "heck."

I sipped soda and readied myself to be the object of curiosity.

True to his word, Damon let me make my escape after the first push of curious onlookers had subsided and he'd introduced me to enough people that the gossip about who I was must have made it around the room.

Apparently I'd been deemed not so important. The people approaching him began to immediately turn the subject to business rather than make small talk with me. Which was rude but kind of a relief. I was happy to fly under the radar.

The atrium had been transformed into a futuristic version of a tropical night. The illusion of a starry sky hung above us, but it had the wrong number of moons and unfamiliar constellations. And the shape of the aircraft that crossed the sky didn't resemble any plane or suborbital I'd ever seen.

Flickering lanterns hung from trees weeping with pale flowers. Some of them were real, but there were holos tucked in among the actual plants, and it was difficult to tell the difference without touching them. Soft music played, not loud enough to drown out the conversations but also not loud enough to drown out the subtler night forest sounds also being fed through the room.

Serenity Falls was set in a futuristic but half-ruined world. I hadn't seen any of it yet, but I assumed this was a taste of what was to come. I hadn't been in the Phenix since it had been rebuilt and reborn as one of the city's most expensive hotels. Before that it had been your standard overly large 4-star corporate hotel. Lots of concrete and bad carpet.

No sign of that now. If I hadn't known we were inside a building, the sense of being at a very swanky outdoor party in an unknown forest would have been complete.

I slipped through the crowd, trying to find Trick's bald head. He was tall enough to spot in a crowd. The atrium was huge, but it was still a crush. Hopefully the feeling of way too many people around me would ease once we went through to the ballroom. If all else failed, I could go in early and see if it was easier to find Lizzie inside.

Riley had set up demo game booths around the edges of the ballroom, giving a very limited preview of *Serenity Falls* for those who wanted it, and the various charities being supported each had a stand as well. Lizzie would be manning Spark's for at least part of the night and, if I knew her, trying to keep an eye on the current and former Spark kids who'd been invited.

But before I had to resort to invading the ballroom, Lizzie said, "Maggie," from behind me. I turned a little too fast and almost ran into a woman in a very frilly white frock that looked like it was made of silk and feathers. The kind that made me thankful it wasn't red wine in the glass I carried. I probably would have spilled it on her, and I doubted her dress was dry-cleanable. I apologized, getting a somewhat frosty smile in response, and ducked around her.

Lizzie, Trick, Yoshi, and two younger women I didn't know stood in what looked like a small grove at the edge of the trees, complete with twinkling lanterns and the scent of flowers. Lizzie waved as I joined them, shooing the others over.

"Let Maggie stand where you are, Yosh," she said. "That way she'll have you on one side and Trick on the other, and hopefully no nosy types will spot her."

I smiled gratefully as I slid in beside Yoshi. "Thanks."

She toasted me with her glass. The bubbly liquid inside it was a pale pink, but I doubted she was drinking when she was working. "How's it going?"

"Okay, I think," I said. "Though my brain hurts already. Lots of names to remember. Lots of people."

"I'll add a couple more," Lizzie said and quickly introduced me to the two girls, Keli and Tisha, without explaining my relationship to Damon. Though possibly they might know already if Yoshi had mentioned it. But if they knew, they didn't seem to care.

The five of us chatted about college. Keli was studying climate engineering, and Tisha was premed. Impressive. The talk eventually turned to the game and the tournament. My cue to find Damon before we were called through to dinner.

I turned to Trick and murmured, "Everything okay?"

He nodded once. "So far, so good. Go find your man."

Dinner went smoothly. The one—okay, two—glasses of the very nice pinot gris I allowed myself over the four courses settled my nerves, but I still felt weirdly exposed. Damon and I shared a table

with the CEOs of Arctos and InX9 and their part-
ners; Simeon, head of Riley's research department,
who I'd met a few times now; and Aries Vea and his
husband, Rafe. Rafe was a drily witty man, as pretty
as his husband, who did something in the more es-
oteric end of finance at one of the global banks that
I didn't really understand when he gave me the for-
dummies explanation.

But he didn't seem to want to talk shop, and the
stories of film sets and adventures that Aries, who
also seemed down-to-earth, sprinkled through the
evening stopped all the tech guys from going down
the business chat rabbit hole.

Rafe asked me how long I'd known Damon but
didn't press for details about our relationship. When
I told him we'd met nearly a year and a half ago,
he'd raised one eyebrow slightly but didn't push. It
was tempting to ask him how he coped with being
the other half of someone famous, but it wasn't exactly the right time with Damon sitting at my side.

"I see you have a chip," Rafe said as a waiter
put a plate of some sort of golden mousse and
pastry confection that smelled like ripe peaches in
front of me. "Does that mean you're a gamer, or do
you use it professionally?"

Simeon turned in my direction, clearly curious to
hear the answer. His department had been involved
in refining the chip technology with InX9, and I was
sure he was dying to ask me how I was feeling after

the surgery, but good manners—and the good sense not to talk about proprietary tech in public— had prevented it so far.

"I game a bit," I said. "Strictly casual. But chip interfaces are becoming more common in lots of industries. And the VR does let you play with infor- mation in lots of interesting ways. Fun for the data analyst types." I'd never worked a job for one of the big banks, so I only had very vague knowledge of the tech they used. But they had the kind of deep pockets needed to fund chips for their employees.

"So they tell me," Rafe agreed. His wrist was bare, no sign of a chip. Aries had one, but he had never hidden his love of games. He'd even done voice work for one of the Riley games, which was why he was MC for the auction and attending the tournament. "They're always upgrading or changing something. Sometimes it makes me feel old. But as long as they're bringing us good information, I can live with it." He grinned. "Aries keeps trying to con- vince me to get one to play with him."

"You don't game?" I asked.

"Not the way he does," Rafe said. "He likes those big, complicated, 'goes on forever' sagas like Damon makes. I have enough big, complicated, 'goes on forever' things happening in the office. If I play, I want easy and uncomplicated. Or a workout maybe. Nothing that needs a chip. But never say never, right?"

I nodded, glad he hadn't asked me how long I'd had mine.

As though he knew what I was thinking, Damon asked Rafe a question about some development in neo-currencies I only half understood. I let them talk and tried the dessert. The food had been delicious, and I wasn't going to deprive myself of the best part of the meal.

I'd nearly finished when Cat came to collect Damon and Aries to start the auction.

CHAPTER EIGHT

DAMON SLID BACK into his seat a few minutes after he finished his speech. Aries was charming the room from the stage, the charisma that had made him a star oozing from him as he laughed and joked and flashed his million-dollar smile.

A holographic list of the auction items had appeared above the table's centerpiece as Aries begun his charm offensive. I hadn't looked. Let the rich people buy the toys. I already donated to Spark regularly, and I doubted anything on the list was in my budget.

"See anything you like?" Damon asked, shuffling his chair closer to mine.

I leaned in to kiss him quickly. "You in that tuxedo."

He laughed. "I'm serious. I have to buy something from the auction. Put my money where my mouth is."

"Isn't throwing this whole thing enough of a demonstration of your commitment to the cause?" I asked. Not to mention his actual foundation and all the other charities he supported.

His smile was lopsided. "Sometimes we have to play these games in public."

Rich people were weird. But I held back my eye roll and turned my attention to the list of items up for grabs. If by "for grabs" you meant "sold to the person who threw the most cash at it."

Jewels, art, wine, fancy spa treatments, meals at some of the best restaurants in the country. Hell, there was even one in Paris, including the suborbital trip to get there. Most of them sounded awesome but weren't exactly the kind of thing Damon needed. Or couldn't just buy on his own if he wanted. I turned to the final page, and something finally caught my attention.

"That one," I said, nudging him to look.

"An after-hours tour of the Lowengraf? You got a hankering for dinosaur bones?"

"What can I say? I'm a nerd." I flicked my fingers to expand the entry. The Lowengraf had been established after the Big One. A smaller field museum firmly focused on giant creatures that used to roam the planet. They had a reputation for innovative exhibits and great learning programs. Nat and I had visited a few times when she'd gotten into *Paleo Titan*, a game involving time travel and dinosaurs. "But I didn't mean for us. You could buy it, then let Lizzie use it. She's always looking for activities for Spark kids. Didn't you have a dinosaur-mad phase as a kid?"

He shook his head. "Not unless the dinosaur was in a game, or maybe surfed."

"Such a California boy." We'd visited plenty of virtual beaches during our "get Maggie back in VR" tour of the world. But so far, we hadn't made it to the real thing. I was hoping when we finally did, I'd just be able to lie around, sip cocktails, and admire Damon in his swim trunks. Though knowing him, he'd probably want to try and teach me to surf.

"Guilty."

"Lizzie would love it. It's the kind of thing rich people get to do, not her kids. They'll appreciate it more. Particularly seeing the off-exhibit areas. You know what the museums are like these days. So much stuff no one ever gets to see."

After the Big One had nearly flattened MoMA in LA and smaller quakes and weird weather patterns had damaged the Met in New York, a lot of the big museums had disaggregated their collections. Established new smaller museums in different locations like the Lowengraf. Or just moved many of the more valuable exhibits into secure storage locations, rotating the pieces between the museums and the offsite storage to minimize the risk.

While that was good for preserving the cultural heritage or whatever, the net effect was that museums were harder to get into, a lot of them weren't free anymore, and it was kind of a potluck as to what you saw when you got there outside whatever their big advertised exhibits were.

Unlike Damon, I *had* gone through a dinosaur phase when I was little. Sara hadn't always found having me around convenient. Single mom of small child wasn't really the image she needed to project to suck people into her shady schemes. The local public library in whatever small-ass town we'd been living in had usually provided an easy—and free— place to ditch me for a few hours.

She'd started doing it when I'd been about five. The first time, she'd taken me to story time and just left me there, not returning for a couple hours. I don't know whether she'd bribed one of the librarians, but none of them called the cops. Instead, they'd just found me more books and fed me crackers and cheese until she reappeared.

By way of apology, when she turned up again about an hour before closing, Sara bought me a stack of cheap books in their library sale—library discards being cheaper than, you know, a kid-appropriate datapad and a reliable netlink—and several of them just happened to be about dinosaurs.

I'd fallen in love with the big critters, though really, now that I'd encountered a demon, I didn't have any desire to meet any giant kill-you-without-thinking creatures. But the Spark kids didn't have my hang-ups, and they'd all been screwed over by at least one of the adults in their lives who were supposed to love and protect them, and they went to schools that didn't have the funding for fancy extras like field trips to private museums. Surely there were some of them who shared baby-Maggie's love of dinos.

I leaned closer to the holo. "Definitely this one."

"Dinos it is," Damon said. He leaned toward the display and then tapped something in against the entry. "I'll tell Lizzie you have to go with them."

"Me?"

"You just got all wistful-looking. If dinos make you happy, dinos you shall have."

"Damon won that museum trip, huh?" Lizzie said about an hour later.

I'd retreated to Spark's information stand after dinner. The auction was done, and the bars had opened. People were starting to fill the dance floor —though most of the moves on display made me think they should spend some of their rich people money on dance classes—and the ten *Serenity Falls* demo booths had opened.

There were even extra food stations in case anyone wasn't completely stuffed after the dinner. One was an ice cream bar complete with ice sculptures of what I suspected were supposed to be exotic creatures to continue the alien planet theme.

Damon was still doing his work-the-room thing, and while I would've braved the dance floor if he'd asked me to, I wasn't going to try it alone. Nor did I want to get stuck dancing with someone who was either trying to get to Damon or see if they could find out more about me.

My cheeks were already hurting from smiling and small talk, and I had the start of a headache from trying to check for magic too often. I wanted a break.

The demo booths didn't hold much appeal. I was curious to see the world Damon had built, but not without him. Plus I still wasn't sure if it was too soon for full VR.

Just as well. Judging by the lines forming in front of each booth, they'd be lucky if everyone who did want a turn got through before the end of the night. Damon's marketing team was clearly doing a great job when even the bored rich folks couldn't quite resist the urge to line up for even just a sneak peek.

"Yeah, I asked him to buy it for Spark," I said.

Damon's first bid for the trip had been ridiculously high, and no one had countered.

Lizzie frowned. "We're already getting enough from tonight. He should buy something he wants."

"He can buy whatever he wants whenever he wants," I said, refilling one of the bowls of Spark promotional candy. There'd been a small but steady stream of people stopping by the stand, so I was trying to be useful and let Lizzie and the other Spark staff do their thing. Right now, there was a lull, giving us a chance to talk.

"And you'll spend that money on sensible things like the meal and tutoring projects and scholarships." Spark ran a lot of fun programs for the kids to get them involved in sports and arts and music, but the bulk of their funding still went to trying to make sure the kids got the education they deserved and didn't go hungry while getting it. A field trip to a museum might be in the cards now and then, but not an exclusive behind-the-scenes experience.

"Okay," Lizzie said, nodding. "You don't have to twist my arm." She reached for one of the cute enamel Spark pins with their shooting star logo glittering over a black base. "You get a free pin though."

I laughed and took it. Lizzie, knowing the audience, had them made with magnet fasteners that wouldn't damage expensive frocks and jackets. I slipped mine into place on the neckline of my dress. "Where are the kids?"

Her smile faltered a little, and she tipped her chin in the direction of the nearest booth. Zee, Yoshi, and a bunch of the Spark kids were waiting in line. Yoshi and Zee in their tuxes looked cute surrounded by smaller kids in more casual clothes. Zee was leaning down to listen to what Liam, one of the youngest, was saying, a gentle smile on his face.

"That's nice of him," I said.

Lizzie's eyes narrowed as she turned her attention back to me.

I held up my hands. "It *is* nice of him. He could be hanging out with his team. He probably *should* be hanging out with his team. I'm not picking a side, but we all have to work together. If you need to take out some aggression, then either run it off tomorrow morning, or we'll play some game where you can shoot people, but you have to play nice."

"You sound like Cassandra," she muttered.

"Pretty sure Cassandra never told you to shoot people." I grinned suddenly. "I can give you the advice she gave me when we first met. About how to 'ground' myself."

Lizzie shook her head so hard I was worried she was going to give herself whiplash. "No, thank you. I've had the sex and stinky herbs speech before."

"You can leave off the stinky herbs. There must

be some cute guys here tonight." I waved a hand at the room to prove my point. It was full of rich guys in tuxes, many of them cute. Who would be charmed by Lizzie with her waves of pink hair and silver mermaid dress.

She folded her arms. "Yeah, hooking up with potential donors is not a great idea."

"Well, there'll definitely be plenty of guys floating around the tournament, too," I pointed out.

After all, if there was nothing between her and Zee, there was no reason she shouldn't take advantage of that kind of target-rich environment. She hadn't dated anyone seriously in the last year, but her tastes ran to gamers and geeks as far as I could tell. The serious gamers all kept in good shape. Game sessions were long, and even though they played lying in game chairs if they used chips, the mental effort of VR took stamina. Not to mention you kind of had to work out to counteract the effects of all that lying around.

Zee was a big guy and clearly strong, but in the pro leagues, he wasn't going to stand out as an Adonis in a sea of weak nerds. He'd fit right in.

"I said no gamers," Lizzie muttered, giving me stink eye.

Okay, she was sticking to that story.

I glanced back in Zee's direction. He and Yoshi seemed to have the situation with the kids under control. I couldn't see Trick anywhere, though I knew Maia would be nearby. "I should leave you to it," I said to Lizzie. She was here to work, not hang out, and another group of potential donors was heading for the booth. I should get back to work, too, and go find Damon.

It didn't take long to hunt Damon down because I asked Maia to find out where he was. An unexpected bonus of having a bodyguard. But even with her assistance, it took a few minutes to weave my way through the crowd to where he stood, just past the last of the demo booths, off to the side of the small stage where Aries had worked the crowd into a series of bidding frenzies.

Damon had his back to the room, talking to an older guy wearing a tuxedo almost as nice as his own. Not someone I recognized from Righteous or even Cat's list of who was who at the gala, but the night had been one stranger after another, so maybe I'd forgotten. Mitch was nowhere in sight, so he, at least, had felt comfortable leaving the two of them together.

But something in the line of Damon's shoulder told me that maybe he wasn't completely enjoying the conversation.

Time for supportive girlfriend mode.

I pasted on a polite smile, studying the two of them as I moved closer. They didn't notice me, intent on their conversation. It was hard to tell in the ballroom's low light, but I though mystery man's tux might be a very dark blue velvet rather than black. Elegant in an old-fashioned kind of way. His hair was a better cut version of the slightly longer shaggy style that lots of the tech guys at Riley had. It might have been dark brown once, but there was gray in it now, streaks of near silver that made me wonder if there was something more expensive than hairstylist handiwork involved in making it look so perfect.

I let my sight slide for a moment, but the deep blue glow of his energy field didn't show signs of an active magic user. In fact, it didn't look any different to Damon's brighter blue one. I let go of the magic as he finally noticed me.

A lightning-quick, mile-wide smile slid over his face, and, well, if I'd been into silver foxes and not dating the man beside him, the focused charm of the expression might have won me over. Light blue eyes in a tanned and handsome face and a flash of very white teeth, along with a dimple in his left cheek, were a good combination, but I got the feeling he knew it.

Damon turned as the older man's smile widened. The smile he directed at me was more one of relief before he schooled it back to polite.

"Found you," I said, tipping my glass at Damon. "Sorry I took so long."

Aka "Do you need an intervention?" It was one of the phrases we'd agreed on. If he wanted to get away from this guy, then I'd run interference like a pro and tell him that an old friend wanted to talk. The gala might be fancy and vastly expensive, but I'd spent enough time in gaming clubs with Nat to know how to get out of an annoying conversation when I needed to.

"Not a problem," Damon said. He reached his free hand out, and I took it and let him draw me in to his side. "Maggie, this is Jack Miller. Jack, Maggie Lachlan. My partner."

Jack's brows flashed briefly upward and then settled as Damon pressed a quick kiss against my temple. I could almost see the wheels turning in his head as he sorted me into "girlfriend," not business partner.

"Nice to meet you, Mr. Miller," I said.

"You, too, Maggie," he said. His voice held a hint of a Southern drawl. "Are you enjoying the gala?"

"Absolutely," I said and lifted my champagne. "Riley Arts knows how to throw a good party."

"They do indeed," Jack agreed. He raised his own glass, a highball holding about a finger of what I guessed was either scotch or bourbon. The good kind. Not that anything else was being served.

"That's a lovely gown you're wearing. And the earrings. The color flatters your eyes. You don't often see that sort of green."

"Thank you," I said, but I didn't mention they were a gift. He was clearly making judgments about me already.

"Did you bid on something in the auction?" I asked when Damon didn't leap in.

Jack chuckled. "A couple things. I won one, but I lost the one I really wanted. That Aries did too good a job. Ah well, it's not like I really needed a holiday at a golfing resort."

"Do you play?" I asked, curious. These days golf was very much the domain of the extremely wealthy. Many cities had banned courses or strictly limited their numbers because they sucked up so much water and other resources to maintain as the weather worsened. Technology and science had come to the rescue with hardier grasses and better fakes, but on the whole, the sport wasn't so widely played anymore.

"Not very often." He sipped his drink. "Hard to justify the expense when I don't have much time. And that's before you work in the other factors."

Like the disapproval of normal people?

"And what do you do, Mr. Miller?" I asked in good supportive girlfriend fashion.

"Call me Jack. Which kind of answers your question. My family says my mama must have had a touch of the sight when she named me. Jack of all trades, you know. I do a bit of this and a bit of that."

Unhelpful. And a vaguer than usual answer. Most of the people I'd asked the same question to tonight had been more than happy to tell me about their very important corporate empires.

"Jack is damning himself with faint praise," Damon said. "Back in the day, he was quite the coder. Got in on the ground floor with one of the early holographic start-ups. They got into medical holos early on."

"Impressive," I said. Holographic training for doctors had been lucrative for a long time. Until VR started to take over. "You didn't want to stay in the medical arena?"

"My mama also gave me a short attention span," Jack said. "I like the challenge of getting things off the ground, not so much the day-to-day grind of running them once they do." He nodded at Damon. "I got out early. Just as well when Damon and his kind have made holos less profitable. I made more getting out than I would have staying in, and I decided to put that money to work."

"These days, Jack does a bit of venture capital work, among other things," Damon added before I could ask another question.

Venture capital? Was he sniffing around Righteous? Searching for weaknesses? Or was I just being paranoid? Maybe he had a company he wanted Damon to invest in.

"So is gaming one of the industries you're interested in now?" I asked.

Jack nodded. "Hard not to be. It's booming. And that's the fun of the tech world. There's always a new part of the game to play. And people are scrappy. They don't give up easy. Look at Damon here, coming out swinging with this shindig."

I stiffened slightly. That sounded like an insult, not a compliment. "Like I said, Damon knows how to throw a party. And he has plenty to celebrate. Are you looking at any part of the industry in particular?"

Jack tilted his glass at me, a tiny toast that might be an acknowledgment I'd hit back at his little dig. "I've been helping out a couple of smaller outfits. Nothing on the scale of Righteous."

There were no other game companies on the scale of Righteous. He was still being vague, but maybe he just didn't want to talk business in front of me. That was fair, considering he had no idea who I was. If he'd been hoping to talk shop, I was thwarting his plans. But he was too smart to try and chase me off. Not when Damon showed no signs of wanting me to leave.

"Here in California? Are you a local?" San Francisco and New Silicon Valley were still one of the global hubs for gaming, but they'd also embraced flexibility, so not the only ones. The Riley campus here was huge and impressive, but they had a whole fleet of staff who worked remotely or in other states or countries.

"Right now, I'm based in Los Angeles, but I've lived all over the country. Even out of it a time or two."

"That must make life interesting." I'd moved around enough for one lifetime. I didn't really understand people who wanted to live like that, but that was hardly the polite thing to say.

"It does," he agreed. "But it's also a case of right place, right time just now. One of the companies I've worked with in the past wanted me to come back and consult on something for them here, and as luck would have it, a junior team I sponsor made the cut for the tournament. "

"Oh? Which one?"

"You game, Maggie?" he asked. His gaze dipped briefly to my wrist.

"A little. One of my friends used to play competitively. So I know enough not to make a fool of myself when the Righteous crew starts talking shop." I aimed a smile at Damon. "And, of course, it's been fun learning about all the teams who are entering the tournament."

"That's a lot to get your head around," he said.

"I have a pretty good memory," I said. "Something my mama gave me, I guess."

He laughed at that and lifted his drink. "To good mamas," he said.

I toasted him back. Maybe I could bore him out of this conversation and set Damon free that way. I curled my arm through Damon's and widened my smile. "You must tell me who made your tuxedo, Jack. It's beautifully cut."

Jack raised an eyebrow, then smiled. "I'll send you the name of my tailor, Riley. Then you can look as pretty as me. To match your pretty lady."

I managed not to roll my eyes. After a few more airheaded comments from me, he finally seemed to realize I wasn't going anywhere.

"I've taken enough of your time," he said, "Riley, let's talk some more during the tournament."

"Maybe," Damon said. "My calendar is brutal, but let's see if we run into each other."

"Well, I do have a lucky streak," Jack said. "I'm sure it will work out." He finished his drink, put the empty glass on the tray of a passing server, and walked away without another goodbye.

CHAPTER NINE

AT MIDNIGHT, the gala ended, and the crowd dispersed rapidly, leaving the ballroom to the hotel staff cleaning up. I helped Lizzie and the others break down the Spark booth, packing everything into the crates the hotel provided so it could be sent back to Spark HQ. It didn't take long, though watching Zee and Lizzie trying to avoid each other in such a small space was entertaining in a weird way.

"We're done here," Lizzie said, latching the last crate. "I'm going to go home and crash." She looked around the group. The younger kids had been taken home a few hours ago. Yoshi, Keli, and Tish looked keen to leave. "Let's get out of here. Maggie, I'll see you tomorrow?"

At the tournament launch. For the next two

weeks, I'd be staying with Damon either in the hotel attached to the conference center or at his house.

"Yep. Sleep well." I hugged her fast.

"Tell Damon bye for me. And thank him. Though he'll get our official thanks tomorrow. Also, tell him he has good taste in bling." She grinned at me, reaching up to touch one of the earrings.

"You've been waiting all night for that, haven't you?"

"Well, it's not every day my roomie gets showered with emeralds."

"Shut up. Don't you need to go to bed?" I made a shooing motion.

"You just want to get back to Damon."

"Well, he looks cute in a tux." I wasn't sure I had energy to do more than admire him. Now that the evening was over and the rush of adrenaline subsiding, I was starting to crash.

As Lizzie and the others headed out, I leaned against the stand's counter and eased out of my shoes, trying to repress a groan of relief—and not entirely about the shoes.

We'd made it through the night. And nothing had happened. I could relax.

One of the hotel staff grinned at me as he whisked a tablecloth off the nearest table. I smiled back, wriggling my toes against the carpet. It was lush and soft beneath my feet despite having been trampled on by hundreds of people for hours, which meant the hotel staff were either cleaning geniuses or it was treated somehow to withstand the punishment.

I gave my toes a minute or so to enjoy being free and then went in search of Damon. Empty of people, the ballroom seemed even bigger. And darker now that the chandeliers had been dimmed and the candles were being snuffed. But there was enough light to spot Damon, standing near one of the demonstration pods, talking to Mitch, a half-empty glass of what I had to assume was scotch in his hand.

"Celebrating?" I asked as I reached them.

Damon raised the glass and sipped. "Too early to celebrate. But I think I earned this. Do you want a nightcap?"

"No." The relief that nothing had gone wrong had me giddy enough. "Let all these people do their jobs so they can go home."

Mitch nodded approvingly. "She has the right idea. It's late."

"You go do what you need to do," Damon said. "We can debrief in the morning."

"It's already morning," I pointed out.

"Later this morning," Damon amended. "Go on. I don't want all of you here until dawn."

"Maia and your escorts are around," Mitch said. "Just call them when you need them. They'll get you out to the car."

"I know the drill," Damon said. "Stop nagging."

Mitch shook his head but left us alone.

Damon took another sip of his drink, surveying the room.

"That went well, I think," I said.

He nodded. "So far so good."

"People were lining up for the demos," I said, nodding at the booth. "And everyone who came out seemed impressed."

"Did you try it?" he asked.

I shook my head. "I figured let the paying customers get their money's worth."

"Do you want to see it now?"

Curiosity warred with caution. "I think Doc Barnard would say I should wait before trying any full VR." I'd seen the surgeon from a distance at one point in the evening, but our paths hadn't crossed.

"This isn't full VR," Damon said. "It's only a tiny portion of the game, and the full effects aren't all enabled. I checked with the doc. He said it would be okay if you wanted to try it."

That was Damon. Always prepared. But was I?

"These systems are safe," he continued. "They're not connected to any external network. Each one operates on its own server, right here. And they're locked down tight. Same security the game pods over at the convention center have."

In other words, demon free. But I still hesitated.

"C'mon, Maggie," he said, voice low and coaxing. "Let me show you this. You know I wouldn't do anything to put you at risk. This is just like the VR you've been trying with me. It's just a made-up place instead of a real one. A very cool made-up place."

He clearly wanted to show off his new toy. He'd been working so hard for this for months. Was I going to let my fears disappoint him?

No. Now was as good a time as any. I reached out a hand. "I know. As long as the doc said it was okay, I guess it can't hurt to take a look."

Relief flashed over his face before it was replaced with a pleased smile. His fingers tangled through mine, and we went into the booth together. He tapped a button by the door to secure it, then pulled out his tiny new datapad. "I'll just let Mitch know where we are so he and the team don't freak out."

Mitch probably already knew, but Damon always tried to be considerate and keep in touch where he could. Maybe it made him feel safer, too. We hadn't talked much about the kidnapping in the last few weeks. Immediately after, we'd both had counseling, individually and a few sessions together, and there'd been some emotional conversations, but lately we'd settled into a routine that didn't seem to factor in talking about it much anymore.

Perhaps because all the security discussions were focused on the tournament, and it was obvious to both of us that Mitch was doing as much as humanly possible to prevent it happening again. Not to mention bringing in things that could be classed as beyond humanly possible by adding witches to his team.

The booth was small. The interior walls were a nonobtrusive pale gray and the carpet a few shades darker. Three black game chairs with silver Riley Arts logos on their backs formed a row in front of a screen about six-foot square that would project what the gamers were seeing for any extra observers into the room. I sat in the chair farthest from the door, dropping my heels beside it and easing back into a comfortable position with the controls. By the time I'd settled in, Damon had done the same in the chair next to mine.

"Ready?" he asked.

I nodded, took a breath, and laid my wrist over the chip interface. "See you inside." I closed my eyes and pressed my wrist down.

:ENGAGE:

The transition was seamless. One second I was lying in a booth in the hotel, and the next I stood in a small room that looked like some sort of rustic hotel. Or maybe an inn. The furnishings were basic, the walls and bed made from wood, but there was a modern-looking screen on the wall opposite the bed and a bulky solar shade across the window, blurring the view slightly.

The room smelled faintly of cleaning fluids and canned air. My clothes, now sensible cargo pants made of sturdy brown fabric with a pale blue shirt and chunky black boots, smelled like horses and dirt and perhaps a few too many days without a shower. A thick leather belt hung with various bits and pieces, including a high-tech-looking water canteen in a leather holder, wrapped around my hips.

So. Drinking water important. Bathing regularly less so. I sniffed again and wrinkled my nose. Then smiled.

The smell. That meant my chip was working. You didn't get scents with a headset. I'd forgotten how real VR felt with the chip.

A grimy mirror hung on one wall. The reflection revealed my hair was braided back off my face and one cheek smeared with something black. The switch from glamour to grunge was a little more jarring than the usual VR transition, and I giggled.

"Everything good?" Damon asked, appearing beside me. His outfit was similar except his shirt was dark blue and the pants gray. So was the waistcoat hugging his torso, a fine gold chain running across from pocket to pocket. A canteen like mine was clipped to his belt, the only thing that looked slightly out of place. All he needed was a bowler hat and he could have stepped out of any old steampunk game.

Of course, on him it looked good. Maybe not as good as the tuxedo had, but I wouldn't object to letting him rumple me up a bit more. He smelled like I did, but underneath it there was still a thread of his usual cologne. Impressive. I wondered if that was programmed in just for him. The thought made me giggle again.

Damn. Righteous didn't mess around.

"I'll take laughter as a good sign."

I nodded and swallowed another giggle. "Where are we?"

"This is where the players first enter the game. It's a hostel in one of the small towns on the safer half of the world. Market day outside so they can outfit themselves."

I crossed to the window, curious. Sure enough, when I wound the solar shade up, the light was glaringly bright. I shielded my eyes, reminding myself there was no actual danger of solar radiation in a game, even if it was worked into the game factors and might impact player stats. It took a few seconds of squinting before the game adjusted my vision and the town outside came into focus.

The market square was packed with stalls canopied in a mix of striped fabrics and various shades of brown leather, propped up by shining brass poles and draped with buntings and flags and emblems that made no sense to me. The stalls were arranged in no particular order, their wares varying wildly from one to the next. Brightly colored fruits and vegetables, glistening blue green fish hanging in what looked to be refrigerated cases, books, clothes, and other things I couldn't name. Even a variety of weapons and tech that had a "cobbled together from parts" look about it.

I couldn't hear much of the noise, but the people, who wore everything from long leather coats and breeches to more modern-looking jeans paired with striped cotton tunics and wide straw hats, moved purposefully from stall to stall, trading and collecting packages, all looking as real as Damon did.

After so much time spent in VR that was empty of other people apart from the two of us, all those sunny beaches and moonlit forest walks and deserted parks, it was something of a shock to be in a crowded game world.

But it all looked fascinating, and to my surprise, I wanted to explore. A reminder of just how good Righteous was at what they did.

Damon held out a hand. "Let's go. I'll take you down to the river. That's the boundary of the demo. It's a nice walk. Less people than the market."

"River it is," I agreed. All those people outside weren't real, and they definitely weren't demons, but after the gala, I wasn't really in the mood for more crowds.

Maybe Damon had set some sort of limits on the game, but none of the characters tried to interact with us as we made our way through the market. The smells of fresh bread and frying foods and mud and sweat and spices and perfumes filled my nose, drawing my attention this way and that as we slipped through the crowd.

Maybe I'd been too hasty. Some of the stalls caught my interest, including one full of gorgeous jewelry made from some sort of opalescent pink stone set in a deep gray metal. The airy pendants and bracelets and earrings almost glowed, looking like sunrise clouds. Not entirely my usual taste, but my fingers twitched toward them.

In a game, they might just be eye candy or a clue or even a curse. But they weren't going to vanish. They'd be here every time I stepped into this world. Or I could hunt down Benji or one of the other designers and see if he knew if there was a real-world inspiration behind the designs.

Damon kept moving, and I followed, not wanting to lose sight of him in the crush. The crowd thinned after a couple of minutes, and not long after that, we turned off the main market street and cut through an alley to cross to another, less crowded road.

"Can you tell me the backstory?" I asked as the

sounds of the market died away. There was still plenty of background noise. Voices and doors opening and closing and the rumble of carts and the odd motorized vehicle trundling over the roads made it clear this was a reasonable-sized town. But I could hear myself think again.

Damon smiled. "I'm not supposed to."

I held up two crossed fingers. "I swear I'm not going to tell Zee. And he's about the only contestant I know."

"I saw you speaking to Alicia earlier."

"Because Zee introduced me. I wished her luck. She complimented my shoes. She's a professional. She's not going to try and wangle information out of me." Well, not by bluntly asking, anyway. Top gamers worked whatever angles they could find, but there were lines the smart ones wouldn't cross. Not at the risk of their careers. Alicia was captain of one of the best teams in the world. She wasn't dumb. "C'mon, Riley. Spill. Entertain me with tales of your creations like a proper master of the universe."

He shook his head, guided me around a spill of something oily looking on the path, then relented. "Okay. But only cause you're pretty."

I snorted. The road ahead broadened out, the buildings to either side houses, not stores and offices. Ahead I caught a glimpse of open space.

"So, this is Serenity Falls," Damon said. "Colony

planet. Colony was doing well, been here almost a century. But about five years ago, something went wrong with the terraforming on the northern continent. The climate reverted to the hotter one it was originally. At the same time, the native flora and fauna became more aggressive. They're getting bigger as they breed. And mutating. The government think they have it contained, but they're worried the problem could spread. And the ship that was supposed to arrive from the home world is two years late. They can't rely on new tech to save them. This is the southern continent. Which is now getting overcrowded and starting to regress."

"And what's the quest?"

"Oh, there are a few," he said. "What would you have it be?"

"Fix the terraforming. Make the other continent safe. Fight the monsters. Go find the supply ship. Wait, do they still have spaceships?"

Damon nodded. "A few. Mostly short range. Some of them are becoming unreliable. And that's just the beginning."

"Which one is the quest for the tournament?"

He wriggled his eyebrows. "That would be telling."

"You're no fun."

"I'm plenty of fun," he retorted. "Do you need me to prove it?"

I looked around. We'd just passed the town limits, the road bordered by dry-looking fields full off stubbly plants. "Not exactly a good place to canoodle. Besides, it's too hot."

It was. The sun was vicious, giving everything a sort of flat, washed-out look. Sweat was starting to trickle down my back.

Should've brought a hat.

And one of the fruity nonalcoholic drinks I'd been drinking since dinner. But the heat explained the canteens.

"The climate is definitely a factor in this game," Damon said. "Next time, I'll remember the hats."

"Next time, I want some minions following behind with a fan," I said. "Or different clothes."

He grinned. "I could put you back in your gown." He raised his hand, fingers poised to click.

"Don't you dare. It would spoil the illusion. How much farther to this river of yours?"

"Not too far, just over that hill and around a bend."

"That sounds like the sort of thing some mystical baddie would say to lure me off into fairy land," I said.

"Well, just as well you can trust me," he said with a wicked grin. The kind that suggested I shouldn't trust him too far. At least when it came to tempting me to do bad things.

"You could be anyone."

He looked affronted. "Nobody else is getting

into this game with you. Besides—" He reached out and pulled me close. "Just anyone wouldn't know how to do this." His lips came down on mine, and for a few brief seconds, the world spun around me as the heat of the sun dissolved in the path of heat of another kind.

Hell yeah. It still startled me, how quickly things burned between us. Would it always be that way?

I pulled back. Kissing Damon was always a pleasure, but kissing was as far as I was going to go. Let him show me the river, and then maybe we could go home and do more than just kiss. Peeling him out of his tuxedo sounded like fun. Though then again, maybe he could stay in it....

"I think you should tell me what you're thinking about." His voice had turned low, raspy. Just the way I liked it. But I had to keep my head.

"I think last one to the river is a rotten egg." I turned and sprinted toward the hill.

Damon caught me just at the crest.

"No fair. You have longer legs," I protested as he cruised past me and picked up speed as he headed down the slope. Clearly there was no way I was going to catch him, but I didn't slow down as I chased after him. Apparently the game didn't want me to break my ankle, and the boots provided remarkable grip on the cracking tarmac. Still, I had to focus to make sure I didn't slip, and it wasn't until I reached Damon and he caught me around the waist to stop me going any farther that I paid much attention to where we were.

"Whoa," I said, taking in the view. River was an understatement. I'd been expecting something relatively tame, but this river was a big one. The water was a sullen sort of blue, with undertones of brown suggesting mud not sand. It flowed fast, the water swirling and foaming, turning the pebbled banks damp and slippery. A wood-and-steel bridge spanned it, looking old and somewhat worse for wear. Though, unless there was another crossing or a different path out of town, it had to be passable. "You expecting people to buy a boat back there in town?"

Damon shrugged. "Up to them. The bridge can work, if you're smart." He gestured at the river. "I wouldn't recommend trying to swim across."

"I wasn't planning to." I liked my water a lot more controlled. I wasn't even that fond of the ocean. Mom had tended to stick to the Midwest. Not much beach time involved. Once I'd come back to California, I'd been to the beach a few times, but these days, with the risk from UV, the whole California beach thing was not so appealing. The currents around San Francisco had grown more treacherous after the quake. Add in the fact that the first imp I'd ever met had come from the ocean, and I trusted the deep water even less than I had before.

There might not be imps in the river, but given this was a Righteous game, I doubted the crossing would be straightforward. Even the banks were forbidding, scattered with large rocks and not offering any obvious easy entry points. Damon took a seat on one of the rocks, and I perched next to him, watching the water swirl past.

"This is all amazing," I said. "I think people are going to love it."

"I hope so. It's the biggest world we've done yet. It has some tricks up its sleeve."

"I'd ask you what, but I don't want spoilers," I said.

"I couldn't give them to you anyway." He yawned suddenly and stretched. "C'mon, it's late."

I blinked at him, startled. The illusion of the world around us was so real, the heat of the sun warming my skin, that I'd forgotten it was past midnight.

Damon laughed at my expression. "You forgot the time, didn't you?"

I nodded sheepishly. "Yes, Oh Tech Genius. Your toy is good."

"And you feel fine? Nothing weird from the chip?"

"Nope. Nothing weird. Just half fried."

His smile widened. "Excellent. In that case, let me take you home and show you some of the other tricks I have up my sleeve.

"So are you happy now?" I asked as we walked into the house. It was late, late enough that the house comp kept the lights low, illuminating our way with the small lights set in the baseboards of the foyer and the hallway beyond. They glowed warm and intimate against the darkened walls. Not quite the fantastical landscape from the hotel, but still enough that it felt like somewhere new, somewhere not entirely of the world. I eased out of my shoes. The floorboards were smooth and cool on my tired feet, and I almost sighed with pleasure.

"Happy it's over," Damon said, tapping something into the house comp screen near the door. "The real work starts with the tournament, of course. Easy enough to get rich people to throw money at an easy cause with a fancy party. But the tournament...that's the big play." He lifted his hand from the house comp panel and came back to me. "At least there will be a lot less talking about businesses I don't care about."

No, at the tournament, he was more likely going to have to deal with Righteous fans rather than those who wanted something from him. He navigated different worlds, this man. God of gaming to Righteous fans. Boss man to the Riley Arts people. Genius CEO in the business world. And then there was the world of crazy money. The one we'd been playing in tonight. I got the feeling it wasn't his favorite place to be.

"Did you enjoy any of it?" I asked.

He smiled. "It's fun, just a different kind. Business is business, and some people will always work the angles. Luckily there are the ones who don't take it quite so seriously."

"Like Pinky. And Rafe."

He nodded. "Even Aries to a degree. He has an eye to his image and works hard for his career, but he remembers where he came from. Unlike some people." He shook his head ruefully, then focused back on me. "I liked having you there with me." His voice went low, and he reached toward his tie.

A small protesting noise slipped from my lips.

He paused, one hand wrapped around the tie. "Problem?"

"I like you in the tuxedo," I said softly.

He flashed a smile. A more relaxed, more real version of the expression he'd been flashing all night. "I like you in the dress."

"I'd be happier in the tuxedo," I said. "The shoes are more comfortable for a start." I'd never been much of a girly girl. I couldn't deny it had been fun to play princess for a night, and I wasn't sure I was ready to take the earrings off. I'd be happy to wear gowns more often if Damon needed me to, but I preferred clothes I could move in.

"You can wear whatever shoes you like," he

said, moving closer to drop a kiss on my bare shoulder that sent a thread of silky pleasure over my skin. "But you can't expect me to prefer you in a jacket and shirt to this."

"You're just being lazy," I said. "You don't want to deal with buttons."

"Wasting time with buttons just means less time touching you." His mouth settled in the curve of my neck, right where he knew it would make me shiver. As I tilted my head to give him better access, it was difficult to remember what we'd been talking about.

"I wanted to do this all night. Everyone wanted to talk to me about the game and the new tech, but every time I saw you, I just wanted to get Mitch to clear the building."

"And waste all that food? Not to mention the ice sculptures?"

"I can think of better uses for ice," he purred.

The vibration sank through my skin, heat blooming in its wake. The boning of the dress meant I needed no bra, and the silk was suddenly too tight across my nipples.

"Ice sounds cold. I'd rather be warm. You want to warm me up?"

"My pleasure." His teeth pressed harder now, just on this side of too much, and a moan slipped past my lips. How did he always know just what to do? What I needed? Like he was the perfect man, stepping out of some virtual reality designed just for me.

I reached back to thread my fingers through his hair, pulled his head closer. He hummed and kissed my neck again, hands sliding up to cup my breasts, hot through the silk.

"Sometimes I feel like I made you up," I said, half dizzy with him. I loosened my grip, pressing my hands against the wall.

His kisses drifted higher. "I'm quite real." The words were soft in my ear. "This is real. This is the only real thing. Not all that nonsense back there. You know that, right?"

There was something almost urgent beneath the words. I straightened and turned so I could see his face. "Know what?" I asked softly.

"Know that if all that went away, I'd still be happy if I could do this." His mouth came down on mine as his hands slipped around my waist and tugged me closer.

The best answer seemed to be just kissing him back. Letting the part of me that burned for him take over. He pressed me back against the wall as the kisses grew hotter and deeper. Urgent. As though he did indeed want to forget everything else.

He pulled my skirt up and my panties down without breaking the kiss. My head thumped back against the wall when his hand slipped between my legs. I widened my stance and let him touch me, eyes closed, heart racing. His thumb found my clit while his fingers stroked. I was already wet, could feel how easily his touch skimmed over me, but I wasn't about to stop him.

Not when he felt so damned good.

Heat rushed through me. Maybe I needed that ice after all. Or maybe I just needed more Damon.

I arched my hips into his touch, purring encouragement in his ear while I fumbled for his belt. It was probably sacrilege to have sex in a gown this expensive, but I couldn't wait any longer. Damon shared my eagerness. He kissed me again, curling his hand around the back of my thighs to lift me.

Then he pushed himself inside me with a groan of hunger that made me clench around him. "Yes."

God. He felt good. Chasing everything else away. Reducing the world to just us as he always did. His mouth, my skin, his taste, my touch. Blurring and parting and coming back together in a rhythm that both of us knew without trying. It wasn't gentle, but it was glorious, and I didn't want to stop. Kept urging him on with sounds that weren't words and trying to pull him closer, deeper. Harder.

Pleasure spiked and echoed through me and around me, and I couldn't resist. Couldn't hold off and make this last. Instead, I came hard, crying his name, seeing stars, only dimly aware of him shuddering inside me, too.

I nearly slid down the wall when he set me down, legs wobbly, body singing. My skirt fell back down to my ankles, miraculously unwrinkled. Serissa had definitely worked some magic on the fabric. Maybe she could do the same for all my clothes. The thought made me laugh, the afterglow making me happy.

"Something funny?" Damon said.

"Just happy." I smiled up at him, then pulled his head back down to kiss him again.

"Have mercy," he muttered.

"Nope." I pulled him closer and then pouted as he stepped back.

"Don't look like that," he said. "If you look at me like that, I'm going to have to do that all over again."

"Sounds good to me."

"I'm not sure you'd thank me in the morning. And that dress is too lovely to destroy."

"Spoilsport."

He grinned. "Oh no. I just have a better idea."

"Oh?"

"Yes. It involves you naked in our bed."

"That is a better idea." I laughed and dragged him toward the bedroom.

CHAPTER TEN

THE LATE NIGHT was catching up with me when we reached the convention center the next morning. Unlike the Phenix, the convention center and the hotel attached to it were your standard, lots of concrete and tinted glass boxy buildings. But on a massive scale. Driving down into the VIP section of the parking lot felt a little like being swallowed by a giant industrial beast.

Which was as good a metaphor as any for the tournament. It was about to take over our lives for several weeks. Hopefully it wouldn't chew us up in the process.

Cat was waiting for us in the parking lot. She looked perfectly groomed and awake as always. Sometimes I wondered if Damon was fooling us all and Cat was actually an android, but I figured if he'd cracked that technology, he'd already be making a fortune selling it. She was just very, very dedicated and good at her job.

Presumably Damon paid her enough for her to buy all the caffeine she needed to stay that way.

I, for one, needed more. We'd had a hasty breakfast at Damon's house, but one cup of coffee wasn't cutting it so far.

Cat led us through a series of utilitarian service corridors to an elevator, which spat us out onto one of the higher floors.

"This is the private floor, for your use, boss," Cat said. "Limited access. You and Maggie. The security team. The execs. You know who. You can give access to others, just let me know. Access is keyed to these." She handed us each a tiny lapel pin. "Make sure you wear them. Though you can scan your palms, too." She pushed open a door and ushered us into a large office. "This one will be your office, Damon."

The dark wood looked expensive. Its surface was clear other than one small silver strip of ports set on the right edge that told me it would produce screens or keyboards or holos on demand. On the wall opposite was a bank of eight monitors, set in two rows of four.

Cat pointed. "Top row can do in-game views of the live heats. The bottom row is the security feeds from the main floor, the team suites, and the game rooms. The desk monitor is for calls or your work, though you can do multi-person calls with the monitors, too."

Damon nodded and sat at the desk, calling up the monitor and keyboard.

Cat's gaze turned to me. "We have some other offices, Maggie. I know you're taking some vacation time, but if something comes up, just let me know, and I'll find you something. There are relaxation suites and a dining room on this level. The penthouse is all yours, too. Your bags will be there by the time we're finished here and should be unpacked. I've sent the details to both your datapads, as well as all the convention center maps and guides."

Penthouse. That took some getting used to. As did the fact that there were staff to unpack our bags for us.

"Damon, there are a few things we need to run through first before we get to the tournament." Cat smiled at me. "Maggie, can I get you some coffee or something in one of the other rooms?"

In other words, would I leave so they could do important Riley Arts biz that wasn't any of *my* business? "I might wander around a bit, start learning my way around?"

"Good idea," Damon said, looking up. "This place is a rabbit warren. You could check out the game again in one of the practice rooms if you want. I'm guessing some of them will be empty. Looks like not all the top league teams have checked in for the day yet, and they're the only ones with access today. Plenty of time if you wanted another look."

He glanced down at my wrist, one eyebrow lifting. There'd been no aftereffects from our session last night. My wrist wasn't even slightly tender. The real question was whether I was brave enough to go into a game alone.

"Is the practice module the same as last night?"

"It has access to the same starting point. Plus a little bit more background on the world available in the systems. Just enough to let them start planning. But you still can't go past the river, and it's still not the full version in terms of sensory input."

In other words, no unexpected surprises.

I nodded. "I'll think about it. Have fun running your empire." He laughed and I left before Cat started ushering me out. Outside in the hallway, I pulled up the hotel map on my datapad.

First priority, coffee. That was easy enough to find. The dining room Cat had mentioned was just a few doors down. It had a fully stocked fridge with all the cold beverages a gal could want, and a gleaming coffee machine set on a counter along with an obliging barista. No one else was in there, but the few minutes it took for my coffee to be made gave me time to work out where I wanted to go next.

The coffee was hot, the scent rich and bitter. I let it cool as the elevator took me down to the practice floor. I couldn't blame the caffeine for the hitch in my pulse.

Damon wouldn't push me, but I wanted to test myself a little. Nothing bad had happened in the game last night. None of the weirdness I'd experienced in *Archangel*.

Another look couldn't hurt. Maybe I'd even wander around the market this time. Check out the jewelry I'd liked. I'd never really gotten to the point of interacting with other characters in *Archangel*.

A safe way to dip my toes in the water.

When I reached the practice floor and put my palm on the scanner just outside the elevator, a chime sounded, and my datapad projected a holo-screen with a map of the floor.

"Hello, Maggie Lachlan," a familiar voice said.

Have AI, will travel? I hadn't realized Riley would be using Madge here. "Hi, Madge," I replied. "How's AI life today?" Officially, AI didn't exist, but Madge was smart enough to give a good imitation.

"I am well, Maggie. Would you like to use a practice room? I can show you a map of the available units."

"Sure," I said, trying to sound more confident than I felt. "Let me see."

"My pleasure," Madge responded. On the holo, a bunch of the rooms turned green. "Room 193 is in the most secure location. Limited access points, and I can advise Ms. Lin of your location. She is on duty."

I looked around. The corridor was empty. No eager gamers in sight. Alone time was going to be scarce for the next two weeks. So was time when I wasn't under the watchful eye of Mitch's team. If Madge knew where I was, they could find me if they needed to. "I think it will be fine. Leave Maia alone for now."

"As you wish." The room in question changed to blue on the screen. "Turn right and then right again at the first corridor."

Clear enough. "Thanks, Madge," I said. "That's all I need."

"You are welcome. Have a nice day, Maggie."

"You, too," I said. Maybe it was weird to talk back to Madge, but it felt rude not to. I'd gotten used to her help at Damon's house and at Riley. She was way smarter than any house comp. Particularly my house comp, which was still somewhat temperamental when it wanted to be. Once the remodel was finished, I was going to have to do a full reinstall.

Room 193 was indeed empty, the door standing open. The panel by the door glowed white. Green would be vacant, red occupied if it worked like the rooms at game clubs. Maybe white was reserved.

I hovered in the doorway. The pod of three game chairs sat in the middle of the floor, innocuous metal and black leather. Only the silver of the interface panel on each arm marked them as anything more than an expensive recliner. For a moment, I wondered exactly why I was pushing myself.

Because last night was fun, and this makes Damon happy. So *don't think*.

It was only a few short steps to the chairs. I trailed my fingers over the leather. The center one rocked slightly, almost inviting, though I knew it was only the weight of my hand setting it into motion.

"Middle it is," I said. But as I walked around, Zee stepped through. He stopped when he saw me.

"Maggie. Hi. Sorry, I thought this room was empty."

I hadn't told the system to secure the room yet. Once I was in-game, the security features would lock it down, and only people with authorization would be able to enter. The private suites in game clubs worked the same way, for safety. Club employees could enter, or anyone the players had granted access to, but other than that, no one could disturb a player while they were connected to the system.

"It's fine," I said. "Come on in. Did you want to play?"

"Need to do another walkthrough of the pregame areas," Zee said. "The others are arriving in an hour or so."

I smiled. "You're keen."

"Out of practice," he said. "I might not be playing, but I don't want to be deadweight. Not when they're doing us a favor." He hitched a shoulder, then smiled. "You were here first. Putting that new chip through its paces?"

"Something like that," I said.

His gaze slid down to my wrist, then back up again. "You had a chip before, yeah?"

Someone had filled him in on my history. "Yes. It didn't end well. Sounds like you know that."

Was that the real reason he'd turned up? Damon making sure I wouldn't be alone in-game, and Zee was on Maggie watch?

But Damon had seemed happy enough when I'd told him I was going to explore. He could have sent Maia with me but didn't.

"I only know the highlights," Zee said. "But seems like it'd take guts to try again."

I looked down, staring at the interface on the chair. "Well, the technology has been refined. Everyone keeps assuring me that the chip won't interfere with my magic this time." I raised my head. "Clearly yours doesn't bother you. Last time it was the bond that was the real issue. That's not a problem anymore."

"Still. Not sure I'd ever go back into a game if I'd tangled with a demon."

"I tangled with it in real life, too. Don't really have the option to opt out of that. Besides, Damon is part of my life now. So"—I waved a hand at the chairs—"this is, too."

"Yeah, I get that." He studied the chairs. "So do I leave you alone, or do you want me to come in with you? Your choice."

"Together sounds good." The words came fast. Perhaps I wasn't as brave as I'd thought.

Zee's mouth quirked. He gestured at the chairs. "Pick one."

"Okay." I settled into the middle chair. Zee took the one to my right, putting himself between me and the door. He tapped a button on the chair, and the door swung closed with a decisive click, the panel flaring red.

Keeping others out, not us in, I reminded my-self. *Just a game.*

"See you in there," he said and settled back in the chair.

I took a breath and lay down. Set my wrist over the interface panel and felt the snap of the chip making contact. Two more deep breaths, and I closed my eyes.

:ENGAGE:

Zee stood by the bed in the room at the inn. Everything looked, sounded, and smelled the same. Even Zee's outfit was similar to what Damon had worn, though buff and brown, the chain across his vest copper. I let out a relieved breath.

Everything was the same. No surprises.

"All good?" Zee asked.

I nodded, then crossed to the window and pulled back the solar blind to check the scene outside. Same bustling market.

"So, I was planning to go down to the river crossing, maybe poke around the market on my way back. Keep things simple."

Zee nodded. "That's good with me. I had a bit of time to explore the market with the kids last night. We didn't leave town though. River sounds good."

Even if he couldn't get past the bridge, it made sense he'd want to get the lay of things before he tackled this with his team. I pulled the blind shut again. "Let's go."

It didn't take long to get through the thickest part of the market, where the noise and smells were almost overwhelming even in practice mode. I led Zee toward the road out of town that Damon had shown me.

We walked in silence for a few minutes, alone on the road apart from the odd bird flying overhead and insects buzzing in the longer dry grass that lined its edges.

"I'm always surprised how real it all is," I said eventually.

Zee nodded. "Yeah. If I think about the games I started off playing, this is almost like magic...better than in some ways." He flung out an arm, sweeping it at the view. "Can't do this with illusion. At least I can't."

"I haven't even tried illusions yet, so I definitely can't," I said.

"Truth? Would've thought Cassandra would have you on that."

"I think she's more interested in making sure I don't accidentally set things on fire. I'm still kind of Witch 101, with a leaning toward defense."

He snorted. "Illusions come in handy for that, too. Or at least knowing how to spot them is the first step. Though not everyone can."

"Maybe you can show me?" I asked.

"Not here. No magic in-game. Can't risk getting pinged for some rule violation."

"This isn't even an official practice session," I pointed out. "But fair enough. You're competing. I'm not." I looked around. "It is kind of magic, isn't it? Though more predictable than magic. Safer, too, maybe."

Zee scrubbed a hand over his head, looking

amused. "I don't know. I've been in some intense situations in game clubs."

"Not the kind of clubs where hot-off-the-press Righteous games are played." The licensing fees for a game club for a new Righteous game were substantial. Too high for the clubs to risk the kind of trouble that came from fights or anything else illegal.

"Didn't spend a lot of time in that kind of club," Zee said with another grin. "But yeah, Righteous games are another level. Your man has an interesting brain. Assuming he still comes up with the ideas?"

"The concepts, yes, he does. For the flagship games. Like this one." The cracked pavement of the road started to curve. "The river is around the next corner. Anything here you want to take a closer look at?" One side of the road was fenced with wire, protecting some sort of golden grassy crop growing in a series of small fields. In the distance was some sort of outbuilding. No sign of any livestock. The other side was scraggly brush. I doubted we'd get very far if we set off cross-country. Maybe in the full version.

Zee evidently came to the same conclusion. "No. There's nothing obvious here. Take me down to the river."

We set off again. The fields were flat, the yellow crop rippling slowly in the faint breeze. The bushes on the other side of the road had spiky greenish-brown leaves. Maybe that was better for the plants under the intense sun.

"Not quite the rolling green hills of England," I said, wiping my forehead with the back of my hand.

"No. But warmer." He squinted at the sky.

The sun was larger than ours and more orange than yellow. The sky itself had a green tinge, and the few clouds were odd shapes. Clearly this wasn't Earth.

"Which is nice," Zee continued.

England, like most countries, was warmer than it used to be but not hot like Serenity Falls. I should have stopped and called up a hat for my avatar. "I don't know. I'd settle for a little rain right now."

"Not sure there's a lot of that here," Zee said. He looked up as some sort of aircraft suddenly streaked across the sky, high above us.

I watched it, too, a grin spreading across my face. I'd never be an avid gamer, but the world surrounding us felt like stepping into one of the old sci-fi movies I'd watched with my grandad. Sure, I had magic, but this was *space*. Humans still hadn't managed to leave the planet in any viable way. The first Mars missions had reached the planet, but so far, we hadn't been able to make it habitable. These days more money was being poured into saving the planet we had rather than escaping it. So VR was probably as close as I'd get to setting foot on a distant world.

"Do you think you'll go back?" I asked.

"England? Too soon to say. But not long-term. Like it or not, the US is home, and I want to be here. My friends are here."

No mention of family. Did he have one? Or rather, one he was willing to claim?

He'd been so good with the Spark kids at the gala, giving them his time without complaint. Careful with the little ones. Joking with the teenagers. Clearly knowing how to handle them. If he'd come from that sort of background, then of course he wanted to finally find somewhere to call home.

Did home for him mean Lizzie? I'd seen her face, watching him when she thought no one was looking. She was clearly mad at him, but there'd been a softness in her expression. Whatever had happened between them, I hoped they could make up enough to be friends again.

I'd never stayed in one place long enough to make ride-or-die friends when I'd been with Sara. And I'd been wary after that. It had taken Nat some time to crack through my barriers, but then she'd been like family, too. Then she was gone.

Lizzie and Zee were both still alive. Hopefully they might be able to fix what had broken between them.

"A home base is good. So you'll keep working for the Cestis?"

"When they need me. But if I'm not doing undercover, I'll need another gig, too." He looked around as we rounded the bend and the view before us shifted to the width of the river and the arc of the old bridge.

"Is there something you want to do?" I didn't know if he'd been to college. I didn't know much about him at all. I assumed he was somewhere around Lizzie's age. Maybe a little older. Young. If he'd been overseas working for the Cestis, especially doing something undercover, it didn't feel like the kind of thing that would also let you hold down any sort of demanding job.

He shrugged. "I've done lots of different things. Haven't really found one that stuck yet." He swept his hand at the view. "This would be fun, but I don't know if I have the skills."

"Game design? Or playing in a league?"

"Design, maybe. I like solving puzzles. Maybe it would be fun to set them. Cassandra always says illusions take imagination. But I don't know."

It took a lot of different skills to build a game. "Well, you're in the right city for that. And the colleges here have some great courses."

That earned me a noncommittal grunt. It felt rude to push him on whether he'd been to school or whether he could afford college. Of course, plenty of the tech companies funded scholarships across the country, but there was a concentration of them here. But Zee wasn't as young as Yoshi, and he wasn't my employee. He didn't need me sticking my nose in.

"Big river," he said as we got closer and the scents in the air changed to water and damp plants and mud. There still wasn't much of a breeze, but the sluggish air currents were slightly cooler.

"Yep." The expanse of water was still daunting. "I'd guess you either get across faster or try to protect it somehow."

"Or blow up after you get across," he said with a grin. We were nearly at the foot of the ramp that went up to the beginning of the bridge. "You could get a small vehicle over it, maybe." He cocked his head, holding up his hand as though trying to measure the proportions.

I nodded. "I think so. The current looks pretty fast. Not sure I'd want to try a boat." I walked around the ramp, closer to the edge of the bank, where the rocks Damon showed me clustered. "Not unless it had a good engine."

"Maybe with a team, you could anchor a rope to the rocks?" Zee joined me at the riverbank.

"There's a bigger one down there." I started to point at the rock I'd stood on the day before and froze. It glowed. That was new. Yesterday it had been just a rock. Smooth and various shades of gray. "Hang on." I headed for the rock.

Zee grabbed my arm, stopping me. "What's wrong?"

I pointed with my free hand. "Can you see a glow?"

"Yes."

"Well, yesterday, you couldn't."

Zee made a displeased noise. I squinted at his face. He was studying the rock with narrowed eyes, one hand worrying the chain at his waist, shoulders tense as though braced for trouble.

"Maybe it's a menu or something," I said. "Damon said this version had a few more features than last night."

That earned me a skeptical grunt. Eventually Zee looked back at me. "Okay. We'll go closer. Slowly. Let me know if you hear or see or feel anything strange. Stay behind me." He let go of my arm and started to walk.

Crap.

I fell in behind him, senses straining. Other than the glowing rock, nothing felt different. The sound of the river, the wet mud and vegetation smell of it and the faint breeze were all as I remembered. My hand twitched, fighting the urge to hit the kill switch and nope out, but if we didn't at least check the rock out, then someone else would have to come back in and deal with it.

And maybe I was overreacting. Maybe this was just a new part of the game.

Even moving cautiously, it didn't take long to close the distance. Zee stopped a few feet away, so I did, too. The glow was brighter, though whatever was making it was on the far side of the stone, hidden from view.

"Do you feel anything?" Zee asked. His mouth was flat, his hand flexing as he stared at the stone. Maybe he had the same idea as me about the kill switch.

But I wasn't going to be the first to pull the plug. "No. And no weird noises." Nothing like my messed-up memories of what happened when the demon had tried to get to me through the *Archangel* beta. "You?" My nerves receded a little. The glow hadn't altered as we moved closer. Nothing had attacked. In fact, what I mostly felt was curiosity. What was causing it?

"Though actually," I said, "I was nervous before. Now that I'm closer, that's gone away. I want to see what that is." It was almost an effort not to step forward, now that I was thinking about it.

Zee nodded. "Yeah. Me, too. So let's be careful. We'll go around, see what's doing that. But whatever you do, don't get too close. And don't touch anything."

I held up my hands and then ostentatiously

shoved them into the pockets of my pants. "Fine by me."

We moved forward again, giving the rock a wide berth as we skirted around it until we could see the other side.

The glow resolved into a symbol, a swirling collection of lines and circles that looked...old. Not like it belonged to the failing tech world of the game. I took half a step forward before I caught myself and moved back instead. "What is that?"

"Nothing good," Zee said. He backed up another step. "System, record."

There was a chime of acknowledgment, and I stayed where I was while he moved slowly around the parts of the rock he could get to without falling into the river. But it wasn't easy. The urge to move closer was still tugging at me. I gritted my teeth, saw Zee start to step forward, then stop.

"Do you feel that pull, too?" I asked.

He bent to study the symbol, hands braced on his knees. "Yes. Which makes me think it's definitely not supposed to be there."

"It doesn't feel like the demon did," I said. I'd had no urge to get closer to the demon. Quite the opposite, in fact.

"There are other things to worry about," Zee said. He stared at the glowing spot on the rock. "We should get Trick and Lizzie. Maybe Cassandra."

My stomach fell. "Do you know what it is?" The symbol was nothing I recognized, the color of the light a pure silver white that almost hurt to look at.

Zee glanced at me. "Maybe."

"Well?" I demanded.

His headshake was decisive. "If you don't know, it's not up to me to tell you."

"I'm going to find out. This is Damon's game. The Cestis aren't going to cut me—or him—out of the loop."

"Maybe. But that's their decision, not mine."

"Something to do with demons?" I asked. I didn't feel any creeping dread and disgust that came with most things demon related. But Zee was clearly worried.

"Like I said, demons aren't the only thing you have to worry about," he muttered.

What the hell did that mean? "That's not helpful if you're not going to tell me anything," I said. "The bigger question is how did it get into the game?" There were things that players could change in VR through their actions. But some of the background objects were fixed. Not editable. And definitely not editable in a sandbox version like this.

Damon was going to lose his shit. Riley Arts had done so much work after the demon to try and make sure their games couldn't be interfered with.

"We should get back," I said. "We're going to need the access logs."

"We're going to need more than that," Zee murmured. "But yes, see you out there."

:DISENGAGE:

I blinked and opened my eyes back in the game room. The light on the arm of the game chair was green, meaning I was logged out and safe to pull my arm away from the interface. I disconnected gently, flexing my wrist. But I couldn't blame my chip for what we'd seen in the game. Zee had seen it, too.

He was already half out of his chair.

"You call Cassandra, I call Damon?" I asked.

He nodded. "That's a good plan. Tell him no one should go into any of the games until we give the all clear."

CHAPTER ELEVEN

CASSANDRA'S GAZE sharpened as she stepped closer to the image on the wall monitor. The rest of us—Damon, Zee, Trick, Lizzie, and me—watched in heavy silence, waiting on her verdict. It had been only thirty minutes or so since Zee and I had left the game, but it felt longer. Maybe because the mood in the room was tense enough that it felt like the air might shatter from the pressure.

Damon had arrived looking grim, and Zee and I hadn't really been able to offer him any explanation for what we'd found. Other than "big glowy symbol on a rock that shouldn't be there." His mood hadn't improved as we'd waited for Cassandra, and now, nobody had spoken for at least five minutes while she watched the recording of the game.

Finally she turned back to Zee. "Does this mean anything to you?"

To Zee? Why should it mean something to him in particular?

He stood much as he had in the game. Shoulders braced, hands shoved into the pockets of his jeans, face unhappy. "Not that, precisely. But it has a certain...style."

The way he said "style" made the hairs on my neck stand up. Lizzie glanced at Trick, one hand tugging at the hem of her orange sweater, the other toying with the end of her pink braid.

They looked no happier than Zee. Which meant they knew something, too.

Crap and more crap.

I moved closer to Damon. I doubted he'd stay quiet much longer.

"Any chance someone followed you home?" Cassandra asked Zee.

Followed? From where? The UK?

Zee shook his head. "Can't imagine they would. My last assignment concluded friendly enough. And they don't travel lightly these days. Particularly not over oceans."

"Still, it's quite the coincidence." Cassandra had her boss lady face on.

Zee just shrugged.

"Is someone going to explain what exactly you're talking about?" Damon asked, the words clipped. He was hanging on to his patience but barely.

I gripped the back of the game chair in front of us, fingers digging into the leather.

"Eventually." Cassandra held up a hand, still focused on Zee. I, for one, wasn't about to interrupt her.

"You want to speed that up a bit? That's in my game." Damon stabbed a finger toward the symbol on screen. "There's a tournament starting tomorrow. And before you suggest it, let me tell you, it would take a lot for me to shut it down at this point. Like that thing being connected to another demon."

That got Cassandra's attention. "It's not another demon."

She sounded certain. So certain that I was sure she had a very good idea about what exactly it was. One of those "other things" Zee had mentioned.

I swallowed, once again very aware that what I knew about magic was only the very small tip of a very large iceberg.

"Then what is it?" I asked hastily before Damon could lose his shit. He wasn't a temperamental guy, but if this turned out to be another magically driven disaster for Riley Arts, I wouldn't blame him if he flipped out.

Triple crap. I didn't want to be back here again. Last night he'd told me that all that mattered was him and me. We'd weathered a demon and the lesserkind together. But when push came to shove, would we make it through if something like that happened again?

Had he really accepted that this was what life might be like with me? I pressed my teeth harder into my lip till it stung, using the pain to stay quiet and let Cassandra talk.

She sighed. "It's something that, by all rights, neither of you should have to know anything about. Maggie eventually, perhaps, but not yet."

Damon crossed his arms, mouth flat. "More secret Cestis business."

"Of a fashion," she agreed. "But it seems, once again, that we have a complication. Zachariah, do you want to explain?"

Zee's eyes flared wide. "Me?"

"You've had more immediate experience of this in recent years than the three of us." Cassandra circled her hand in a motion that took in Lizzie and Trick.

"But I'm not Cestis," Zee protested.

"If I think you're going too far, I'll let you know. Go on."

He glanced at the door as though contemplating whether to just make a run for it. I was fairly sure that Damon would tackle him if he tried. Just what we needed.

I rocked forward slightly, ready to step between them, but then Zee seemed to find his ground again, his shoulders set, arms folded. He jerked his chin at the screen. "That there. It looks like Elder sign. Though not a glyph I know. I'd have to do some research. Or there are...people...I can ask."

"Assume for a minute," I said carefully, "that Damon and I have no idea what Elder sign is." Because that assumption would be 100 percent correct. "Do we get an explanation?" I glanced at Cassandra, expecting her to shake her head, but she just made a "keep going" gesture at Zee.

He shoved his hands deep in his hoodie's pockets. "The Elders. They were here before us. Some say they gave witches their magic. They're not here much anymore. Other than in the stories."

I was still confused. "Stories? Like monsters?"

Zee winced, and Cassandra said, "Not monsters. Well, not in the sense of claws and fangs and scales."

Not exactly reassuring. But she'd said it wasn't a demon. Cassandra and Lizzie and Trick weren't panicking, despite Zee's clear unease. So I wouldn't panic either. But I reached for Damon's hand.

He'd come up close and personal with some of the worst aspects of magic, and I had a bad feeling we were going to take another step into one of those parts of the magical world we'd be happier not knowing about.

"Is there another sense?" Damon asked. "Just tell us what is going on."

"It's not quite that simple," Cassandra said. "Dealing with the Elders takes...delicacy. Negotiation. Protocols. Rules."

Something about how she spoke the words dredged something up in my mind. "That sounds like something out of a fairy tale."

Cassandra hitched a shoulder. "They don't like that word. Though there are reasons there are tales."

"You're saying fa—"

"Don't say it," Zee said. "They don't really like that word."

I snapped my teeth shut. Blew out a breath through my nose. "You're saying there is a basis for some of those stories we were told as children? That the *people* in the tales are real?"

"Something like them, yes."

"And I'm just hearing about this for the first time because?"

Cassandra bristled. "Because you, Margaret Lachlan, are barely past newborn in magical terms. And you arrived bearing a demon in your wake. Demons take priority over all else. Not to mention that you did your best to ignore us for nearly a year after we had dealt with your demon. The fact that you have rejoined us and are finally learning to use your magic doesn't entitle you to all our secrets at once."

I flinched inwardly, trying to keep the expression off my face. Damon's hand tightened over mine.

This was Cassandra in scary mode.

A reminder of who she truly was.

I'd seen her spew magic from her fingers and take down a lesserkind. A power to be reckoned with. One who, when it came to magic in this country, could be judge, jury, and executioner if she chose. She bore a burden in wielding that power, but she didn't, as far as I could tell, let that stop her from doing what she thought was right.

Her expression eased. "We do not share the truth about the Elders with anyone who does not need to know because that is part of the agreement we hold with them. We leave them alone, and we make sure they are mostly undisturbed. In return, they leave us alone, too. As I said, they are powerful. Not malevolent or actively trying to take back the world from humans, but not to be trifled with. Occasionally there is need to interact—such as the last job Zachariah had in England—but we do our best to keep that to a minimum. Which is better for all of us."

Fairies were real. Or perhaps Fae? Those were the ones with the scary folk stories involving blood and pain and death and people being stolen away for years, lives ruined. Fairies conjured up images of tiny, cute beings with wings. I didn't think tiny, cute beings with wings were likely to be something the Cestis would treat so warily.

"If they are supposed to leave us alone, why is one of them leaving"—Damon pointed at the symbol—"that in my game? Leaving aside the more immediate question of *how* one of them left it."

Zee nodded. "I'd like to know that, too."

"The Elders are rarely straightforward. And they have to be careful how they do things in our world. That is also part of the rules between our races. It may be that one of them is merely curious," Cassandra said. "That something you have done has caught their attention." She turned to Zee. "Though I have not heard of any being so keen to embrace something quite so modern. What did you see in England?"

"That was some of the *tanai fol*," Zee said. "Kin. Not full bloods. We had to do business with one of the Elders at the end, to resolve the matter. But they didn't seem too interested. Mostly just satisfied the job got done. Didn't see any of them out and about in the world.

"But the tanai, those with diluted blood—well, those who choose to be out in the world—seem chill with tech. They use datapads and computers. Go to clubs. Most of them have to work. Some game." He glanced at Damon. "Not that I was hanging out in game clubs. But I saw gamedecks.

No chips. The Elders are said to like stories and music and art. The humans they get tangled up with tend to have those kinds of talents, if you believe all the stories and rumors. VR is just another form of storytelling, so I guess it makes sense. The tanai—most of them—are fast and smart. They'd make good gamers."

"So now I have to deal with other kinds of magical gamers, not just witches?" Damon asked, the words clipped.

"Yeah. Well, not that that's new. I mean, if there are tanai gaming, they're already in it. But there aren't many of them," Zee said with a shrug. "The Elders don't tend to have many children, and those who go outside their realm and end up with a tanai child—that's rare. Of course, even the tanai tend to live a long time by our standards, and those who marry tend to marry humans, so there are enough of them. With varying degrees of power. But I don't think you have to worry about many of them being pro gamers."

"But you can't rule out the possibility?" Damon asked.

"No," Cassandra said. "The Elders and the tanai are supposed to abide by our laws when they leave their realm, but historically, they have been somewhat flexible in their interpretation of 'abide.' So I don't know if they would declare themselves under your usual rules. Though the tanai don't seem to cause much trouble these days."

Damon stepped away from me, his fingers sliding free of mine as he stalked closer to the screen. "Fuck. Just what we need."

I didn't disagree. And Cassandra couldn't be telling the whole truth about the tanai or whoever they were staying out of trouble if Zee had been sent to England to deal with a situation involving them. But pointing that out wasn't going to help the current situation. "Don't panic," I said. "We don't know that it was necessarily one of the competitors who did this."

"Yeah," Zee agreed. "It could be anyone who can access the game booths, or the systems. I guess we don't know which until we work out what that is. Could even be one of the guests at the gala. Elders like the good life, and from what I've seen, that's true of the tanai as well."

"Great, let's add another thousand or so suspects to the pool." Damon scowled at the screen.

"Can't we narrow that down? The servers from the gala were transferred back to here, weren't they? Is this room one of those?" I asked.

"The ones set up for chips might be on the floor," Damon said. "The ones still using headsets are being set up for the junior teams."

That made sense. Younger kids didn't get chips. At least not yet.

"Madge, where did the server from this booth come from?" Damon asked.

"The server was transferred from the Phenix last night," Madge said, her cool, emotionless voice almost a relief. "It was in demonstration booth ten at the gala. System checks were completed upon transfer when it was connected to the game chairs. No anomalies detected."

"Apparently you weren't testing for fairies in the code," I said. Nobody smiled.

"Don't say that word," Cassandra said. "If this is Elder magic, then they could even be listening to us now. Even if it's not, it's a bad habit to get into. Names have power."

Perfect. Magical eavesdropping.

"Mostly the power to annoy, in this case," Trick added.

Cassandra nodded. "I prefer not to annoy them. Historically, it doesn't end well. Respect goes a long way to preventing incidents. Or accidents."

"This doesn't seem very accidental. Someone put that thing in there," Damon said.

The question was who.

"Is it easy to spot an Elder? Or one of the tanai?" The word was strange on my tongue. It sounded, to my admittedly clueless ear, vaguely Gaelic. Maybe that wasn't so strange. Plenty of Fae lore in Celtic countries.

"A full-blood Elder, yes. I would know if I met

them face-to-face. But they take care to look human when they move among us, so I don't think you could identify one just from security footage," Cassandra said.

Did that mean they didn't look human the rest of the time? Maybe I should have read fewer dinosaur books and more fairy tales in those libraries. I knew the stories from animated movies or fantasy retellings, but I wasn't familiar with the old, wilder versions.

"The tanai are even harder to detect," Zee said. "Most of them look human, anyway. Their magic feels a bit different to human magic, but not as different as the Elders'. You have to know what you're looking for."

"Just what I wanted to hear," Damon muttered. He moved closer to the screen, studying the symbol, hands on hips. He'd rolled his shirt sleeves up, and the muscles in his forearms flexed as his fingers twitched.

Trying to resist the urge to touch the screen? Or punch it? Or wondering what the hell trouble I'd brought to his doorstep now? The tournament hadn't even started and already magic had thrown a spanner into his plans.

"What do you think they want? And how the hell did they leave that?" Damon pointed at the screen. "In my game? Is that magic? Or did they manipulate the code somehow?"

"That might take some time to figure out," Zee said. "I can go back in and take a closer look." He grimaced as he offered. "Though it would have to be you or Maggie who came with me. No one else has a chip."

"Right," Damon agreed. "But each room is an isolated system with a separated server array. Same setup as last night. Designed to stop someone hacking in anywhere from inside the game. But as Maggie said, we didn't program against certain elements. So let's hope that thing hasn't shown up in all of them. That would be a bigger problem."

He wasn't wrong. Magic that could infect multiple separated systems would definitely be bad news. Nothing to mess with. Though Cassandra had said the Elders weren't malevolent.

"Can you check the systems without going into the game in each one?" I asked.

"We can run the feeds," Damon said. "That gives us visuals. Big glowy rock isn't that hard to spot. We can start with the rooms that have servers brought across from the hotel."

"So maybe it's better if you check the feeds and I go in with Zee?" I asked. My stomach rolled at the thought. Had I really just offered to go back in a game that might be infected with magic?

I wrenched my mind away from the immediate image of the demon's face. Not a demon. And

Damon needed this taken care of. If Righteous pulled the plug at this late stage, it would be devastating.

Nothing really happened in there. Big glowy rock. That was all. It hadn't hurt us.

Damon must have seen something in my expression. He came back to me, threaded his fingers through mine. "I don't want you doing anything dangerous."

Taking care of me. Well, I'd return the favor. I forced a smile that felt distinctly lopsided. "I'm not going to touch anything or try to do anything," I said. "Zee knows what he's doing. I'll just be there for backup." Like, I could hit the kill switch and yank us both out of there if something happened. If anything else happened that was bad enough to take Zee out, I doubted my magic would be much use. Not in-game. And not even in the game room. So far, in a panic, I tended to default to fire. Not such a good idea in a small, enclosed room.

"I can go in alone," Zee offered. "It should be safe enough. That thing didn't do anything more than glow at us."

Cassandra pursed her lips, shaking her head. "No. I think Maggie's right, two heads will be better than one. Lizzie would be the better choice, but she doesn't have a chip."

"That's decided, then," I said before I lost my nerve. "Zee and I will go in, Damon can look at the feeds, and Trick and Lizzie can help. And Cassandra, maybe you should stay here with us. You'll be able to see what we're doing on the screen." I pointed at the monitor. I had no idea what she knew about gaming. "That way you'll know if anything happens. Well, anything that's visible. We'll show you how to use the kill switch to pull us out if you think you should." There, another layer of backup. That should at least make Damon happy.

He squeezed my hand.

I squeezed back, trying to channel all the reassurance I didn't really feel at him.

Maybe it worked, because his grip eased.

"All right. That's our plan," he said. "But I want to start checking the feeds first. If we find that thing in any of the other iterations, I don't think it would be a good idea for the two of you to go back in."

"That's fair," Cassandra agreed. "How many game rooms are there?"

"Over two hundred between booths and rooms. But it's early. The techs might not have pulled some of them online yet. It's only the top league teams that are getting a more detailed preview today, so they've been the priority."

The top league was where the big money was. The lower leagues had smaller prizes. Enough to still be a nice chunk of change for the competitors and their sponsors. But most of the lower-tier players would be competing to show off their skills, maybe impress a higher-level team or a bigger sponsor. Pro gaming at the top level was mostly a young person's sport, but the inclusion of tech and strategy members on the teams meant players could extend their careers at the elite levels longer. Competition to progress was fierce and could be cutthroat.

The tournament was wrapped in layers of rules and security to try and prevent dirty dealings, but it was impossible to prevent it completely. Crappy humans always found a way to be crappy.

The winners of each of the lower leagues would get a chance to compete in the final, but the likelihood of one of them actually winning over a pro team and walking away as champions was slim. But between the actual prize on offer and the potential for lucrative sponsorships, there was enough money at stake that some people would inevitably risk skating close to the edge of legality. Or try to get away with jumping off that edge entirely.

"Start with the booths from the gala, like Madge said. If there's nothing in any of those, then Zee and I will go back in. If it's in the other systems, then we may need a plan B."

"That your professional opinion?" Damon asked.

In other words, what was my computer whisperer mojo telling me? "Hard to tell. But it seems sensible to me to start cautiously. This feels like it has to be just one booth or all of them."

"Either that or that symbol is keyed to only activate for particular people," Cassandra said. "There are ways to do that. I'm not sure exactly how it would work in a game, but maybe it would be possible." She looked at Zee and me. "Though to do it, the person in question would have to have met both of you."

"I met a lot of people last night. I'm sure Zee did, too. And he already knows other gamers." Which didn't narrow it down. Madge had picked the game room for me this morning, and I hadn't known Zee would join me.

Damn. If the spell was targeted, then it might have to be in multiple versions of the game. But also a targeted spell—assuming it was aimed at me or Zee—should present no danger to anyone else, and maybe we could declare it safe for the tournament to go ahead.

Depending on what exactly was targeted. Which none of us knew.

I sighed. Theories would only take us so far. "Basically, we have no idea until we go back in. Unless you find something in the feeds. We can stand here and argue about what we're going to do, or we can just do it. Either way, we're up against the clock. Damon?"

He nodded, face grim. "Lizzie, Trick, come with

me. We'll go up to my office. Mitch can meet us there."

Of course. He had to tell Mitch what was happening.

"Okay. We'll wait here until we hear from you," I said.

"Do not even think about going back in until then." He looked at Zee and me.

I held up my hands. "We won't." I didn't really need the warning. It was going to take almost all my willpower to get back in one of the chairs, knowing what was waiting for us inside the game. I had zero desire to do it any sooner than I had to.

Damon, Lizzie, and Trick departed, Damon throwing me one last reluctant look over his shoulder before he pulled the door shut. Which left the three of us behind, still staring at the glyph or whatever Zee had called it glowing from the screen.

"Now that Damon's not here, is there any more you can tell me about the Elders?" I asked. "I already agreed to secrecy when you gave me access to the Archives. I won't tell him anything you don't want me to. Not unless it becomes necessary to keep someone safe."

I didn't like keeping secrets, but Cestis business was Cestis business. Which Damon understood, to a degree. "Anything that might be useful. More about their magic? Or what they might want?"

"I can't help with the second part," Cassandra

said. "They're never very predictable, and this isn't something I've come across before. In all the years I've been on the Cestis, we've only had to deal with them directly here in the US a few times. But I've studied what we have in the Archives and what the Cestis who have more contact—like in Europe—have to share.

"The Elders are highly skilled with glamours and illusions. Better than any witch. They are also masters at enticements. At least when it comes to dealing with humans—even animals, according to some texts. There's a reason why fa—" She caught herself. "—the tales talk about being charmed away."

"And when they're not dealing with us?"

"Their magic is more elemental than ours. They can manipulate their realm to suit them, to some extent. The most powerful can change it completely, or so they say. Move the earth, literally. Call the winds. Part the seas."

"Can they do that here?" A demon had moved the earth. Set off a fault line and killed thousands and thousands of people. Wrecked a city. I didn't want anything to do with anyone who wielded that kind of power.

"They can't change things the same way. Though they seem to be able to manipulate natural things easily. An Elder would likely be able to call lightning far more precisely than you did, for instance. And I'm sure there are other things they can do that we have no idea about. After all, they manage to hide their realm from humans, and that takes powers we just don't have."

"Is their realm like the demon one?" I asked.

"Not exactly." Cassandra shrugged. "The demon realm, we know, is another world. The Elder realm, well, since they hid it, it's hard to know what to call it. But it is, at least, definitely connected to ours. In a way that the demons would like theirs to be. Fortunately for all of us, they have not yet been able to make that happen."

I shivered. "But the Elders have?"

"Well, they were here to begin with. Perhaps it's easier to think of it as them having taken part of the world as it was then and removed our access."

"And when exactly did this happen?"

"Centuries ago," Cassandra said. "When our numbers began to grow. Human numbers, that is. Not witches. If it had been just us, then maybe the Elders wouldn't have left. But they learned the hard way about the less pleasant aspects of humans and their need to control and take. Even before we began to build the machines and fill the world with iron."

"So the part about iron is true?"

"They don't like it," Zee said. "At least the full-blood Elders don't. It's not like in stories where it will make them really sick. Stab an Elder with an iron knife and they'll still be perfectly capable of making you sorry you did. But they find it unpleasant, and they don't choose to spend time around it when they can avoid it. The tanai, well, most of them are fine with it."

"So no Elder equivalent of demon stone?" *Damn*.

Cassandra shook her head. "We don't need one. An Elder in our world can be killed or injured by normal weapons. They heal fast, but they're not invincible. They are hard to kill—harder still if you try it in their realm—but it's not impossible. That's part of the reason they withdrew from our world. As Zee said, the tanai are weaker, but I wouldn't want to put it to the test. Their powers are unpredictable. Of course, that's not something we usually have to worry about here."

"Why not?"

"There just aren't many tanai here. A lot of them left after the Big One."

"After the demon." Couldn't blame them for that.

"Yes," Cassandra agreed. "The Elders told us they were closing the door to the realm here. Though they didn't say if the demon had damaged it somehow or if they were just making a strategic retreat. There have hardly been any hints of them in the United States since then. I certainly haven't heard about any Elders being seen. At least, not one who has caused trouble enough to draw attention. The tanai who live here seem to be mostly law-abiding. More so than their English cousins, anyway." She looked at Zee.

"And how did Zee get tangled up with the English...cousins?" I asked.

"I was working over there," Zee said. "The Cestis in London needed someone who knew how to play the outsider and still fit in. Cassandra suggested me."

Before I could ask any more, my datapad dinged.

"Damon," I said as I scanned the screen. "So far nothing in any of the other booths. He's going to run a code comparison, see if there's been any obvious tampering from that end. That will take a while. I guess we stick to the theory that it's either just this one or set to trigger for certain reasons."

Neither Zee nor Cassandra offered an alternative.

"Is there anything that would help us work out what the glyph is for once we get back in there?" I asked.

"Well, we could send someone into one of the other setups and see what happens. That's always an option. But that just seems like making more work. We should start with this one," Zee said. "No point potentially messing up another server. You ready to go?"

No. But refusing wasn't exactly an option, so I nodded. "What do you want me to look out for?"

"Not sure." He tapped the controls by the monitor, rotating the game recording through the full view again. "I can try a couple things, but mostly I want to see if there's anything we missed the first time."

More magic. Great.

If the Elders were as good at illusions as Cassandra said, we might have missed something. Though I wasn't sure what the point of hiding another spell might be. If they were trying to send us some sort of message, then surely it made more sense for it to be easy to find?

"Okay, I'll follow your lead."

"Good. Tell me if you notice anything weird at all. Anything else different than before. Or even last night." He walked over to the chair on the right and settled back into it.

I gave Cassandra a quick overview of the controls on the screen menu, including how to use the message system to contact us if she wanted to. I left the most important one until last. "This is the kill switch." I pointed at the button on the wall next to the screen. "If you see anything on the screen that you think is wrong, or if we start acting strangely, hit that, and it will shut down the game and disconnect us. We should wake up right away."

Not that gamers were asleep, exactly, but VR

was as close to a waking dream as anything else, and I couldn't think of an easier way to explain it.

"If either of us don't sit up, or don't answer you or anything like that, then ask Madge to get help. Don't touch us."

"No," Cassandra agreed. "I'm not in the habit of blundering into unexpected magical consequences without thinking it through." She touched my shoulder briefly. "Go on. I know what to do. You'll be all right. Zee knows what he's doing, too."

As much as anyone trying to deal with a possibly fairy-infected game could know, I guessed.

I gritted my teeth as I lay back down in the chair, breathing through my nose.

"Ready?" Zee asked.

"See you in there." I laid my wrist against the panel.

CHAPTER TWELVE

:ENGAGE:

I opened my eyes. Back in the room at the inn.

Zee blew out a breath, stretching his arms and wriggling his fingers as though reassuring himself everything was working normally. He looked the same as before, which was encouraging. I glanced around. Everything else seemed the same as well, including my reflection in the old and dirty mirror. So at least whatever we'd set off with the symbol, it didn't seem to be messing with anything else.

So far.

"This is where it would be good if we could jump around in the game. But I guess it's another walk to the river," Zee said.

"Yeah. I don't think we have access to anything to get us there faster." I should've asked Damon about that. There were nearly always shortcuts built into games that the coders could access easily. There were probably more than most in this version, built for a tournament. It needed to be easy for Righteous to put the teams wherever they wanted them in the world and lock and unlock options and game areas as needed. Along with managing the difficulty levels and all the other differences between the versions the different leagues would be playing.

We walked fast, the sun beating down on us. Apparently practice mode was stuck in the one time of day rather than progressing through time like the game normally would. That made things easier, as we weren't going to have to do this in the dark. Though nighttime might have been cooler. It didn't take long for the sensation of sweat trickling down my back to start being a distraction.

"Which one do you think it is?" I asked when we reached the edge of town. "Random magic or trigger?"

Zee sighed, shading his brown eyes to glance back at the town. Was he worried about someone —or something—following us?

I didn't want to ask. I didn't want to *know*. I was jumpy enough as it was. I couldn't blame all the sweat on the sun. Some of it was pure nerves.

"Probably a trigger. The Elders don't do these things on a whim. Not anymore. If they are doing something to alert us to their presence, there's a reason."

"Good reason or bad reason?"

"I guess that's the harder part to figure out."

"You're not making me feel better."

He kicked a stone in the road, sending it skittering ahead of us. "I'm not making me feel better either. But the only way to feel better is to work this thing out. So we keep walking."

I humphed at him but did as suggested. "If it's a trigger, it might be in all the games?"

"Maybe. Or as many as whoever it was who set the spell was able to access. That might be useful, you know. Assuming someone did this last night, Damon could search for any of the guests who had more than one turn at the game."

"Unless they glamoured themselves in between. Changed what their appearance."

"Yeah," Zee agreed. "But it's worth a try. None of us noticed any magic last night, so however this was done, it was slick. Subtle. People were going into the game in groups, and the sessions were time limited, so they must have been with other people. The elders and the tanai are good at magic. A human might not notice them doing anything, but they couldn't pull off anything that would take a long time to set up."

"Assuming it's not in the code," I said.

"Yeah, that's the other path of attack. But I'm

not sure how you'd do that from inside the game, and I'm assuming Righteous had all the servers at the hotel locked down tight. So that seems less likely. I haven't thought of a way I could do it yet."

Did that mean he thought he might be able to given enough time? Interesting. What exactly had he gotten up to in his younger days?

"Cassandra said Righteous is hiring witches?" he continued.

"Yep. But no one was looking for...you know who." No, just demons. I could only imagine Mitch's face when Damon told him there was a whole new category of magical threat to worry about. Maybe I could avoid him for the rest of the tournament.

"Never a dull moment around the Cestis," Zee said, wiping his forehead. "Man. This is going to be a tough environment. Health stats gonna be shaky."

"Unless the characters are adapted," I said, happy to think about anything other than the fact that the Fae were real and putting magic in VR for a few minutes.

His brows drew down. "Too recent if this is from the terraforming breaking down. The colony hasn't been here long enough to have made any significant adaptations according to the backstory. Unless they have gene tech or something. I guess everyone will have to get used to sweaty avatars."

I rubbed my damp palms over my pants. "They

were never going to make it easy. Righteous always try to do things bigger and better."

"True," he said. "Where's the fun in easy?"

"In games, I might agree with you. In life, well, I'd be perfectly happy with some boring easy times."

"You've had a lot going on," he said. "Doubt you're going to have to deal with anything like that again."

"I hope not," I said. "But the magic part isn't going anywhere." I waved an arm at the road ahead. "I mean, it's why we're here."

Zee nodded. "I guess, but this still might be nothing."

I snorted. "If you believed that, you wouldn't be in here. Besides, I'm allowed to be a little rattled. After all, I just found out that, well, you-know-whats exist. I swear I'm going to read every damn book in the Archives. I'm over the surprises."

"That would take a while. And some of those books might do you more harm than a you-know-what might. Careful what you wish for."

"Now you sound like Cassandra."

"She rubs off on people. You'll see."

We were nearing the river. "Did you meet her through Lizzie?"

He nodded. "Yeah. I didn't know I had magic. Not really. But Lizzie knew she did. Not that she told us. We stumbled into a situation the Cestis were involved in. Lizzie kind of gave herself away. Cassandra took over from there. Which was good for all of us, particularly Lizzie. The Cestis got her asshole dad squared away. Not sure what Cassandra did, but he's never tried to bother her since."

That was more than Lizzie had ever told me about her past. Maybe I shouldn't have asked. "Cassandra can be scary when she wants to be."

We reached the top of the hill, and I paused, staring down at the river, trying to spot the rock. It wasn't hard. None of the others glowed.

I pointed, and Zee nodded.

"How do you want to handle this?" I asked.

"We go down, not too close. See what we can see. Get the system to take more pictures. I'll see what the magic feels like. You watch and take notes."

Fine by me.

We walked down the hill cautiously. Nothing like the headlong charge I'd taken with Damon. I sighed.

"Something wrong?" Zee asked.

"No. It's just...well, I've kind of had a hang-up about VR since the...since my chip glitch." Mitch and his team knew about the demon, and so did certain other Riley employees, but I had no idea who might watch this at a later date, so I wasn't going to flat-out say "demon" right now. "I was just getting over it. Feeling like gaming might be fun again."

"This isn't fun?"

"I'm not one of the Cestis," I said. "I don't leap into weird-ass situations for fun."

He grinned. "You get used to it. But okay. This isn't all bad."

"Really? Explain to me what part of magic in a game is good news."

"You're a programmer, right?"

"Sort of. I mostly troubleshoot. I don't build things from scratch."

"Well, that means you're good at problem-solving. Working out puzzles. This is a puzzle. Even kind of a tech puzzle. Think of it that way rather than, you know—" He made a vaguely magical swishing gesture. "That might help."

"Maybe," I agreed. But it did help a little. Zee was right. I was good at figuring out problems. I could handle this.

We reached the point where the road curved up to the bridge, and he stopped.

"Now what?" I said, studying the area around us. Still no change in the rock or the glow.

Zee snapped his fingers, and a system menu appeared. He punched one of the options. "Okay, this is recording my avatar viewpoint. You do yours."

I copied what he'd done. The system would already be recording the full game view, but individual views might help. It was something the gamers did all the time so they could study a game from different angles. Nat used to watch hours of game recordings. Me, I'd never been that into it. Which was why Zee had thought of it and I hadn't.

"I'm going to walk closer," he said. "But first, do you feel any magic?"

"How do I check that here?" I asked. "This isn't me, after all." I looked down at my avatar. It felt real, but it wasn't.

"Just do whatever you usually do. The chip is interacting with your senses. The way you see magic is just another way you use those."

"If you say so." Maybe he was right. Magic must work in the games or the gamers with magic wouldn't be asked not to use it. But the knowing how a person might use magic in-game to cheat was different to knowing *if* there was magic being used. Usually I could see the change in someone's energy field if they used magic. But in here, everything—and everyone—was really just energy. What would that look like?

No way to know without trying.

I closed my eyes for a moment and tried to summon the sensation of opening myself to the energy field. When I opened them again, everything seemed faintly brighter. Including our unfriendly rock.

Zee had a faint purplish tint around him.

"I can see the energy. I think. That's a start."

He nodded. "Good. Watch mine." The purple light around him flared for a few seconds, then subsided.

"What was that?" I asked.

"I tried a cooling charm."

"Did it work?"

He glanced up at the sun. "That still feels damn hot, so maybe not. But you saw it, yeah?"

"Yeah," I agreed. I wasn't entirely sure how that worked. Maybe the magic was translated to an extra layer of pixels in his avatar or something. But I didn't have to understand it if I could see it. I didn't really understand how I saw the energy in the first place. I should just file this under the same "because, magic" part of my brain and figure it out later.

"Okay. Now we look around, see if anything stands out."

"Almost everything glows in here," I said. "Not like outside. Usually it's just the people who stand out." Inanimate objects had energy fields, too, but not generally bright. Unless they used electricity.

"Like you said, in-game, everything is energy. You have to look for something active."

Gah. "I suspect that's one of those things that sounds easier than it is. But let's get this over with." I scanned the surrounding area. But nothing stood out to me other than the rock with the glyph. That made me want to squint. But it had made me want to squint before. "I don't see anything."

Zee nodded, his fingers tapping the canteen at his hip as he considered.

"I'm going to move closer," he said. "Wait here."

That was an order I was okay with.

He moved slowly, pausing every few steps to stop and turn in a circle so the recording would get a full view before standing still facing the rock. Checking for magic?

I strained my senses, watching and listening. But there was nothing but the sound of the river rushing past and the breeze and the shifting pebbles under Zee's feet. Nothing that stood out.

He paused a few feet away from the stone, on the side with the glyph, and crooked his hand, beckoning.

I swallowed, muscles tensing. Taking the first step was an effort, my instincts yelling at me to stay away from the damned stone. I moved slowly, like Zee, mentally ready to hit the kill switch. I stopped when I was halfway to him and circled around, to keep some distance between us. He wasn't blocking my view, and the swirls of the glyph still made my eyes hurt. But it wasn't any brighter than it had been before.

"Feel anything? Or see anything?" Zee asked.

I shifted my senses again. The glyph shone

brighter, but not with an intensity suggesting active magic. But if Elder magic was different to ours, maybe it wouldn't.

"Anything in particular I'm looking for?" I asked. "What does their magic look like?"

He shrugged. "I've never seen it. Tanai a few times. That wasn't that different to ours. Though it looked...ripply somehow."

Ripply? Not helpful. But the glyph wasn't moving at all. "Like a shimmer rather than a glow?"

"I guess." He glanced back at me. "I don't see a shimmer here. Do you?

"No. It's brighter than everything else, but I can't see anything moving."

"Me either." Zee sounded frustrated. "I'm going closer. Come here and stand where I am. That way you can record."

"Is that really a good idea?"

"Maybe not, but I don't see much choice. Either we try this, or we go back out with no more idea about that thing than we had before."

I took a few steps forward. "Now what?"

He shrugged. "Try some in-game things, see if it interacts with those."

"Like what?"

He bent and picked up one of the pebbles. "Like this." He tossed the pebble toward the rock. It connected and bounced back with no discernible effect.

"That was risky. And it didn't work," I added.

"No." Zee took a step closer, bent to pick up the pebble where it had landed. It hadn't changed, still rimmed with a faint white glow like mist or smoke, but nothing like the glyph's brighter light. "It looks the same." He dropped it back down onto the ground.

"Anything else you want to try?" It felt like pushing our luck to keep going, but Cassandra hadn't pulled us out or sent us a message, so apparently she didn't disagree with Zee's approach. I was in no position to second-guess either of them.

"Water, maybe?" He reached for the canteen hanging from his belt, opened the lid, and sniffed. "I think this is water."

"You think? Shouldn't you be certain?"

"Seems like a water canteen would be standard equipment in a hot world like this. In fact, it is standard equipment. I didn't choose anything custom for my avatar, did you?" He pointed at my belt. "You have one, too."

I shook my head and reached for the canteen strapped to my hip, lifting it to study the small indicator panel on its side. Some sort of purifying system, maybe. Which seemed to suggest water over anything else.

Zee was right. On a hot and hostile world, water was a key commodity. I undid the cap and sniffed. "Mine smells like water, too. I guess we could do a test. You try what's in yours, and I could empty this and refill it from the river. That should be fresh water." Fresh muddy water, but there was no smell of salt in the air. I didn't know anything about the oceans on this world, but salt water was salt water. And river water smelled different. "If I lie on the bank, I think I can reach the water."

"Right," Zee said. "Let's try mine first."

"Okay. You going to pour or try and splash it from where you are?"

"I'll try a splash. Keep some distance. If that does nothing, we can pour some from yours."

He turned back to face the stone and swung the canteen. The water arced, some of it turning to spray in the breeze, but some of it hit the stone. I thought for a moment that the glyph flared, but it happened so fast I couldn't be sure. The rock looked darker where the water dampened it but otherwise no reaction. I moved closer, curious despite myself. "Did you see anything?"

"No. Which maybe helps rule out this being coded in the game. In-game, there'd be some sort of reaction, I think."

"Not if you're not trying the right thing," I said. "It might only react with certain substances or touch or something."

"Well, neither of us is going to touch it."

"No argument from me." The glyph was elegant and strangely appealing. Something in the way the light played over the stone made it look smooth to touch. My hand flexed a little, itching to see if it was. I shook off the sensation. "Definitely no touching." I looked at him. "Though I kind of feel like it would be nice to? Are you getting anything like that?"

"No," Zee said. "Not so far. *That* sounds like Elder magic though. Some sort of lure. Though it's not very strong if it's not just pulling you over there and making you put your hand on it."

"Maybe it's just supposed to make us feel like it's safe," I said. "Which means it's probably not." I glanced over my shoulder at the river. "Let's try river water. If that doesn't work, we'll think of something else. We could ask Cassandra?"

"If she's thought of something, then she would have sent us a message. Let's try the river."

"River it is," I agreed.

The pebbled bank looked dry enough, the drop to the water below only about a foot. I eased closer to the edge and crouched, peering down at the water. Up close it was still muddy blue but not completely opaque. I could see a couple feet down from the surface. No sign of any fish. Or predators. Then again, this was just a preview. It wouldn't give away anything like a giant crocodile equivalent lurking in the river, so I was probably safe enough.

"I'm going to lie down," I said. "How about you

hold my ankles, just to make sure I don't take an unexpected bath?"

Zee nodded. "Sure."

I wriggled into position, moving my hips close to the edge so most of my upper body and torso hung over the bank. "Okay, grab on."

There was a soft thump as he went to his knees beside me. Then his hands closed around my ankles. There was a flash of gold, and the air chimed.

"Fuck," I said before the game dissolved around us.

CHAPTER THIRTEEN

"DON'T MOVE, EITHER OF YOU."

Cassandra's voice.

Okay, good. Some of the panic flaring through me eased. If Cassandra was talking to me, we must still be in the game room, and whatever had happened hadn't transported us somewhere else entirely.

I opened my eyes. "Define 'don't move.'" Nothing hurt, which was another plus.

Cassandra stood in front of the chairs, hands on hips, frowning. "Don't move off the chair. Don't touch anything else. Or anyone else."

She turned her attention to Zee. "That was careless, Zachariah."

I turned my head carefully toward Zee.

He was keeping still, too, still cradled in the

game chair, but the look in his brown eyes was sheepish. "Yeah, sorry. But I was being careful. Nothing happened when I first touched the pebble. Or even when I picked it up again."

"The pebble?" *What did the—* "Oh, you think the pebble somehow carried the spell? Zee touched it and then touched me." Then we'd been kicked out of the game. Or had we? Had Cassandra pulled us out? Maybe it didn't matter. What was important was what the heck the magic had done. "Does this mean I was the target?"

Cassandra shrugged. "I can't be sure."

What the hell did the Fae want with me?

I looked down at my arms, letting my gaze shift. A silvery glow surrounded me, the color reminiscent of the glyph. "What is this? Can you both see it?"

Zee stared, mouth turning down.

"Elder magic," Cassandra said.

"I think it's a summoning," Zee said. "Or something like it, at least."

"What sort of summoning? What are we supposed to do?" The only summoning spells I knew about were the kind that called imps or demons. This couldn't be the same or we would have been taken wherever the Fae wanted us to be, surely?

"You're supposed to stay right there," Cassandra said firmly. "How do you feel?"

"Normal," I said. "Freaked out. But normal. Zee?"

"I don't feel any different."

"That's something, I guess," Cassandra said. "Zee, what do you think they want?"

He grimaced. "There's no compulsion. Maybe just to talk?"

"They could have just asked," I muttered.

"Maybe they needed to know something before they could tell if they needed to talk to you," Zee said.

"Then they could have sent one of the tanai to talk to us," Cassandra countered.

"Don't blame me," Zee said, sounding cranky. "I didn't make the rules. And I'm not them."

"Arguing about it isn't going to get us any-where." I lifted a hand to hit the button to change the position of the chair, then froze. A glyph glowed in the center of my right palm, pale gold against my skin. "Zee. Show me your hand."

He held them both up, palms out. A matching symbol glowed on his right hand. "Well, fuck."

That sounded about right.

My heart pounded as I flexed my hand carefully. I stopped and took a breath. I didn't want Madge triggering a medical alert and calling in the doctor. The fewer people who knew about this the better.

Less freaking out, more thinking.

"Is this the same glyph as in the game?" I asked.

Zee squinted at his hand. "No, I think it's different." He sat up, twisting toward me. "Let me see yours."

I stretched my arm, not leaning any closer. Touching him again seemed like a bad idea.

"They look similar," he said. "Maybe not exactly the same?" He squinted at his hand again. I did the same. The glow made it difficult to decipher the exact lines of the glyph.

"Wonderful," I said. "What do we do now?"

Cassandra held up her datapad. "Right now, I'm going to call Lizzie and gather everyone to come back down. We can ward you while we figure that out."

Telling Lizzie meant telling Damon. "Do we have to?"

"We need an answer," Zee said. "I can't sit here all day. The Diablos will be looking for me. They'll freak if I don't show. They need me."

"They're going to have to wait a little longer," Cassandra said, eyes steely. "After all, you joined them so you could keep an eye out for any magical problems. This is a magical problem."

"Yeah, but I'm guessing it's not one you want me to share with them." Zee's expression was just as set as Cassandra's.

"No, but they knew there might be some demands on your time."

"Tonight's the launch session," I said. "The teams will be mostly in the audience. It's only the team captain and seconds on stage during the in-troductions, right?"

Zee nodded. "Yes. But there will be eyes on the team. Cameras. And I'll be missing our practice runs before that."

"Well, you weren't going to be in-game," I pointed out. "They'll have to make do for now. We should be able to get out to the launch. But it's not going to be the end of the world if you're not around for a few more hours." I lowered my hand, curling it into a fist so I wouldn't have to stare at the glyph. "What happens after the ward?" I asked Cassandra.

"We decide on the next steps. You'll know when I do."

"That's not reassuring," I said.

"Sorry. But it's the truth. For now, you're safe. You just need to stay put."

"I'd like to move sooner rather than later. We should work the problem while we wait. Is there any way to find out what this glyph means?"

"We have some records back at the Archives," Cassandra said. "But we can't exactly take you there."

"Yeah, this is where Damon's idea about having the Archives online starts to sound pretty good," I said.

"If you ignore the fact that we're actually dealing

with a spell active in a digital form," Cassandra retorted.

True. Though right now I was more worried about the spell in the physical world. Aka on my hand.

I unclenched my fist, forcing myself to study the glyph. It didn't give off any sensation of heat or weight. If I hadn't been able to see it, I wouldn't have known it was there. Which didn't make it any less creepy.

"Okay, so that's a no to the slow route and looking it up in books. Which leaves us with the faster approach." I waved my hand at Zee. "He's the one with the recent connections to the Elders. Can't he ask someone?"

Cassandra raised a brow. "That's not necessarily—"

"It's fast," I interrupted. "The worst they can do is say no, right?" I shrugged and turned to Zee. "*Is* there someone you can ask from England? One of the tanai? Or did you burn all your bridges back there?"

His brows drew down, and he didn't answer immediately. After a pause, he hitched a shoulder as though shaking off a bad memory. "There's someone. I don't know if they'll tell me anything, but I can try."

"Will that cause problems?" Cassandra asked.

"I understood things were delicately balanced over there."

Clearly she knew more about whatever Zee had been doing than I did.

"I don't think so. They just won't help me if it's going to make trouble." He reached for his datapad, lying next to him on the other arm of the game chair, calling up a bank of icons. He tapped one I recognized, a privacy shield that would blur the other side of the call so we wouldn't be able to hear it properly.

Protecting his friend's identity, maybe? Or making them feel secure?

"You sure about this?" he said to Cassandra.

She nodded, and he tapped a number into the datapad. "It's me," he said. "Sorry, weird time." His accent had shifted, definitely more British to my ears. Or what you'd get if an American had spent a lot of time there and was trying to fit in.

He listened to the response. "Calling for a favor. You owe me, yeah?"

Another response, which resulted in a satisfied nod. "Right. So. If I needed to talk to the family here in San Francisco, where would I go?"

This time the answer on the other end was louder and sounded surprised, even though the words were muffled by whatever program Zee was using.

"Yeah, I'm aware," he said. "But in this case,

there's not much choice." He pulled the datapad away from his ear and held his palm up to the screen.

Another surprised-sounding squawk.

"Just lucky, I guess," Zee said. Then he paused. "Yes, there are two." He listened another moment. "Okay. We can try that. Thanks. Enjoy dinner."

He ended the call, dropping the datapad onto his lap.

"Well?" Cassandra asked.

"They agreed it's a summoning. Said if we touch the two glyphs together, we should know where to go."

"Or you trigger whatever the spell is actually supposed to do," Cassandra said.

Zee shrugged. "Sure. But honestly, they could have snagged us in the game if they wanted to do something bad. Or glamoured us and snatched us out of the party. This is a fairly polite invitation, I think. Not the straightest path, but you know, if they're trying to skirt around the rules, it's going to be weird. Elder logic and all. I guess they have their reasons."

"Their reasons being they enjoy being mysterious," Cassandra said.

Zee's mouth quirked. "And they're well up on the usefulness of a reputation as hardasses. Same as the Cestis."

Cassandra smiled reluctantly. "All right. Well,

we'd better be prepared for a drive. As far as I know, they closed the door to their realm here after the Big One. Don't try anything until Lizzie is here and we set up a ward—"

"I can do that," Zee objected.

"No you can't. Not while you're carrying a glyph. Even if you can ward yourself against a spell you already bear—and if you can, then that's another discussion we will need to have—you don't know how Elder magic might affect yours. Let's not make the situation worse."

He subsided with a mutter.

"So, we're going to do some Elder magic and then go and visit them. Awesome," I said, fighting the urge to curl into a ball and try the "if I can't see them, they won't see me" approach to get me out of this.

Cassandra smiled tightly. "Sarcasm isn't becoming, Maggie."

"You get sarcasm or me freaking out at this point," I said, trying to breathe deeply. "This is not the plan. This was all supposed to go smoothly." My voice tipped into whiny territory.

"Expecting the unexpected is often a good idea when it comes to magic," Cassandra said as the door opened.

"Yeah, that will go down well with Damon," I replied as Lizzie walked in.

"Judging by the language he and Mitch were

using earlier, probably not," Lizzie said. "But good news: so far, no sign of your symbol in any of the other booths. That calmed them down a bit." She dumped her purse on the carpet near my chair. "He wanted to come down with me, but I told him to stay put. That didn't really improve his mood. You might have to do some boyfriend soothing. I suggest hot sex to distract him."

I held up my palm. "That's not exactly an option when Cassandra says I shouldn't touch anything." Not that I thought it would necessarily help as it was. Sex wasn't the solution to this problem. This seemed to be a fairy tale, not a romance.

"Huh," Lizzie said, taking in the glyph. "Yep. I'm guessing that would kill the mood." She flashed me a smile. "But hopefully that's only temporary. Damon sent you a message."

"My datapad is in my bag, over there," I said. Unlike Zee, I hadn't thought to pull it out before we'd gone into the game.

"You can check that later," Cassandra said when Lizzie took a step toward my bag.

"Or I could pull it up on the room comp," Lizzie said. She turned toward the game screen and stopped. "Huh. Where's the glyph?"

"What?" I focused on the screen. Sure enough, the image there, frozen from when Cassandra had hit the kill switch, showed our avatars by the river, surrounded by a golden glow. But in the background, the rock where the symbol should have been looked like just a rock again. "It's gone." I hadn't actually paid much attention to the screen since we'd been yanked out of the game.

"Guess whatever it was transferred to you," Lizzie said. She smiled, then started rummaging through her purse. It was bright purple and nearly as big as the backpack she often carried. "That's good news. That means it was magic, not a change to the game."

The whoosh of relief made me glad I was sitting down. If it was magic, then we could take care of it. Do whatever the Elders wanted. And the games would be fine. No reason to delay the tournament. "Is there any way to know for sure?"

"Yes," Cassandra said briskly. "We ask the Elders when we see them. Which we can't do until we set this ward. Then we'll see what happens when you two take Zee's...friend's advice."

Lizzie's head snapped up. "What friend?"

"Zee talked to someone in England," I said. "About how to get in touch with you know who."

Her gaze fixed on Zee. "Interesting friends you have." She started hunting for whatever it was she was looking for in her purse again, mouth flat.

Zee wisely kept his mouth shut.

The silence stretched until Lizzie and Cassandra started casting the ward. They worked fast, and I couldn't follow everything they did. Zee watched intently but didn't interrupt. When they were done, they stepped back.

"Right," Cassandra said. "Let's try this."

I tensed. I really didn't want to. But we didn't really have a choice.

I looked at Zee. He looked back at me. Then we stretched out our hands and pressed our palms together.

There was another chime and flash like there had been in the game. When my vision cleared, I blinked. Hanging in the air above us, like a perfect miniature holo, was a familiar sight.

"Is that the Rose Garden?" I said, puzzled. The Berkeley Rose Garden had been reestablished after the Big One, the roses rescued or replaced, the terraces rebuilt. Even the trellises had been restored.

"They do like gardens," Cassandra said, peering at the image. "Though I wasn't aware they'd reclaimed a link to their realm there." She didn't look pleased. Was this a breach of whatever the agreement was between the Elders and the Cestis?

"The door was in the Rose Garden?" Lizzie asked.

"Before they left, yes."

"Roses show up in their stories a bit," Lizzie said. "Maybe there's a reason."

"I'd still like to know why they want to rejoin the party again, now. Mad urge to game?" Irritation spiked my voice. When was this all going to end? I stared at the tiny garden. The illusion was perfect, right down to sunlight chasing across the roses. Impressive. And suddenly I was very eager to be there. I started to swing my legs off the chair.

"Stay still. We haven't released the ward," Lizzie said. "Then we probably should ward you once you're off the chairs."

"Why? We know what they want." I pointed at the illusion.

"Some of it," she said. "But hey, your hand is glowing, so let's be careful."

"What more could they possibly want?" I muttered. It was an effort to stay still, the urge to get moving growing.

"Perhaps they'll tell us when we get there." Cassandra patted her bun for a minute, still frowning.

"Get where?" Damon's voice came from the speakers.

"To Berkeley. We have some people to discuss this matter with," Cassandra said.

"You mean the people you talked about before?" he asked.

"Yes. Generally, it's best not to keep them waiting."

"I'll be down in five minutes."

"You need to stay here, finish your checks," Cassandra said. "I am fairly certain that your game is safe, that they have gotten what they wanted, but better to be safe than sorry. Lizzie and I can handle this."

"I want to—"

"You were not invited. Maggie and Zee were. I have a certain status because of the Cestis. Lizzie does too. You do not. Better for you to stay out of it. We don't want to complicate this any more than we have to. We'll tell you what you need to know when we get back."

I winced, glad Damon wasn't using a vidlink.

"I could lock you all in that room, you know," he said. I didn't need the vidlink to know he was only half joking.

Cassandra rolled her eyes. "Yes, dear, but then you'd have to delay your tournament, because you're not going to put your gamers at risk and let them into the game while you don't know what's happening. I don't think you want to do that, so in this case, you may have to, as Lizzie would say, suck it up and wait for news."

"I totally wouldn't tell you to suck it up," Lizzie said, grinning at the screen.

"You totally would," Damon said, but he sounded less annoyed. "All right. Can I send Maia with Maggie?"

"Do you think Ms. Lin has skills that Lizzie and I lack?" Cassandra asked.

"Pretty sure she's a better shot than either of you."

"Trust me, you do not want her shooting an Elder. The consequences would be unpleasant. Besides which, Zachariah is not such a bad shot, I
believe. So we have all the bases covered. Stop
stalling, Damon, and let us do our jobs."

The drive to Berkeley in Cassandra's neat red
hatchback was silent until we crossed the bridge
and I stopped worrying about what Damon was
going to say when I got back and started worrying
about what was about to happen before that.

The urge to get to the Rose Garden was still
strong, but it had eased back now that we were
heading in the right direction. Maybe I should have
been more freaked out, but I was more worried
about the upcoming meeting than why I was going
there.

Meeting with the Fae. Who were *real*. Part of me
wanted to laugh at the idea. Part of me was
curious.

The rest of me was having a minor meltdown. I
had no idea what to expect. Everything I knew
about fairies came from books I'd read as a kid.
Hazy memories at best. Though what I remembered
was that to do well when it came to dealing with the
Fae, it was important to keep your wits about you

and make whatever rules there were for the en-counter work in your favor.

I had no idea what the rules were. Other than don't say "fairy." My pulse started to pound, the car suddenly hot.

Freaking out wasn't going to help. I needed something to focus on.

Rules. Right. What are they?

I leaned forward in my seat. "I'm going to take a wild guess and say there are rules for talking to the Elders? Protocol or something? To make sure they don't get, what did you call it, unpleasant?"

"Yes," Cassandra agreed, keeping her eyes on the road. "Many. But they have asked for this meet-ing, so that gets us around some of them. The es-sentials boil down to: be respectful, do what Lizzie and I tell you to, and answer their questions care-fully. Don't make any promises, don't ask them for favors, don't tell them anything more than you have to. If you can let the three of us do most of the talk-ing, that would be best."

Zee, squashed into the back seat with me, grunted something that might have been agreement.

"Do you have any advice to add?" I asked him. "Seeing as you've had more to do with them than the rest of us?"

"Don't piss them off, don't believe everything

you see. Don't eat or drink anything they give you," he said.

Wait, what? "Now that *is* straight out of a f—a story."

Lizzie, who'd been doing her best to pretend there was nobody in the back seat, twisted around in the passenger seat. "The tales aren't all wrong."

"No," Cassandra agreed. "The food might not tie you to their realm, but it could very well knock you out long enough for them to take you somewhere you can't escape from. Or poison you. And the stuff they drink is going to make Sandman or black market stims look tame. You don't want to be tripping and trying to deal with them."

I tried to picture Cassandra high and failed. I had to assume she'd always stuck to the rules in her dealings with the Elders.

"Shut up, be nice, and don't eat or drink. Got it." I hunched down, arms crossed, my palms tucked beneath my jacket so I couldn't see the glow from the glyph. The image of the Rose Garden had vanished once Zee and I stepped away from the game chairs, but the symbols on our hands hadn't budged. I was going to have to come up with some excuse to wear gloves a lot if whoever we were meeting didn't make that stop.

It didn't sound like I could actually ask them to do it. That would count as a favor, wouldn't it?

Cassandra parked the car near the entrance to the garden. "Lizzie, set up a stay-out ward. I'm sure the Elders will be discouraging anyone from feeling the urge to stop and smell the roses while we're here, but we might as well back that up. The last thing we need is someone blundering into the middle of this."

Now that she mentioned it, the street was strangely empty. And there wasn't anyone in the gardens. Which, on a nice sunny morning, was un-usual. There hadn't even been cars coming the other way down the hill as we'd driven up.

Lizzie nodded and got to work setting the ward.

I studied the garden. I drove past often enough but hadn't spent much time in it. Lizzie and I had come here once when we'd been talking about plans for the backyard, and she was trying to work out what roses might work nicely with the survivors of my gran's tea roses. As far as I could tell, it hadn't changed since then. Only some of the bushes were flowering, which made sense given the time of year, but other than that, it matched my memories.

No handy sign reading "This way to Fairyland." I tucked my hand back into my pocket just in case there *was* somebody else here. Zee stood with his hands deep in his pockets, too.

"Come along. We might as well get this over with." Cassandra urged us all toward the entrance.

"Do you know where this door or whatever is?" I asked.

She pointed toward the trellises, covered in white and red blooms. "My guess is over there. It's a sheltered spot, less obvious when someone needs to cross the threshold."

It made sense. The trellises were the only sub-stantial structures in the garden. Presuming some sort of magical door wasn't just going to appear in the hillside itself as it might in a fairy tale. I trailed behind Cassandra, dread building in my stomach with every step.

As we reached the trellis, someone stepped out of the shadows. Someone I recognized.

"Pinky? What the hell are you doing here?"

CHAPTER FOURTEEN

PINKY GRIMACED APOLOGETICALLY before straightening her shoulders, her face settling into a serious expression. In the shadow of the white and red roses climbing over the trellises, her hair wasn't quite so bright, but the green eyes were even more vivid. Last night I thought she'd had the color enhanced, but now I wasn't sure.

"Hello, Maggie." She wore a long white linen dress with loose sleeves falling to her wrists and braided leather sandals. The outfit seemed more like something out of an old movie about hippies than what I'd imagine a woman with a taste for pink hair, tattoos, and dragon scale dresses might choose.

So which was the real Pinky? The friendly woman I'd met at the gala or this one, standing before me, who clearly had some connection to the Fae?

"What are you doing here?" I asked, trying not to snap the words. Best not to anger the Fae before we even began. But I couldn't help feeling stupid. I'd *liked* her.

"The High Ones, my Elders, requested I bring you to them." Her attention shifted to Cassandra. "Lady of the Cestis, welcome."

Cassandra bowed slightly. "Thank you."

"May I know the names of your companions?" Pinky asked.

That phrase was far too formal. But a good reminder that I needed to let the experts handle whatever was about to happen. I bit down the questions burning on my lips. Like what the hell a composer was doing playing intermediary for the bloody Fae?

"May I know yours?" Cassandra countered, voice cool.

Pinky nodded. "Pinky Andretti. Your companions, Lady Cestis?"

"Do you guarantee them safe passage and safe return?" Cassandra asked.

"I do. No harm shall befall them from me and my kind."

"What about your Elders' kind?" I blurted, unable to stop myself. She had to be tanai rather than full Fae, surely?

Pinky grinned. "New to this, aren't you?"

"I think you know that already."

"Ladies," Cassandra said in a warning tone. "We shouldn't keep anybody waiting."

"No," Pinky agreed, her face resuming its more formal expression. "In answer to your question, no harm shall befall them from me or my kind or the Elders. Safe passage and safe return. To this time and place," she added when Cassandra made a soft noise. "They only wish to talk."

"Very well." Cassandra made a peculiar motion with one hand. "You know Maggie already, it seems. This is Zachariah, who has met with some of your far kin before, in England."

"His name is known to us."

Zee grunted softly and bowed his head in acknowledgment.

"And this is Elizabeth, also of the Cestis."

Names. But not full names.

Though it was entirely possible Pinky already knew them, as she knew mine. She'd been at the gala, would have been sent all the information about Spark. Lizzie's name wasn't hard to find on the Spark website. And Zee was on the list of players. But maybe knowing them and saying them had a different level of risk in this situation. Either way, if Cassandra was being cautious, best to follow her lead.

"Welcome, Elizabeth of the Cestis," Pinky said. "May I see the summoning?"

Zee and I looked at each and then held out our hands.

Pinky inspected the glyphs for a moment. "Thank you. Stay close with me. We will only be going a short way into the realm, but sometimes the spaces within are...capricious. Do not stray. I have promised safe passage, but if you try to travel within without me and get lost, I won't be able to help you."

"If this is just a discussion, then there is no reason for us to get lost, is there?" Cassandra asked.

Pinky bowed her head slightly, holding up her hands. "No, Lady. But as I said, the realm can sometimes be difficult. The link here is freshly bound and still remembers the harm before. It makes it nervous."

The *realm* was nervous? That sounded...not good. What the hell were we walking into?

"Very well," Cassandra said. "Let us enter."

Pinky nodded and turned to face the trellis. A solid bank of rambling roses hung down from the wooden structure. Studded with thorns that were easy enough to see even from a distance. Not something I wanted to tangle with. Freeing my gran's roses from the overgrown wilderness the backyard of my house had grown into had left me with a few scars. They were much smaller than these, but most roses had teeth. What sort of bite might come from a rose that guarded the entrance to fairyland?

Stop calling it that.

Safer to just think of it as the realm and stick to that until someone gave me a better term for it.

Pinky gestured slowly at the roses, her hands tracing a complicated shape in the air. Light shimmered over the flowers, and suddenly they became a door made of golden wood, silver hinges fastening it to a carved doorframe. No handle. It gleamed in light that shouldn't have been there, given we were under the roof of the trellis. The door swung silently inward. More lights shimmered beyond.

I took a breath. Light was better than darkness. I doubted a door into the demon realm would shimmer prettily.

Pinky's hands lowered, and she pressed them together and bowed to the door, then straightened and turned. "We may enter. But remember, please stay close. It isn't far."

Wonderful. This was not what I'd had planned for my morning, but apparently it was what I was going to be doing anyway.

Pinky went through first, and Cassandra followed without hesitation. Lizzie turned and smiled encouragingly before she followed.

"You go," Zee said. "I'll bring up the rear."

On the other side of the door was a hallway that looked normal until you noticed the glowing balls of light, each about the size of a baseball, hovering at intervals along the walls with nothing supporting them.

Fae magic.

Something about them made me shiver. I looked for a sign of normality.

The walls were painted wood, decorated with plants and flowers and shapes in twining patterns, and the floor beneath our feet was slate tiles. The air smelled faintly of flowers. Not roses. Something headier and sweeter. Gardenias. Or jasmine maybe? Or something that bloomed here and not back outside the door.

Still, it seemed...welcoming, even if it was odd.

It could all be an illusion, but if it was, I was going to take it as a good sign that whoever was waiting for us wasn't trying to scare the crap out of us.

True to Pinky's word, we walked maybe twenty feet down the corridor before she stopped in front of a door on the right. She pressed her hand to the wood, and it swung noiselessly inward. Pinky smiled and swept a hand toward the doorway. "Please enter."

Cassandra walked through. I exchanged a look

with Lizzie, who just shrugged. She looked more curious than intimidated. I guess it helped if you had at least known that all this existed for more than a few hours. My heart was thumping hard enough that I was surprised none of them could hear it.

Maybe Lizzie could, because she squeezed my hand briefly before following Cassandra through the doorway.

"Safer if I bring up the rear," Zee said.

For the first time, the thought struck me that he possibly knew more about all of this than he was letting on. And if he was somehow working with the Fae, then this was a very neat way to deliver us to them and get away scot-free.

But he'd do it at the risk of pissing off every Cestis in the world. Cassandra was intimidating enough on her own. I wouldn't want to be the person facing down multiple wrathful versions of her.

Besides, Cassandra and Lizzie knew Zee. I was being paranoid.

Just a door.

The fact that it led into a room where some vastly powerful magical being was waiting for me was a minor detail.

One small step for witch, one giant step for me. Or something like that.

I lifted my foot.

And stepped into a forest.

Or something close enough to it. Tall trees with long branches of fluttering silver-green leaves ringed a small glade, dappled with light, the air ripe with damp and green and life.

In the middle of the circle of trees, a woman sat in a chair that looked more grown than made, the wood twined into shape, first gold as the outer door would be, then more silvered like the trees. Her hair echoed pale shades of the leaves and the branches, caught up at her brow with a braided leather circlet and falling down her shoulders in a river of soft browns and greens. Her skin was pale and seemed green-tinged, too, though that could be a trick of the light. But the startling silver shade of her eyes was no trick.

The light playing over her skin made her seem as much part of the forest as the trees or the smaller bushes and plants between them or the unseen bird trilling a song too perfect to be from our world from somewhere above.

How much of this was real?

I had questions. Questions I couldn't ask. And I didn't dare try to use magic to so much as look more closely. Not when I had no idea what the rules were.

Pinky approached the woman and made a complicated bow. "Lady," she said. "The ones you wanted. And the Lady of the Cestis and another of her circle." She moved to stand beside the chair, folding her hands in front of her in a practiced gesture. The white dress looked right here, not out of place as it had outside.

But she looked human, at least. There was nothing otherworldly about her, other than those green eyes. Her hair was still pink, her curvy figure very human beside the slender Elder.

"Cassandra Tallant?" The woman's voice was as beautiful as her face, as beautiful as the birdsong and the wind moving through the trees. *Too* beautiful.

Anything too perfect shouldn't be trusted. Not blindly anyway.

"I am the Lady of the Cestis," Cassandra said as she stepped forward. She didn't bow as deeply as Pinky had, but the movement was respectful and practiced. Like she had done this before. Or at least had been taught what to do.

"You are welcome in our realm," the woman said. "And which are the two who were marked by my magic?"

My stomach clenched, but there didn't seem to be another option. Zee and I stepped forward, holding our palms out. The glyphs flared briefly, then faded back to a glow. Zee bowed quickly, so I copied him.

The woman studied us for a long time, her eyes searching our faces. Her face was young, but the weight of that gaze felt old. And deep. Cassandra's eyes told a story of her power. This woman's eyes *were* power.

I didn't want all the power in those eyes focused on me. Especially not when the expression in them was hardly what I'd call friendly.

If only we'd had more time for Cassandra to tell me about the protocol here. I had no idea what I was supposed to do, so the smart thing was to keep my mouth shut and let the others take the lead.

"Come closer." The Elder beckoned with a slender long finger, hand heavy with silver rings.

Cassandra stepped forward, moving in front of us, and Pinky's eyes widened. "Stay where you are." Cassandra bowed again. "Lady, we must discuss terms first. These two are under the protection of the Cestis. I would like to understand what you want with them before we proceed. As is my right under the terms between our peoples."

Her objection didn't warm the expression in those cold eyes, but after a moment, the Elder nodded. "Very well. We are concerned, Lady Cestis, with the events of recent years. We felt the return of the demon. But you took care of that rapidly, as you are tasked to do. We have felt, too, the movements of the smaller darknesses."

Did she mean the imps and the lesserkind? And what the hell did she mean by "tasked"?

"We have those under control as well," Cassandra said.

"And yet they keep coming," the Elder said. "It has taken us no little time and effort to mend our realm after the earthquake fractured the anchor. We did not take the decision to reopen a door here lightly. We would not care for it to be disrupted again."

"I don't think there is much danger of that. There is no sign of even a lesserkind in the city at the moment."

"Perhaps. My kin, some of them have visions. Disturbing visions. A darkness over the city. Coming from elsewhere. There were those who did not wish for the door to be made again here because of it."

I barely stopped myself from flinching. *Fuck.* The Fae had felt darkness, too? Like the witches with their premonitions. I swallowed hard as my stomach rolled and avoided looking at Cassandra.

"Forgive my bluntness, Lady," Cassandra said, "but if there were concerns, why did you not speak to the Cestis? Here or elsewhere? We could have reassured you. The Cestis have not failed. The demons do not walk freely in our world. We have defeated them every time."

"We have our reasons."

Cassandra shook her head. "No. I'm sorry, but if you want something from us, then I need to know more. I know you and your people want the protection of mystery, but I am not an enemy, and we can help you more ably if I know what is wrong."

The woman tilted her head, considering. "That is a fair request. But I have a counter to it. Before I can speak more openly, we have to address the matter of the summoning."

"Why?"

"Because that spell was set to trigger to identify those who have been in recent contact with a demon or their kin."

What the hell? I bit my lip, trying to hold the words back. Beside me, Zee flinched.

Cassandra was shaking her head. "These two triggered it. They are nothing to do with demons. He"—she pointed to Zee—"is known to your kind. He did your kin in England a favor recently. Don't you think they would have noticed if he carried any hint of demon taint? As for her, well, she has been tested. The demon stone has cleared her twice."

The Elder's gaze fixed on me. "Tested twice. That is unusual. Am I to assume, then, that this one has indeed had some contact? Is she the one connected to the most recent demon? The one who was bound?"

"How do you know about *that*?" Cassandra asked.

"Our realm is not unconnected entirely from

your world, Lady Cestis. You know this. News of demonkind travels."

Between who exactly?

"I see," Cassandra said. "Very well. I asked you for honesty, and I will give you honesty in return. Yes, she is the one who was bound. But she was freed and, as I said, has passed the test of demon stone more than once. She has had no contact with even an imp for months now. So if your summoning was triggered by either of these two, then it must be sensing something else."

I really hoped it was. And it wasn't two times, it was three. Damon and I had been tested with demon stone again in the aftermath of the lesserkind's attack, just to make sure any hold it may have had on either of us had died with it.

I shivered at the memory. One encounter with demon stone was bad enough. Three was more than I wanted in my lifetime.

"Our magic is rarely mistaken," the Elder said.

"I'm sure that is true," Cassandra said. "But rarely is not never. Perhaps there is another reason your spell found a target. But I will give you my word and my oath that these two are no threat. And remind you that they are under my protection."

The Elder's eyes flared brighter for a moment, the silver near incandescent.

"Our summoning was set to find those who

have touched the demonkind. Or had contact with one who has."

"Everyone in the Cestis has had contact with someone like that. It does not mean we are tainted. Any more than these two are."

The woman straightened in her chair. "Do you think us so foolish? It was set for recent contact." There was an echo to her voice, and the birds in the trees went silent.

Great. Now she was mad.

"I haven't seen an imp for years," Zee said.

"And it's been months for me," I added hastily.

"So you say. Yet you bear the mark of our magic."

I lifted my chin. Scary Fae lady or not, I wasn't going to stand there and not defend myself. "There were nearly a thousand people at the gala. I shook hands with lots of them. Zee probably did the same. Maybe it was one of them. Is that possible?" I didn't like the idea that someone I'd met last night was dealing with demons, but it was better than the Elder thinking *I* was.

"It is possible," the woman said slowly. She turned to Pinky. "Rosaline, did you sense anything last night?"

Her name was Rosaline?

"Not when I shook hands with Maggie," Pinky said. "I didn't touch him." She nodded at Zee.

"You can sense demon taint?" Cassandra asked.

"I would know someone who was under a demon's control if I met them," Pinky said. "If I touched them. I am from the line of those who fought back the demons from the realm long ago. They set the knowledge in the blood to know if such a thing was tried again. But for we of the tanai, it is a chancy power. For me, it requires touch. And no, before you ask, I didn't shake hands with many people at the gala. I was trying to be inconspicuous."

I glared at her. "*You* planted the summoning in the games?"

"In the booths I could get to," she said unapologetically. "I was hoping for more, but those lines were crazy. I didn't think we were likely to find anyone with so few set. Yet here we are."

"Why now? The demon..." I trailed off, wondering how to avoid saying "the one I was bound to". "The demon was taken care of more than a year ago." The Elder hadn't blasted me for talking to her yet, so I might as well ask the question.

That brought the silvery gaze back to mine. Well, I'd faced down a demon and a lesserkind. I could face a Fae.

"You ask for information?" she said.

Cassandra moved half a step forward. "This is part of our discussion. It is not a favor. You can, of course, choose not to tell us why. But we are here now. And we may be able to help, as I said. But only if we know the truth. And only if you deal fairly."

The Elder smiled at that. It made her face even more beautiful. Easy to see why humans may have lost themselves to the lure of the Fae. "So fierce, Lady Cestis." The birdsong began once more.

Cassandra snorted. "There is an agreement between your people and mine. Things are best for both of us if we hold to that agreement. So perhaps you could answer the question. I will admit, I share her curiosity. Why the sudden interest?"

The Elder shifted in her chair, her hair rippling over her shoulders. "Time does not pass the same in our realm as it does yours, Lady Cestis. Since the door here was closed, we have busied ourselves with securing our realm. With strengthening it. But we found without the anchor here in California, there remained a certain instability. And so we discussed our options. Reform the old door. Find a new anchor point. It was a matter of contention. There were risks to both, just as there were risks to doing nothing."

I wanted to ask what those risks were, but I'd probably already pushed my luck far enough.

"Go on," Cassandra murmured.

"Eventually it was agreed that we would reshape

our door here. So we set to work. Which took time. It proved more difficult than anticipated. We were in the midst of the process when word of the second demon passed to us from the parts of the realm anchored elsewhere. But by then it was judged too late to stop the work. It may have made everything worse to try and unwork the magics at that point. And so we continued. And some of our kin dreamed of the darkness while we worked. When we finally had the door in again, naturally we sought news of the outer world before we ventured forth. We spoke with our kin like Rosaline here and elsewhere. And we learned that the newest demon may have had a connection with these games you mortals play."

The Fae grapevine, it seemed, was good. I was going to have questions for Cassandra about that. Later.

"I see," Cassandra said.

"And then the tanai told us of a great tournament, of many gathering in one place to try these games again. Combined with the dreams of darkness, it seemed to us that we should be wary before we ventured out. So we sent Rosaline—who works in that world—to the gala, to see what there was to observe. To see if any marked by the darkness might be there. As she said, she did not encounter such a one, but still, something triggered the summoning."

"And you want to know who," Cassandra said, sounding somewhat resigned.

The Elder nodded. "You have told me that these two are not the ones we would seek. In that case, yes, it would be best to determine who is. And deal with them."

Did she mean them or us? From the little I'd been told so far, it seemed as though the Fae had retreated and left the humans to deal with the demons alone. Yet Cassandra was wary of their power.

"I see," Cassandra said. "Then yes, I agree. This is something the Cestis should know about."

"Good," the Elder said. "Now that the door is here again, we will defend it if necessary."

I didn't like the sound of that. Nor, judging by the wince Pinky tried to hide, did she.

"And will you help if need be?" Cassandra asked.

The Elder shrugged. "We will aid where we can. Much of our strength here is supporting the realm while it settles back into this place. It will grow stronger with this anchor available to it again, of course, but these things take time. And I think you would not argue that you want a weak door. So there may be limits to the assistance we can pro-vide. Not without falling foul of the rules between us.

"But you have proved equal to the task before

this. And we have given you the information you lacked. That the creatures may be planning once more." She tipped her head at Pinky. "Rosalind will offer her aid. And keep me informed. She had told us much of these games since we returned. We are curious about the dreams they create. They call to our tanai kin, it seems."

I looked at Pinky. "They do?"

"A lot of us game," she said. "But then so do a lot of people."

"There are those closer to us than you, child," the Elder said. "The half kin who wish for powers they cannot have. The discontented ones. I suppose it might give them a sense of what those of us who have full blood to the realm can do."

"Such as?" I asked. More information was good. Damon needed to know if he was somehow building fairy traps in his game. Or doing something to annoy the Elders.

The woman lifted a hand. "Like this." The forest shivered around us, then vanished, replaced by a meadow full of flowers shoulder high and as wide as my hand. Their colors were more like jewels than any plant I'd ever seen, shining in the light. "Or this." The scene shimmered again, became a night sky above us blazing with stars and galaxies. The earth beneath my feet turned to marble. "Or this." Another twitch and we were in a grand room, gilded wood and carved stone and silk banners sur-rounding us.

The scent of the air had changed, carrying woodsmoke and cooking and some sort of incense. If it was an illusion, it was impressive. If it wasn't and she could move us through her world, or per-haps shape the world around us, so easily, it was terrifying.

But I got the point. VR definitely gave players the ability to manipulate their environments. There were whole games built around that premise where the players could build houses or towns or whole worlds to their specifications. Human beings had always chosen to escape into their imaginations. It should have come as no surprise that those born of human and Fae did, too. Particularly those who didn't have the magic they might consider their birthright.

"And is that a bad thing?" I asked.

"Not necessarily. Not if it is helpful. For some, I might imagine, it is a comfort. For others, it may only increase their discontent. And when they are discontented, some will turn, as humans do, to sources that promise them more power."

"Demons," I said.

"Or their servants. Since your games were brought to our attention, we have filled the gap in our knowledge. You are connected with the man who owns the company that makes these games.

The one who had troubles that coincided with the demon who was banished so quickly. But we have not found out more. We must know if there is a connection. If these games put us in danger." Her hand flexed against the end of the armrest. "We will not allow the demons to find a new route into the world we have worked to seal against them."

Did she mean our world or theirs?

Cassandra cleared her throat. "There was a connection with the games. But the door that demon used has been closed."

"Are you sure?" the woman asked.

"As sure as we can be," Cassandra said. "None of us want a demon. The...part of the game...that allowed the demon to make contact has been closed. The lesson was learned. The technology has been altered."

"And how do you know there isn't another path?"

"There haven't been any more demons," I said. "That seems like good evidence."

"But that does not explain why the summoning was triggered," the woman said. "Or the dreams. The darkness is moving."

Or it could just be a coincidence. If I ignored the witches. I clenched my jaw. Cassandra should be the one talking, not me.

"The tournament is well protected," Cassandra said. "They are watchful for such threats."

"Good," the Elder said. "Find the one who triggered the summoning. Deal with them."

And after that? What the hell would happen then?

"Very well," Cassandra said. "But these things are not simple."

"The witches have succeeded thus far, Lady Cestis. As the humans grew and as those of us here before retreated, you have kept the world safe. You should not fail now. If indeed we were called to face down the darkness directly, I fear my people may be moved to do something...extreme."

"The tournament has attracted thousands to the city. Tens of thousands. There were more than a thousand people at the gala last night alone. It will take time to pursue this."

"Do what you will," the woman said. "But now that the realm is connected here again, there will be others of my kind who begin to pay closer attention to the human world. They will hear the news of what has happened here. They may not be so patient. The demonkind extracted a heavy toll on our kind already. We will not be harmed further."

CHAPTER FIFTEEN

"YOU WANT to explain who that was, *Rosaline*?" I said to Pinky once we were safely back in the Rose Garden, blinking in the California sunshine.

"You mean Grandma?" Pinky said. Behind her, the door vanished, leaving only the undisturbed roses.

Cassandra stepped closer, one finger stroking the petals of one of the flowers, as though somehow it might tell her how the door worked.

Lizzie joined her, looking curious.

Zee had already walked away from the trellis to stand in the light several feet away. Was he worried he might be pulled back in? I couldn't blame him.

But I was more concerned with Pinky.

"She's your grandmother?" The Elder looked the same age as us.

"Great-great. Maybe throw in a few more greats. Once upon a time, her daughter fell in love with a human. She had a baby. After that, more generations. You know how that works."

Well, yes. But most of the time, when you got a few more generations down the track, the original matriarch of the line didn't still look like she was in her twenties.

Or cause birds to go silent when she was angered.

How old was she? And how powerful? Once we got out of here, I was going to have a *lot* of questions.

I stared at my hand. The glyph was gone. The Elder had touched me briefly, to remove the summoning, or so she said. Her magic had been cool, like a breeze over my skin, gone so quickly I would barely have noticed it if I hadn't been paying attention. I'd smelled roses briefly, and then the symbol had vanished.

"And her daughter? Did she return to the realm?" Cassandra asked, turning back to us.

Lizzie let go of the rose she was studying and came to stand next to me.

"Yes, once her husband died. She looks in on the family from time to time. Or she did until the Big One. The Elders have mostly stayed away since then." Pinky glanced back at the roses nervously.

"Look, I'm happy to tell you what I can, but let's do it somewhere away from here, yeah?"

"You think they might be listening?" Cassandra asked.

"I think better safe than sorry," Pinky replied.

"Good idea," Lizzie said. "But where? Neutral ground would be best."

I couldn't disagree with that. I didn't want Pinky at our house, I couldn't imagine Cassandra would be keen to let her anywhere near the Archives, and now that I knew who Pinky really was and what she'd done, I didn't trust her enough to go to her house, wherever that was.

Pinky nodded. "I have a friend who lives not far from here. He's away, and I've been watering his plants. He's a sculptor. Works in metal. Lots of scrap iron in his studio."

In other words, somewhere the Elders were unlikely to follow.

"Lead the way," Cassandra said.

The drive only took ten minutes. Pinky pulled up in front of a Tudor-style house. Knowing Berkeley real estate, if her friend was a sculptor, he was doing okay if he could afford to live here. Cassandra parked behind her. We all trooped up to the front door, and Pinky let us in, releasing a distinctly re-lieved sigh when she closed and locked the door.

"I don't think the Elders know about this place," she said, glancing back toward the door. "They know where I live, of course. They know where we all live, it seems." She pulled a face and then pointed down the hallway. "Studio is that way."

"Do they really know where all the tanai are?" Lizzie asked as we walked through the house.

Pinky didn't stop moving. "Well, they lose track sometimes, and there must be babies now and then that no one learns about, especially as you get more removed from the actual Elders, but yeah, they find us if they want us." She pushed open a door and ushered us through.

The room we stepped into had a vaulted ceiling, lots of windows, and was, as advertised, filled with a lot of scrap metal. And tools. And workbenches of various sizes. It smelled of oil and metal and dust and sun-warmed air. The five of us clustered around the biggest one. A metal file lay on the battered wooden surface in front of me, and I picked it up. I had no idea if it was iron or steel, but it made me feel better.

Zee lifted an eyebrow at me but didn't speak. He'd been quiet since we'd left the garden, and it didn't seem like that was changing any time soon. He'd chosen to stand on my left, putting me between him and Lizzie. Pinky and Cassandra faced us across the bench.

Pinky didn't seem bothered by the metal at all. In fact, she looked relaxed for the first time since we'd first seen her under the roses. So maybe what Zee had said was right about iron not affecting the tanai.

"How long has the door been open?" Cassandra asked.

"I'm not exactly sure," Pinky said. "First I knew of it was when my presence was requested last week. I hadn't heard anything about them being back before that, so it can't have been long. That kind of news travels fast." Her mouth twisted.

"Is it considered good news or bad news?" I asked.

Pinky waggled a hand. "I'd say views are mixed. Those of us who stayed when the Elders left, well, let's just say we've gotten used to a bit more freedom without them. Among my kind, it can be complicated. Some families are closer than others. Though where the ties were tightest, the tanai went with them. The ones who stayed were mostly happier for things to stay distant."

Did that mean Pinky and her, well, grandma—seemed as good a term as any—didn't get along?

"And now?"

"And now, I guess from time to time I'll be providing such assistance as they request." She pushed a hand through her hair impatiently, the movement frustrated.

"Like booby-trapping Damon's game?" I asked.

Pinky winced. "Yeah. Sorry about that. But we don't really have much choice when the Elders ask."

"Was she telling the truth about why they're so concerned about the demon?" Lizzie asked.

Pinky turned to Cassandra. "You probably know more about the history than I do. I was away at college when the Big One hit. Our house was damaged, and my mom—she's tanai—was more focused on that than the Elders in the aftermath. By the time she found out the door was gone, she was still dealing with all the shit from the house and trying to find somewhere to live. But from what I heard later, there was a lot of drama.

"The people who were the most freaked out about it were the ones who left to follow the Elders. Those who stayed got on with life. Mom was an only child of an only child. Her magic isn't that strong, so I guess she didn't really care. She told me about it all when I was young. Seven. Told me what it meant and what our obligations are, and I went to the realm to meet Grandma and some of the others a few times before the quake, but since then, my heritage has been pretty academic." Her mouth quirked. "Never expected I'd meet one of the Cestis officially, so to speak."

"Well, now you've met two of us," Lizzie said. "If it helps, I'd never met an Elder before today. Neither had Maggie."

She didn't say anything about me not even knowing they existed. Was that a hint that I shouldn't mention that part?

"So that's a super fun morning for everyone," Pinky said. "Which brings us back to why my relatives have decided to return home. If they're so worried about demons, why not just stay away?" She was looking at Cassandra again.

Cassandra pursed her lips. "What do you know of nexuses?"

"They're places of power around the world," Pinky said.

"Right. They were considered powerful even before human tradition. Places where...well, it might be easiest to say that the magic runs deep. Places that those with magic are drawn to. Some of them are well known. Like the henges in England and Ireland. Glastonbury. Cairo. Easter Island. Many more. Others are more hidden, their locations only shared among the magical communities."

Why did I get the feeling she didn't just mean witches?

"San Francisco is a nexus," Cassandra continued. "No one really knows what makes one, though there are various theories. But the Elders tapped into them somehow when they first separated their realm from the world. Used the strength of the nexuses to shore up their working. Not just here. The Elders around the globe worked together to do that magic. At least, that's what our histories say."

"Ours, too," Pinky said. "Though I'd guess they might have different perspectives."

"The lady—your grandmother—said something about an anchor. Did she mean the nexus, then?" I asked.

"Yes," Cassandra said. "I think so. The easiest points of access to the realm, the oldest and strongest doors, are near nexuses. The realm is a place of deep magic, too. Perhaps the nexuses help it. It would explain why the Elders needed to reopen the door. If the realm is somehow weaker if it isn't connected at all the nexuses. Maybe they didn't understand that when they first closed the door."

"And the Big One? It hurt the door somehow?" It was a lot to get straight in my head.

Pinky nodded. "That's what my mom told me. They closed the door. Though, honestly, I don't know whether that was entirely due to the damage or the fact that a demon had gotten so close."

"If they're powerful enough to make something like a realm, why are they so worried about a demon?" I asked.

"Demons feed on energy," Cassandra said. "It's why they are drawn to humans and witches. Elder magic is more powerful than ours. They're a tempting target, I guess. Given how much power there would be in the realm for a demon to feed on, I don't think it would end well for any of us if one got inside. That was always part of the agreement between us when they left, that the witches would guard against demonkind."

My spine crawled at the thought of demons drinking the kind of magic that had let the Elder change the world around us as easily as calling up a holo.

"Now they seem to think there's a threat again. Or else they want to be sure there won't be one. Which makes me wonder what has been happening in the realm while the door has been closed." Cassandra's golden eyes fixed on Pinky.

She shook her head. "I, for one, am not volunteering to ask. But they do seem quite adamant about protecting the door. We don't want them to do anything drastic." She exchanged a look with Cassandra.

Not a good look. I tightened my grip on the file, the rasp of its surface against my hand distracting me from the fear. "For those of us playing along with very little idea what's going on, how about you try and define drastic?"

"Well, I don't think they could take out the human race now. There's too many of us—" Pinky said.

"You think of yourself as human, not tanai?" Cassandra interrupted.

Pinky nodded. "Yes. My power is only a small part of me. One I rarely use. I don't think it makes me less human. Any more than yours does."

Fair point. But I was more interested in the answer to my initial question. "You were talking about worst-case scenarios," I prompted.

"They could turn the city, or a good chunk of it, or more perhaps into a realm," Zee said. "Couldn't they?

"What?" I only just managed to stop myself from shouting the word. As it was, it seemed to echo around the room.

Lizzie gently took the file out of my hand, tucking her arm through mine.

Cassandra ignored me. "Do you really think they could do it?" She was talking to Zee, not Pinky. "Did you hear anything like that while you were in England?"

He shook his head. "No. But the tanai over there, they tread warily around the Elders. Respect their power. Well, the smart ones do." He tipped his chin at Pinky. "Seems she does, too, if she leaped to do what they wanted the first time they asked."

Pinky glared. "You think I had a choice? I have responsibilities. Obligations. Just like you working for the Cestis. Only the Cestis probably aren't going to be quite as harsh if you cross them. Like you just said, it's smart to respect them. I prefer not to live out my days as some small furry thing in some forest in the realm."

Was she serious? Could the Elders really turn her into a...? I swallowed, feeling sick. I'd joked about Cassandra turning people into frogs before, but I'd never really believed it was possible. But Pinky seemed to think it was.

Cassandra held up a hand. "Let's not fight about that. Zee, Rosaline—"

"It's Pinky," Pinky said. "No one calls me Rosaline."

No one but her terrifying grandmother.

"Pinky, then, is right. She has obligations, Zachariah. You know that."

Zee shrugged. "Sure. Sorry, it's chill. I was just saying they're not the ones to be messing with. So yeah, power. Lots of it. Can they do what they did when they first made the realm now? Who knows? Do we want to gamble with pissing them off? Probably not."

"I agree," Cassandra said. "I got the feeling that there may be internal politics within their world at play, too. Which complicates things. What do you think, Pinky? Have any other tanai been summoned?"

"Not that I've heard," Pinky said. "But they wouldn't talk about it if they were told not to. I didn't see any tanai I know at the gala. Not that I know them all. And I guess it makes sense that Grandma would be given the task since her family have always been defenders. She didn't tell me anything about what's been happening in the realm. Just that they needed to make sure things were safe."

"So we don't know what they're capable of if they think that isn't the case," Lizzie said.

"No. But they did something when they locked the realms away the first time," Pinky said. "No one really knows. Humans weren't exactly keeping good maps of the planet at that point. But they didn't create the realm out of nothing. Our lore says once, all the upper land—that's our world—was theirs, and now they only have part of it. But it's a point of pride. That others retreated and hid, but we kept part of the world. That suggests they took some of it into the realm with them. So I wouldn't want to bet that they couldn't do that again if they decided it was necessary."

Others retreated? What others? I filed that one away. There'd been enough new information for one day.

"Necessary   to   keep   them   safe   from demonkind?"

"Or to keep the nexus safe, perhaps?" Pinky said. "There are others who know more about the Elders than me. I can ask, but it will make them curious about what's going on, and we don't want anyone else meddling. We need to focus on keeping the door safe, if that's what the Elders want."

"We can hardly stop demons from trying what they try," Cassandra said. "They will always have more lesserkind to walk the Earth for them."

"I'm not sure they're expecting demons to go away completely. But two attempts in what—for them—is a very short period of time must be worrying."

"Okay, so we find whoever it is they think they're sensing and deal with them," I said. "Then they can chill, and everybody can just get on with life."

"Good plan," Lizzie agreed. "But it's not quite that simple, is it? The tournament is huge. Hunting for someone who has some sort of connection to a lesserkind or demons sniffing around is like looking for a needle in a haystack."

"Well, if Pinky set the spell to detect demon contact, surely she can do that another time?"

"It was Grandma's spell," Pinky said. "I just placed it.

"Didn't you say you could sense demonkind?" I protested.

"If I touch them. Someone who was fully under the influence—bound or something—then proba-bly," she said. "Or an imp or a lesserkind. One of the small darknesses. But someone who may have just had dealings with one, I'm not so sure. And I can't just walk around the convention center randomly bumping into people for days."

"Then we need more of Grandma's spell," I said.

Pinky raised an eyebrow, shaking her head. "You want to go back and ask her for a favor? If she wanted to give me the magic, she would have done so."

"Why wouldn't she?" Lizzie asked. "If they're so worried about the demons, why not just stop them themselves?"

"It's a test," Zee said. "That's what it seems like. We fix this problem, and we prove we have things under control and will hold to the terms of the agreement. Which is the second part of the reason they might not want to step in. Without proof of a demon actively here, they probably can't just interfere." He looked at Cassandra. "Isn't that right?"

"Yes. They're supposed to stay out of things, unless we ask. Or fail."

Failing sounded bad. But surely asking couldn't hurt? "I vote for asking."

Cassandra shook her head. "No. Zachariah has it right. They're testing us. The Cestis cannot be indebted to the Elders. That provides too many opportunities for any Elder who may have an agenda to try and get around the agreements."

My head was starting to ache. I dug my fingers

into the muscles at the base of my neck, longing for some ibuprofen. Or to wake up and find out that this was all just a nightmare. Some sort of chip-induced hallucination. But it wasn't. "Then what do we do?"

"Come up with a plan," Cassandra said. "If we can figure out what a demon or a lesserkind might want with the tournament, that would be a good starting point."

"Something to do with the game?" Pinky said. "Rumor has it—among my relations—that there was a connection to the games with this last demon." She pointed at me. "The fact that the last demon was connected to Maggie and she's dating Damon Riley tells me maybe the rumors aren't completely crazy."

I frowned. "That's something we can't discuss. Secret Cestis business. Also secret Righteous business. If it did involve them, which I'm not confirming."

"Oh, we can discuss it," Cassandra said, looking stern. "But first we're going to need one of Damon's NDAs."

CHAPTER SIXTEEN

BY THE TIME Pinky lifted her hand off the palm scanner after signing the NDA, I'd recovered enough from dealing with the Fae and other revelations of the morning to realize I was starving. It wasn't even midday yet, but my stomach had had enough.

We were back in Damon's office at the hotel. Only now there were eight people—Mitch and Maia had been waiting with Damon when we'd returned —crowded into the room. The silence of seven people waiting for the eighth to read through a long and complex NDA was kind of loud. Just as it had been while Damon was arranging said NDA.

He'd responded to Cassandra's announcement that Pinky needed to sign one before we discussed anything with the steely kind of politeness that told me he was unhappy with the situation.

The discussion we needed to have now that Pinky had been sworn to silence, or rather to as much silence as her obligations to the Fae would allow, would go more smoothly if none of us had to add "hangry" to the list of emotions we may or may not be feeling.

But Cat, it seemed, was two steps ahead of me. Before I could suggest a lunch break, the door opened, and she came in and announced that she'd arranged for lunch in the meeting room next door and that the security features of that room were in operation. She turned and left again before any of us could say so much as "Thank you."

I voted with my stomach and headed to the meeting room before anyone else said anything. Apparently I wasn't the only one feeling hungry, because the others rapidly trailed in after me. Pinky hovered by the door, looking wary as everyone chose sandwiches and seats around the table.

I got up again, plate in hand, and went over to her. "Not hungry?"

"Not really." She grimaced. "I haven't had a chance to say I'm sorry."

I shrugged. I didn't love what she had done, but I understood being in a position of having to do what someone more powerful than you wanted. The Cestis were gentler with it than my mother had been, and, to date, I couldn't argue that they hadn't done their best for me, but I also knew they would act to protect whatever they saw as the best interests of the country and magic when they made choices.

And they expected the rest of us to go along.

I couldn't blame Pinky if she had to go along with the Elders, too.

"You did what you had to do. Maybe it's for the best anyway. If there's another demon sniffing around, better we know about it." I sounded casual, but the thought was still enough to briefly squelch my appetite. "Get something to eat and come sit with me."

"Aren't you going to sit with Damon? I'm not sure I'm his favorite person right now." Her eyes flicked to Damon. He was scowling at the tray of sandwiches with enough intensity that I was surprised they didn't shrivel up.

I patted her arm. "I'm not sure I am either. But coming up with a plan will help with that."

Everybody ate quickly and silently. Apart from the odd request to pass a paper napkin or the jug of water, no one seemed to want to be the first to break the ice. I sat between Pinky and Damon, wondering who would be the first to crack.

In the end it was Zee who shoved his plate away and said, "I need to get back to my team. Let's do this, yeah."

"Not much point going back to your team if there's not going to be any game play," Lizzie said. "Damon, did you find anything in the game booths?"

"Not so far," he said, putting down his sandwich. "Do you think we will?"

Everyone turned their attention to Pinky, who shook her head. "No, I only did a few. I can tell you which ones."

Damon nodded once. "This conversation might go faster if we go back to the beginning. Pinky's signed the NDA. Somebody tell me what she has to do with all this."

Cassandra put down her sandwich. "Pinky is tanai fol. That means descended from the Elders. She was the one who set the spell in the game on their behalf."

"I see," Damon said, tone was distinctly cool.

I put my hand on his thigh and squeezed. "She has reasons."

Across the table, Mitch was watching Pinky with narrowed eyes and an expression that suggested he was fighting the urge to bundle her out of the room and far away from Damon and me. Though the "me" part might be debatable. He hadn't looked too pleased to see any of us when we'd arrived.

"They'd better be good," Damon replied, but he put his hand over mine.

I squeezed again, a little more gently.

"Cassandra, why don't you tell me the rest?" Damon said.

She nodded and gave him a neat recap of our time in the Rose Garden.

Mitch bit back a curse the first time she mentioned the word "demon," but after that he stayed quiet and let her finish.

"All right," Damon said once Cassandra fell silent. "So the...Elders...are real, and they are back in San Francisco, and they don't like demons."

"Can't blame them for that," Maia said before Mitch shot her a look.

Damon nodded. "That might be the only thing we all agree on. So now, explain to me what this has to do with the tournament and what the hell she did to my game." He fixed his gaze firmly on Pinky.

Who, to her credit, raised her chin and glared right back.

I pushed my chair back slightly, not wanting to be in the line of fire. I mean, I was definitely going to be in the line of fire, because once again, Damon had been dragged into magical shenanigans, but I'd wait my turn.

"She," Pinky said, "didn't *do* anything to your game."

"I think Maggie and Zee would beg to differ."

"Neither of them is hurt."

"According to you."

"If the Elders wanted to take any of you out, you'd be dead already," Pinky said. "A summoning was perhaps weird and a bit inconvenient, but they're fine. And so is your game."

Damon's mouth flattened. "That still doesn't explain what you did."

"I set a spell. One provided to me. Don't ask me how it works. It's not magic I can do on my own."

"What can you do on your own?" I asked before Damon could jump back in. A chance for him to take a breath and calm down couldn't hurt.

Pinky took a bite of her sandwich, chewed, and swallowed. Maybe she thought a slight pause in the conversation would help, too.

"I don't have a lot of magic. I can set a ward, though I'm guessing most of you could break it if you tried. I'm good at finding lost things. I see better in the dark than most people. I can sense demonkind up close, but you already know that part. Maybe I could do more, but my mom always said I had to rely on my human skills, not magic, so she never wasted much time trying to teach me about it. Hers is probably weaker than mine anyway. It works that way, sometimes."

Pinky's mom sounded nicer than my mom.

"And the music," Lizzie asked. "You're a composer, right? Is that an Elder thing?"

"I don't know. Are there Fae who are musical? Yes. But there are plenty of human kids who are good at music. I was one of them. Even when I was tiny. I wasn't a child prodigy by any means, but I practiced, and I'm good. I have no idea if magic has anything to do with that. Grandma told you what my family is good at."

"Demons," Zee said.

"Yes. Who don't, from what I've heard, tend to care about the arts."

Zee snorted across the table and Cassandra smiled briefly.

"As fascinating as this family history is," Mitch said, "the important question is, are the games safe? Can the tournament start tonight?"

"Yes," Pinky said. "The summoning has been removed."

"Which is good. No more glowing hand." I held up my palm for him to see.

He looked closely, making a grumbling noise under his breath before he leaned back.

"If they can put a spell in my game that detects demons, why can't they just use a spell to detect whoever it is that they're worried about?" Damon asked.

"Because there are rules in place about what they are allowed to do in our world. Agreements I'm not willing to let slide. We don't want them back in the world, running roughshod over humanity," Cassandra said.

"They used their magic to set this summoning," Damon retorted.

"Technically, they used Pinky to do that," Cassandra said. "The tanai are allowed to use their magics. And a detection spell is also within the bounds of what the Elders are allowed. It falls under the need to protect their realm."

"So they've shoved the problem into our laps, and now we have to solve it?" Damon asked.

"That about sums it up," Cassandra said. "Convenient for them that the first people who set their spell off were witches."

I frowned at her. "You think they wanted witches, not demons?"

She shrugged. "I don't know. Do I believe they're worried about something, yes? But do I believe their spell was designed specifically to detect those touched by a demon? I don't know. We use demon stone for that. They have powers beyond ours, but if it was easy to detect demon taint with magic, our job would be a lot easier. And it's never a good idea to take what they tell you as gospel— no offense, Pinky."

Pinky nodded. "None taken. It's the truth. They play long games, and it's best to tread carefully. But I think they probably could detect a demon or its influence if they wanted to."

"It's a moot point anyway. They want us to deal with it," Cassandra said. "The summoning could just as well have been set to find someone with magic. After all, Maggie and Zee were the only ones caught. I know the odds, based on how many people attended last night, are that they may not have found anyone. But it's interesting that they chose to make you put something in the game."

"It's a gaming tournament," Pinky said. "It makes sense. It's not like I could just go around shaking hands all night."

"They could have sent more of you," Damon said.

"Your party was expensive," Pinky retorted. "And hard to get an invite to. There's not that many of us who I know about who are connected to this industry."

"Who you know about being a key part of that sentence," I pointed out.

"True." She nodded. "But still, with the rules in place, they couldn't just flood the gala with magic. And so far Grandma hasn't told me about anyone else triggering the spell. She hasn't given me another one to set, so it doesn't really matter what the fuck her motivation is. What matters is that she's expecting a result."

"A demon," I said.

"Not necessarily. Someone working with a demon, maybe. Or a lesserkind."

"We've seen no sign of another lesserkind in the area," Lizzie said. "And we've looked."

"Good. But that doesn't mean the Elders' visions are wrong. There are thousands in town for the tournament. From all over the world, right?"

Damon nodded.

"So this could be a whole new party. It doesn't matter how good a job you've done running lesserkind out of town if someone has just arrived who can just invite a new one in."

Lesserkind could be sent by a demon. Or, supposedly, summoned by a human. If a human was strong and stupid. My mother had made a bargain with a demon. She'd thought she could outsmart it, presumably. The mysterious car accident that killed her a few months later after she'd sold my powers to it suggested otherwise. Ajax had worked with a lesserkind, and he'd wound up dead, too.

"Okay, so we have to look," I said. "But that's not easy. We can't go around stabbing people with demon stone. So how are we supposed to find whoever this is?"

"Try to figure out what they want and work the problem from that angle," Zee said. "Get ahead of them. Which we already are, in a way. They have no idea we have any reason to suspect anything. Whatever they're planning, they're not going to be on high alert yet."

"Well, no higher than anyone coming to this town, presuming they know about the Cestis, would be," Trick said. "After what's happened the last few years, you'd think the demons would be wary."

"Demons are not known for their logical thinking. If they want something, they keep coming. There's a reason the Cestis has been fighting them for centuries," Cassandra said.

"But why do they keep coming here?" Pinky said. "I signed your damn NDA. I know something happened at Righteous. Something triggered the recall. Was there a demon involved in that? Are the rumors true?"

"Rumors?" Cassandra asked sharply.

"There were mutterings in the tanai. But no one knew anything for sure. I didn't hear anything concrete even through the gaming grapevine. Just that there was some problem with the tech."

I looked at Damon. "It's yours to tell if you want to. She did sign the agreement."

Across the table, Mitch leaned forward slightly, ready to spring into action. I don't know what he thought was going to happen, but the man was nothing if not prepared. Maia, on the other hand, looked relaxed, though that was probably deliberate. Her expression was more intrigued than tense.

Damon shifted in his seat. "The rumor mill was right. There was a problem with the tech. One of the elements we use in the game lowered the barriers to mental susceptibility. Somehow a demon worked out how to use that to get to people."

It wasn't the whole story, but if that was the part he was willing to tell, then that was his right.

"I see," Pinky said. "And the recall was to remove that element?"

"Not exactly. We hadn't rolled out *Archangel* yet. It was to check there was no way something similar could happen with the older versions of the tech."

Righteous had spent millions replacing game cartridges and decks. All just in case. The algorithm that had been changed in the beta of *Archangel* hadn't even been released. But Damon had wanted to be sure. Not everyone would have made the same decision in his place. Though my guess was, at that point, the Cestis would have stepped in and made sure things were taken care of. But Damon had done the right thing without any prompting.

"It hasn't happened again," I said. "The problem was fixed."

"But demons are persistent," Pinky said. "Which makes the question whether they're trying to get their hands on that algorithm or whether they think the new game could have something similar."

"We haven't used anything like that filter since. We've found new ways of deepening the experience, but they work differently. And we've had the Cestis and some healers helping us. There's no indication that using the new game would make anyone more susceptible to demons. Or lesserkind or whoever. We've had no problems in the betas."

"And there are no versions of the old algorithm lying around?" Pinky asked. "Nothing tucked away?"

Damon shook his head. "We deleted everything. And my research divisions are under strict instructions to avoid going down any similar paths. There's nothing to find."

Obviously he thought it was true. But knowing how big and complicated Riley Arts was, was it really possible to be sure he'd erased all hint of the code that had caused all the problems?

"It doesn't really matter whether or not there's something there to find," I said. "Maybe all that matters is that somebody out there thinks there is. I mean, it makes sense to me that that might be the target. Hell, even without the algorithm, there's plenty of stuff worth stealing from Riley."

"Of course," Damon said. "We deal with that kind of thing regularly. People trying to hack their way in or bribe their way in or whatever. But that's people. Not demons. And that's what the Fae said, right? That they were worried about demons."

"Yes," Cassandra agreed. "Though demons are usually assisted by humans."

Very stupid humans.

"Which brings us to what we do about it?"

Mitch said. "The tournament is going ahead. So how do we keep everyone safe?"

"Maybe we need to wait and see what happens, at least for a couple of days," I said. "Like Zee said, whoever this is, they don't have a reason to worry that we know they're coming. Maybe they'll give themselves away."

Lizzie looked at Pinky. "What do you say to that?"

She shook her head, the motion small but firm. "I think we need to have a plan in place. Grandma is going to want updates."

Right. Grandma. Who might react badly if we didn't sort this out. "Is there anything we could do to try and force their hand? Dangle something under their noses?"

"Like what?" Lizzie asked.

"Well, if they want the technology, maybe we need some rumors that Righteous still has it somewhere." I looked at Zee. "Think you and Carlo could work out how to plant some seeds in the teams? Something about the old algorithm."

He nodded. "Gamers love gossip. We could figure something out. Carlo knows a lot of people not playing, too."

"Maybe Yoshi could do the same with his friends. He's hooked into the game clubs. He's going to the hackathon. Maybe he could start something about the challenge being around the old algorithm." I looked at Damon. "It's not, is it?"

He shook his head. "Definitely not. But that's a good idea." He tilted his head, watching Mitch. "What do you think?"

"We're prepped for the hackathon. The kids know there are consequences, but there always seems to be one idiot each year who thinks they can really hack us. Between that and the tournament, we've already layered up the security. So many gamers in town, it's inevitable some of them are going to get drunk and try things. Maybe drunk enough to come up with something crazy that works. A right rumor would definitely make them try harder. We could even set up a decoy server, something that looks like it's connected to the Riley systems but hidden away. Hackers love that shit." He folded his arms. "Until they try us."

Hacking Righteous would definitely be a feather in someone's cap. People must try every day, but Mitch was right, it would be doubly tempting to do it during the tournament. Big kudos in the darker side of tech if you could break Riley during something so massive.

"What do you think?" I asked Damon.

His hand lifted from mine. "Do I want to dangle my company as bait? Is that what you're asking?"

"Yes," Cassandra said bluntly.

"Doesn't seem like I have a choice, does it?" he

said, voice tight. His leg flexed beneath my palm, and tension crept down my spine. Just how pissed off was he?

"Is that a yes?" Cassandra asked, not blinking an eye.

"Yes."

"Good." She looked around the table. "Then we should get going. Zee and Lizzie and Trick, you stay here and talk with Mitch and Maia. Work out what you think this rumor should be. Lizzie can talk to Yoshi about it once you're done. Pinky, you can come with me. I have a few more questions about your grandmother."

Pinky's shoulders slumped, but she nodded. "Yes, ma'am."

Cassandra nodded. "Good. Then that's settled. Let's get going."

She hadn't given me a task. Which made it clear that mine was making sure that Damon calmed down and played along. I reached for a water bottle, cracking it open as the others cleared the room at record speed. Leaving me with Damon.

I sipped, trying to think. Let him vent or try to talk him down?

Before I could decide, Damon pushed back his chair and stood, the move so fast the chair fell over with a crash.

"Fuck," he said.

"You could throw it at the wall," I suggested as

he bent to grab the chair. "It would only go on your bill, after all. What's one more chair after all this?"

His head snapped up and he straightened, leaving the chair where it was. "You don't think I'm allowed to be pissed off about this?"

"Sure. But being pissed isn't going to help. So throw the chair. Maybe you'll feel better. Then we can get on with things." I kept my voice neutral.

"Perhaps you could give me a few minutes to get my head around the fact that fairies are fucking real, they messed with my fucking game, and that another fucking demon might be sniffing around?"

"You knew that last thing was a possibility." I sipped water again. I needed it. I was somehow sounding casual, but my heart was thumping.

"Maggie, this tournament is important. Riley Arts needs it. There's a lot riding on us getting things back to normal. No more weird shit."

"I understand that."

"Do you? Do you know what it's like to be re-sponsible for something like Righteous? To have thousands of people who depend on you for their livelihoods?"

"No, but I understand having your life fucked up by magic. Dead mother, remember? Dead best friend."

We glared at each other.

Not helpful.

I looked away, took another drink. I didn't want

to fight. But I needed to know if he could handle this. If he was going to crack and run again, better to get it over with. I put the bottle on the table and stood. The chair lay on the carpet between us.

"Okay," I said. "I get that you're mad. But here's the thing. You made a choice. You chose me. You did it with both eyes wide open this time. This is part of that choice. And really, to be fair, this was happening before I even came along. Demons were sniffing around your games before I got tangled up in them."

He opened his mouth, and I held up a hand. "No. You're going to hear me out. You stumbled across that algorithm that let the demon in all on your own. Your beta testers were having issues before you even knew my name. And at that point, the demon wasn't after me." Because it still had control of my power.

"So, sure, I've landed you in some trouble and brought some things to a head. But to balance that, you also know about this whole other world and the threats it brings. You can prepare. And you have the Cestis on your side. Magic is still going to throw you some curve balls, sure. Hell, I'm not that happy about finding out that fairies are real either, but you built one of the biggest companies on the planet, and you don't do that without being able to deal with curve balls.

"Last night, you said all that mattered was us. If

everything went away, that we were what mattered. You need to decide if that's really true. Because this"—I gestured back at the meeting room—"is part of my life. I can't make my magic go away, nor do I want to. So if you want me, you have to be able to handle all of this. I'm not going to walk on eggshells around it, and I'm not going to feel guilty every time something magical comes up." As the words left my mouth, I realized they were true. That I was sick of feeling guilty. "I don't want to have to worry about you and me every time this happens. Either we're together or we're not. But if we are, then this is part of your life. Hell, even without me, it might be part of your life."

I blew out a breath as his face twisted.

"So, you can be mad about this stuff. And I get that. It's shitty, and you wanted the tournament to go smoothly. You get to be mad. You don't get to be mad at me though. Or the others. You can vent at me. You can ask me to take you to bed and help work off some of your frustration. You can come to me for care and comfort. And demon smiting. But not to be a scapegoat and not to be your whipping boy. My mom treated me like crap, like an inconvenience, like it was my fault when we got run out of town or one of her idiot boyfriends got mad and dumped her before she dumped them. I was a kid then. I didn't have a choice. But I have a choice now. And you know I want to choose you. But only if you choose me, too."

I snapped my mouth shut, chest tightening suddenly. I wasn't going to cry.

Damon stared down at me, breathing hard, too. Then he stepped over the chair and pulled me into him. "I choose you," he said. "Sorry. This isn't your fault. I choose you." He bent and kissed me, somehow gentle and fierce at the same time. Then he pulled back, resting his forehead on mine, his breath coming fast. "I'm sorry. Maybe *you* should throw the chair."

I snorted. "Don't push your luck, Riley."

"My luck is right here," he said and kissed me again.

"Good. Then let's go work out how to fix this."

CHAPTER SEVENTEEN

THREE DAYS LATER, our plan had gotten us precisely nowhere, and I was beginning to feel stir-crazy in the hotel. Nothing was happening. The launch had been completely uneventful, much to Damon's relief, and so far the heats had been running like clockwork as well. Which I knew all too well as I'd spent hours watching game play and game tape, looking for any signs of magic use when I was there in person and just anything weird in the tape.

Combined with attending all the various events Damon had to attend for the tournament—winner ceremonies, meet-ups, VIP drinks, team meals—it was exhausting. I couldn't even sneak back home for a few hours for a break. Since my appearance with Damon at the gala, paparazzi had staked the house out. Lizzie had been forced to move into the hotel after the first night.

They'd lose interest sooner or later. At least I hoped they would. But according to the security team, not yet. Apparently, despite the fact that there were plenty of celebrities watching tournament heats live at the conference center, some of them had decided that trying to get some candid shots of Damon Riley's new girlfriend at home was more interesting.

My house didn't have a massive convenient fence like Damon's. Mitch had sent a team out a few times to chase the vultures off, and the house comp hadn't pinged any attempts to get inside, so at least no one had tried to break in. But I'd lost my own patch of private life for now, and it grated on me more than I'd expected. But after yelling at Damon about him choosing me, I couldn't complain.

I'd chosen him. So I'd chosen this.

Knowing that didn't make it easier to adjust to, but it meant I couldn't stop trying.

Which left me stuck in the hotel. The penthouse was gorgeous and luxurious, tastefully decorated in shades of white and beige and pale blues. It had everything a gal could want, including a lap pool, a small gaming room, an entertainment system that included a massive screen that slid down from the roof if the huge television wasn't big enough for one's movie-viewing pleasure, and even a damned helipad on an adjacent section of the hotel's roof. But it wasn't home.

And I couldn't relax when I did get a break. Not when I had no idea whether or not we might be fighting a demon at any minute.

I stared out the french doors that led to the small terrace. Outside, the sky was blue, and the clouds were white and fluffy, and the city hummed away as though nobody had a care in the world.

Nice for it.

I shook my head at the thought. I was being ridiculous. What I needed was some of that fresh air. Then I'd go back down to the tournament.

The terrace was too small to satisfy my restlessness but there was a rooftop garden on the roof of a lower part of the building. It was currently reserved for Riley Arts use. There'd been a cocktail party there after launch night, but so far, every other time I'd gone there, it had been empty. It seemed most people were more interested in the tournament happening inside the conference center than sunning themselves.

Damon was working in his temporary office a few floors below. Part of me wanted to go down and try to tempt him out with me, but I didn't want to bother him. Or risk picking a fight because I was feeling nervous. Lizzie was at Spark, and Cassandra was probably at her store, though she and

Trick and Radha and Ian had spent plenty of time playing audience at the tournament and trying to spot any trouble over the last three days, just like me.

No doubt that would be causing some talk for any witches in the audience who knew who the members of the Cestis actually were. Before I'd crossed paths with an imp, I'd known about the existence of the Cestis, and I'd known Cassandra's name. I'd never seen her face though. Which made sense. The kind of business where the Cestis had to step in in any significant way was the kind that got dealt with as quietly as possible.

They didn't seek out publicity. Probably so they could do exactly this kind of thing without being mobbed.

If *I* didn't want to be mobbed, then I was going to have to choose the garden or go crazy.

I got as far as the foyer five floors below the penthouse where I needed to switch to the elevator bank that would take me up to the garden and ran into Zee, just stepping out of one of the elevators.

"Hey," I said. "Taking a break?"

He nodded and hid a yawn behind a hand. "Sorry. Long days." He hadn't shaved, and his red T-shirt and black cargo pants were both wrinkled, as though he'd already been sitting for hours.

"Yeah," I agreed. "You guys are doing great though." Trueno Diablo had the second highest score in the top league so far, only a couple of thousand points behind the current leaders. Third and fourth were more than twenty thousand behind them. There were still some great teams to come, but unless a couple of them pulled off amazing runs, they were looking certain to make it to the finals.

"Thanks. It's intense." He stretched his arms behind his back, yawning again.

"So I gather. So, mental health break?"

"Yeah. There's only so much strategizing to do until we get the next levels. And we've watched the replays of our runs so many times they're singed on my eyeballs."

The teams were allowed to replay their own runs but not see what the other teams were doing in the first heats until they'd all completed the first round.

"I'm heading up to the rooftop garden," I said. "Want to come with? There's fresh air, at least. Or fresh as it gets in the middle of the city."

"Sure," he said, "If you don't mind the company."

"Nope." I hit the button to call the elevator.

It arrived quickly, and we headed up and then out into the garden.

It was planted to look more naturalistic than formal, proof the hotel chain had plenty of money to throw at it. It was well done, only revealing glimpses of the cityscape between the trees and shrubs set out in a series of small open spaces separated from each other by screens and more plants. It was prettiest at night, when there were garlands of twinkling lights in the branches, but even in daylight it was lovely. Not exactly Golden Gate Park, but it was as close to nature as we were likely to get on the top of a hotel. Zee pulled a pair of gold-rimmed sunglasses out of one of the pockets in his pants and slid them on.

We walked a lap of the garden in silence.

My favorite spot was a couple outdoor sofas arranged by a small pond with tiny darting orange fish and a small natural-looking trickle of water that ran over the surrounding rocks and added just enough noise to make the fact that there were aural blockers up hiding the city sounds less obvious.

I pointed it out to Zee. "Keep walking or sit?"

"I already worked out before breakfast." he said. "Let's sit."

We settled into place. I tried to think of a topic other than the tournament and the plan. If there'd been any developments, someone would have told me—both of us, really—already. But I still didn't know Zee that well. We'd bonded a bit through our experience with the summoning, but he was a quiet guy, and I'd hardly seen him the last few days because he'd been with the Diablos. He fed updates to Trick but so far had nothing to report.

I didn't do sports, and I doubted he'd had time to pay attention to anything other than the tournament in the last few days. And I couldn't talk to him about how the other teams were doing. That was definitely against the rules.

"So," I said eventually. "Do you think what the Elder did in the realm was all illusion?"

He lowered his sunglasses a moment, peering at me over the rims. "That's an interesting choice of subject." He slid the glasses back into place.

"You're supposed to be good at illusions. We can't talk about the tournament, and I don't want to talk about Grandma business—unless you do?"

He shook his head. "Hell no. Okay, illusions." He settled back on the chair, crossing his long legs. "If I had to guess, I'd say some of it was illusion. At least, I hope it was. Otherwise, well, that's some seriously jagged-up magic."

"Yeah," I agreed. "I'd really prefer to stay on Grandma's good side."

"Maybe start by not calling her Grandma," he suggested.

"What should I call her? She didn't tell us her name." Nor had Pinky. Or a title.

"Names aren't something they give out easily."

That much I'd figured out.

"Could you make an illusion like that?" I asked.

"That fast? No. With some prep time, could I

build something that would fool most people for a while? Yeah."

He could? Just how good at illusions was he? "Most people?"

"Normal people. Some witches. Depending on how good they were at illusions. Or spotting them. Probably not a tanai fol. Even the ones without much magic seem to be able to spot an illusion pretty fast."

I frowned. "I thought you went to the UK because you were good at illusions. How did that help if they can spot them?"

"I was working with them, not trying to fool them. Being able to hold my own gave me the in."

Right. That made sense. "You might fool me. What I know about illusions would barely fill one of those espresso cups." I nodded at the coffee station built into the rocks behind the pond and the delicate white china stacked around it. One of the reasons I liked this part of the garden.

His head tilted. "Right. You're still just learning. That must be—"

"It's weird," I said. "I grew up believing I had no magic, and now I have to try and learn stuff that most people my age would have been doing for fifteen or sixteen years."

"You're strong though," he said. "You took out a demon and survived."

"Yeah, if you want a lightning strike, I might be

your girl. If you get me panicked enough." I glanced up at the sky, blue and placid above us. "Maybe not just at the moment."

"Lightning is big magic. That's the hard stuff, the real stuff. Glamours are just smoke and mirrors. Here, then gone." He blew a breath out, opening his fingers, and a tiny shower of multicolored sparks flew outward, then dissolved.

Pretty. And impressive.

"Illusion is probably more useful day-to-day."

"Maybe. If you're into fooling people." His mouth turned down.

"You could make a fortune as a makeup artist to the stars."

He snorted. "Not my thing." He looked around and waved a hand. "There might be a few sprinkled in around this garden. Too many plants for them to all be real. Gotta be careful with weight on rooftops."

"Maybe, or holos," I said. "Hotels aren't going to pay for magic when they can use tech." I looked around, but if any of the trees and plants were virtual, they were seamless from a distance.

"Yeah, probably."

"Can you show me how to do that spark thing?" I asked.

"That depends. What have you been learning?"

"Controlling fire," I said. "Seeing as that seems to come naturally for me. Seeing the energy flows.

All the building blocks. Some basic wards. Lizzie says I'm doing okay on those."

"She would know." His shoulders hunched, his expression turning briefly unhappy.

"Then there's lots of reading. Herb lore. History. I'm well up on imp identification."

He raised his eyebrows. "Cassandra does like solid basics. The imps usually come later, but I guess for you, it's no secret they exist. Okay, then, if you can do a ward, then you might pick this up. Hold out your hand."

I obeyed and reached my hand toward him, palm up. I still half expected to see the summoning glyph glowing there every time I looked, but it hadn't returned.

Zee held his next to mine. "Right. A ward is magic surrounding an object, protecting it, yeah? The basic form of a glamour is magic surrounding an object and disguising it. Illusions are more complicated and require more magic. You can build an illusion from nothing if you're good enough. Kind of like VR. Illusions make people see things that aren't there. A glamour makes you see what is there differently. Like a filter on a photo. Or augmented reality. Does that make sense?"

I nodded. "I guess."

"Good." He hitched a hip and dug one of the tiny boxes of mints that were everywhere in the convention center out of his pocket, then shook one of the mints into my palm. A small white ball of sugar, about a quarter inch in diameter if it was lucky. "Okay, that's nice and small. Let's make it look like something else."

"Like what? And don't say a candle or I'll smack you."

He laughed. "Cassandra drills, huh? No, not a candle. That's way too big for this. It would have to be more illusion than glamor. We need something small. Like another candy. Go on. Make it a Skittle. A red one."

"How old are you again?" I asked. But I saw the sense in what he was saying. A Skittle was a bit bigger than the mint and a flatter disc shape but, in essence, pretty similar.

"You hang out with gamers and game coders. I'm sure you know what a Skittle looks like, too."

My own tastes ran more to chocolate or sour gummies, but I couldn't argue. "Sure. What I'm not so sure on is how to make this look like one."

"Imagination. It's kind of like a ward. But build the magic in the shape of what you want it to look like. And it doesn't have to do anything more than just look like that. You can combine the two, of course, put a ward in a glamour, but that's way more complicated. For now, just make it look different."

I stared down at the mint, chewing my lip. Then let my sight slide into the magic. Zee glowed a soothing sort of smoky purple. The mint just looked like a mint. Maybe slightly brighter.

Which didn't give me a lot to work with.

I pulled my sunglasses off with my spare hand, then lifted the mint, bring it closer. Maybe there was a tiny gleam around it.

See the energy, change the energy. I tried to picture it as a Skittle instead. Or maybe inside a Skittle. A shell being built around it the way I'd seen Damon's animators build a character over a frame. I closed my eyes, trying to hold the image steady.

"Not bad," Zee said. "Though, last I checked, they didn't come in pink."

My eyes flew open. For a moment, I just saw the mint, but then it morphed into what was clearly a hot pink Skittle. Slightly lopsided but at least recognizable.

"Okay, let go of it," he said, tipping a mint into his palm.

I let the magic die away, and the Skittle turned back into a mint. "Huh," I said, feeling stupidly pleased.

"Kind of cool, right?" Zee said. He held his hand up. "Can you feel the mint's energy field?"

"I can see it, just. Not sure I feel anything," I said, studying it.

"Yeah, sorry. Small is easier to glamour, but some things don't give you a lot to work with. Right, now close your eyes."

I obeyed.

"Now open them again."

I did. There was a bright green Skittle sitting in Zee's palm. So perfect that it was hard to believe he hadn't actually replaced the mint.

"Can you feel the energy field now?" he asked.

I stared at the Skittle. It glowed a little brighter, but there was a feeling. I hovered my hand just over his. Was that a faint vibration? "Maybe? Sort of a buzzing sensation? Or maybe I'm just imagining things."

"It takes practice," he said, nodding. "This is a good start."

"Just what I need, more homework," I groaned.

"Does it help if I remind you that demons use illusion too? And lesserkind."

"Not really," I said. "Mostly it creeps me out."

"Only until you realize that it's possible to be able to spot them that way."

Huh. He had a point. I straightened. "You have my attention."

"Good," Zee said. Then he pointed at the mint. "Try again."

"Enjoying the show?"

I blinked, startled out of my thoughts. I'd been replaying Zee's illusion lesson in my head, trying to remember everything he'd shown me. Jack...Miller —that had been his name, right?—had taken the seat to my left in the bank of spectator seats in the small auditorium. After my lesson with Zee, I'd come back down to keep up my share of the surveillance. I'd chosen one of the lower leagues this time. The top leagues were impressive to watch, but sometimes the mistakes and sheer wacky ideas of the less polished teams were more fun.

"Yes. Nice to see you again, Mr. Miller." He wore jeans and a sports coat over a white Henley today rather than the midnight blue velvet, but something about the way they fit him told me they were probably nearly as expensive as his tux had been.

"Now, Maggie, I said to call me Jack." He flashed that charming smile, and I felt myself smile back.

"Sorry, Jack." I searched my memory for what we'd spoken about at the gala. It had only been four days ago but felt like half a lifetime already. Technology, investor, and...sponsor. That was it. "Is the team you're sponsoring competing in this heat?" I looked down at the stage at the front of the auditorium, where a large screen was set up. It was currently powered down, the white shape of it standing out against the deep red backdrop. The next heat wasn't due to start for a few minutes.

He nodded and pointed up at the smaller display off to the side of the screen that displayed the competitors and game times. "Yes, the Rainbow Rexes. They start in an hour or so."

I smiled at the name. "Checking out the competition?"

"Something like that." His smile widened. "Truth is, the kids like to focus in for a bit before they start, so they chase us old fogeys out of the room."

I left the obvious response that he wasn't an old fogey dangling. His smile was charming and the face to go it with handsome, but the thing about charming men was that they sometimes didn't know where the line was. Or didn't get told often enough, perhaps.

My cynical side said he could be trying to charm me to see if I'd let something about Damon or Riley slip, or charm Damon by sucking up to his girlfriend. Of course, my cynical side could just be too damned paranoid, but either way, friendly but with no chance of misunderstanding was what I was aiming for. There weren't many press or tech bloggers at this heat, which was part of the reason why I'd chosen it, but I didn't need to add any drama to the current situation by giving one of them a photo op that could be spun the wrong way.

"Gamers like their little rituals," I agreed.

He nodded, tilting his head at me. "You sound like you're familiar with competitive gaming. Something you've dabbled in?"

"I had a friend who did," I said. "So I learned enough along the way."

His expression turned sympathetic. "Had?"

I steeled myself not to wince as the familiar pang of guilt hit me. "She died."

"I'm sorry, Maggie. That's a hard thing, losing a friend. Especially at your age."

"Thank you," I said. "That's kind of you to say." I nodded down at the screen. "She would have loved all of this."

"I can imagine," he said. "My team have talked about little else since they qualified. They're a great bunch of kids." His smile and the pleasure in his voice seemed more genuine when he talked about them.

So that was a safe subject to stick to. "What got you into sponsoring a game team?" I asked.

He hitched a shoulder, then spread his hands. "Well, I have plenty of money and plenty of curiosity for new tech. I have a soft spot for the young and enthusiastic. It's why I like investing. Seeing what might happen. Sponsoring a team is just another way to do that." His mouth quirked. "The children's charity Damon was supporting with his gala the other night seems like they do good work."

"They do," I said. "They make a difference in those kids' lives. I know one of the women who works there."

"Maybe you can introduce me," Jack said. "I'd

be happy to make a more regular contribution. It's hard for people who don't get the right start in life."

"You sound like you know a bit about that."

"Well, my folks weren't rich. But they were kind and supportive. And luckily for me, something in their genes gave me a good brain. That got me the rest of the way I wanted to go. But there were a few people who helped me along the way. I like to give back."

"Well, I'd be happy to introduce you to Lizzie," I said. "Spark can always use more supporters. Do you have kids of your own?"

He shook his head, held up his left hand. No wedding ring. Not that everyone wore one. "Never did convince anyone to marry me. So, no. Not that I know of." He flashed another grin, and I wondered whether he was single by choice or circumstance. Maybe I was reading his charm all wrong, and he was gay or something. Not that that was a barrier to marriage and a family, but I didn't think so. A good-looking, flirty, rich, straight, white guy who had never married. That was probably a choice, unless he was way more of an asshole in private than he was in public.

"And how about you?" he asked. "Looking for the family and the 2.5 kids?"

Damn. But I'd asked him, so it was only fair that he got to ask me. "I guess I'll see how things turn out," I said.

"You're not looking for a Riley diamond?"

I frowned, and he held up his hands. "No insinuation. Just when a guy like Damon goes public with a relationship, it's usually fairly serious."

"We're serious," I said. "But we're not at the diamond stage."

He raised an eyebrow. "Fair enough. I won't push."

I hitched a shoulder. "I've never really believed in the whole fairy-tale wedding thing. My mom never married. My dad wasn't in the picture. It's not the model I grew up with." Not exactly true. I'd had my grandparents' marriage as an example of the good that came of two people who loved each other and stayed together a lifetime. But these days, that seemed like the exception rather than the rule. And why was I telling a relative stranger these things? Jack Miller was definitely a bit too easy to talk to. That charm thing again.

Perhaps it was time to go back to talking about the tournament. But before I could think of a neat segue, I spotted Yoshi and Pinky down on the lower level, standing near the bottom of the stairs that connected the tiers of seats. I leaned forward to wave an arm and see if I could catch their attention.

"See some friends?" Jack asked.

I nodded as Pinky looked up and smiled. She said something to Yosh, who turned his head toward me, too, and waved. "Yes, Yoshi works for me. And do you know Pinky Andretti? She's a composer. She's worked for a few of the game houses and done a couple movies."

"Ah, no, I don't believe I've had the honor," Jack said. He stared down at the bleachers at Pinky. Her hair didn't really stand out in the tournament crowd, but between it and Yoshi's ever-interesting fashion sense, which today featured a shirt in a neon yellow and green plaid, the two of them made an impression.

I made a little come-on-up gesture, and Yoshi nodded. But instead of both of them heading up, Pinky turned and walked away. Maybe she thought both of us in one section of the convention center was a waste of effort in the keeping an eye on things department.

Yoshi bounded up the stairs and dropped into the empty seat on my other side. "Hi, Maggie. Pinky went to get snacks."

The two of them had clearly hit it off. I hadn't intended to mix him up with the whole Fae problem, but he already knew about magic and bits and pieces of my world, if not the whole story, so it wasn't as though his life was completely normal. And we needed him to do his part spreading rumors. Which, apparently, he had.

"Hey, Yosh," I said. "Having a good day?"

He nodded. "Icy." He looked past me at Jack.

I introduced them.

"Jack Miller? Like from the Sec18H holographic engine?" Yoshi asked, seeming impressed.

Jack's brows lifted. "That's me. You been reading dusty memoirs of Silicon Valley old-timers, son?"

Yoshi grinned and pushed his thick red-framed glasses up his nose. "I'm doing history of holographic tech at school, so I've been boning up."

"Yoshi's at UC," I added. "It's his first year." Not that it wasn't possible that he'd have known who Jack was anyway. The kid was a bit of a tech savant and knew more about the history of the gaming industry than I did.

"Well, hopefully they'll move you on to some more interesting subjects fast," Jack said with a smile. "You young guys need to focus on the future, not the past."

"Oh no," Yoshi said, shaking his head, face set in one of his usual serious expressions. It gave him a cute tiny wrinkle between his dark eyebrows. "I like understanding the history. It's interesting. Helps me think about how ideas work. How things come together."

"Sounds like a coder brain talking to me," Jack said.

"He's good," I said, smiling fondly. "Actually, he's doing the hackathon at Righteous this week. Got in all on his own. Didn't even tell me—or Damon—he'd applied." The hackathon was being run by one of the research divisions I hadn't had much to do with. And Damon had kept himself out of the selection process, having had too much to do already with the tournament. If whoever was in charge knew who Yoshi was, it wasn't because of anything we'd done.

"Congratulations," Jack said. "I hear that had stiff competition to qualify. My team's vice captain's big brother tried to get in and didn't, and he's a junior."

"Thanks," Yoshi said, looking pleased. "It's going to be fun."

"Do you know what the project is yet?" Jack asked.

"Only bare bones," Yoshi said. He launched into a description of the specs. After a minute of tech chatter that wasn't really my thing, I stood and made him switch seats so the two of them didn't have to talk across me.

Down on the stage, the display was still in holding mode, the countdown to the next team's run the only thing moving. My datapad showed no messages, so I let my mind wander, trying to relax. Maybe Grandma had been wrong. Maybe this was as exciting as it was all going to get.

Yeah, and maybe that's wishful thinking.

As though summoned by my thoughts, Pinky wandered back into view along the main aisle and then started climbing the steps.

I nudged Yoshi, who was still bending Jack's ear, and said, "Snack patrol is here."

Yoshi broke off midsentence, head turning. He still ate like any teenage boy, and the arrival of food was always a distraction. Beside him, Jack stood.

"I've taken up enough of your time, Maggie," he said. "I'll leave you to your friends." He held out a hand to Yoshi. "Nice to meet you, kid."

"You, too, Mr. Miller," Yoshi said, shaking it politely.

Jack nodded and stood, making his way out across the row in the opposite direction. I watched him for a moment, then turned my attention to Pinky and whatever she had that smelled so damned good.

CHAPTER EIGHTEEN

MANY HOURS LATER, I stood with Damon at the side of the main auditorium stage and pictured flickering candy shapes in my head as we watched the MC give a quick wrap-up of the pro teams' performances for the day. Only one of them in the top league had scored well and found themselves sliding into third. The other two had made a few mistakes that had cost them points, and they were hovering just outside the top ten.

I leaned into Damon, trying not to yawn. As fun as *Serenity Falls* was, after watching at least thirty runs of the first heat versions in the last few days, I was looking forward to the next rounds where the teams would have some new levels to play with.

At least Zee's suggestion to practice imagining different shapes had come in handy. I could do that and still look as though I was half paying attention to the games. Damon had seemed a little distracted himself, though he'd sat in the VIP box with me and watched the runs until Cat had come to escort us downstairs so he could shake hands with the teams who'd just competed.

"Tired?" he whispered.

I nodded but kept smiling as camera flashes went off in front of the stage. Technically anyone with a media pass wasn't supposed to take pictures of what happened side stage, but the vidstreamers did have permission to shoot B roll backstage stuff. I didn't want to see my face looking bored plastered all over the newslinks tomorrow.

"Not much longer," he said. I nodded and slipped my hand into his.

The lights went out.

"What the fuck?" I said before I could stop myself. Hopefully the power had cut off the vidstream feeds and there were no mics.

Damon already had his hand to his ear, presumably listening to whatever the security team were saying. I'd taken my earpiece out while we'd been watching the game, finding the background chatter too distracting. It was tucked in its case in my purse, but I wasn't going to fumble around in the dark trying to find it.

"Power's out all over the hotel," Damon said

quietly. "Mitch wants us to stay right here." His fingers curled tighter around mine, and I moved closer still, straining my senses. Shouldn't there be backup generators or something kicking in by now? The hotel and the convention had their own separate power grid with solar batteries. From what I remembered from the emergency protocol briefings, the power was supposed to switch over fast if there was an outage in the city supply.

My spine started to crawl as the lights stayed off. Here and there, the darkness was broken by the glow of datapad screens, both backstage and out in the seats, but the roof in the auditorium was high, and I was uncomfortably aware of the cavernous dark space above us.

Where anything could be lurking.

"C'mon," I muttered, and Damon squeezed my hand again.

"Don't worry."

I really wanted that earpiece, if only to hear Cassandra or someone reporting in. Instead, I grabbed my datapad and tapped a message to her and Lizzie, the light from the screen somewhat comforting.

The crowd was growing noisier, wondering what was going on. I couldn't blame them. Where were the damned lights?

After a few minutes, one of the hotel staff came out on stage with a megaphone and told everyone to stay seated and that the lights would be back on shortly.

I hoped he was right. It would take hours to empty the auditorium by flashlight. Hours in which security systems would be down and communications difficult.

Just when I was starting to consider telling Damon that we should leave before things got chaotic, the lights came back, dazzling bright. I shielded my eyes for a moment, blinking and trying not to show just how relieved I felt.

Damon blew out a breath. Out on stage, the MC was back on his mark like the professional he was, one hand to his earpiece, listening to the broadcast director or whoever was talking to him. Damon tapped his own earpiece.

"Mitch, how about an update?" he said softly. The response didn't take long. Damon listened intently, then focused back on me. "They're going to wrap up fast, go to the replays. We're going to go meet Mitch and get a report."

Fine by me.

My datapad buzzed against my palm, and I saw a thumbs-up from Lizzie flash up on the screen. Good.

Maybe it had just been a blackout after all. Nothing more than that.

Still, I paid extra attention to the surroundings,

on the lookout for any sign of magic, as Maia arrived to escort us upstairs.

Mitch's report didn't take long. So far, they'd found no signs that anything unexpected had happened during the blackout. All systems green, so to speak.

Damon's shoulders relaxed, and he nodded approval. "Good. All the same, I think Maggie and I will go back to my place tonight."

Excellent plan. After what had happened with Ajax, Damon's home security, which had already been next-level, was probably better than just about anybody's other than presidents and royalty. Maybe better than theirs, too. He probably had a bigger budget to play with.

A night in a familiar bed sounded divine. Maybe I'd finally get a good night's sleep.

"Are you sure?" Mitch said. "The hotel says the systems are all back online."

"I trust our systems more than the hotel," Damon said. "Unless you think I shouldn't."

Mitch shook his head. "No. No signs of trouble there.

"Good. Then wrap this up, and make sure you get home, too. I'll see you in the morning."

A thunderclap woke me a few hours after we got home. Beside me, Damon barely stirred, which told me something about how tired he was.

We'd returned to his house and practically fallen into bed, both of us barely keeping our eyes open long enough to say good night.

I rolled over, turning toward the window. The familiar scents of the room and softness of the mattress beneath me made me feel safe despite the storm. It was nice to be home.

Home?

That thought made me sit up as another thunderclap boomed overhead, followed by a flash of lightning that lit up the edges of the curtains. Damon still didn't move, and I stared down at him, wondering when I'd started thinking of his place as home.

And wondering what he'd think about that.

Probably a conversation for a time when we weren't worrying about whether a demon was going to try and disrupt his tournament or whether the Fae were going to annex San Francisco if we couldn't find it before it did.

My brain started to whir.

Crap. My chances of getting back to sleep were falling fast. And I'd toss and turn if I just lay in bed, trying to sleep. Which would wake Damon up. No need for both of us to suffer.

I slid out of bed and grabbed my robe, then slipped out of the room.

Tea, maybe. Put some of that herb lore to use and brew myself something soothing. I headed to the kitchen on autopilot and flicked on the small light over the stove. Between that and the lightning, I'd be able to see well enough to make tea.

I filled the kettle and grabbed some of the herbal teas from the pantry. There was a small herb garden not far from the kitchen door, but another crash of thunder was enough to convince me that now wasn't the time to go out and snip some fresh mint. Having seen what being on the wrong end of a lightning strike had done to a demon, I had no desire to ever experience it myself. I'd make do with what we had.

I brewed the tea, poured it into a mug, and walked over to the window, watching the storm. The last thunderclap had been followed by rain, and between the water streaming down and the wind making the trees and plants dance, it was hard to see much. But the flickering movements were just random enough that my jumpy nerves kept thinking maybe I saw *something*.

I stepped closer to the window, watching more intently. Maybe I was paranoid, but we'd had an imp get through Damon's defenses once before. Granted, that was before his defenses had been

upgraded to Fort Knox-worthy and magically forti-
fied, but still.

"Maggie?"

I jerked, almost dropping my tea as I spun
around.

"Shit. Sorry," Damon said, holding his hands up
in apology. "I didn't mean to scare you. I thought
you must have heard me."

I shook my head, trying to slow my heartbeat
down. "No. You were sleeping pretty hard back
there. I didn't expect you."

"How long have you been awake?"

"Not long." I turned back to the window. "The
storm woke me up."

"Wouldn't have taken you for a storm watcher,"
he said, coming to stand next to me. He was only
wearing black boxer briefs, and against the darkness outside, his body was reflected in the glass, a
perfect mirror image of his muscles and long limbs
on display.

Now *that* was an illusion I could get behind. Or
in front of. Or on top...and *nope*. We needed
sleep.

"Just keeping a lookout," I said. "Feeling a bit
jumpy after the hotel, I guess.

"It was just a power outage," he said. "Mitch
gave the all clear. There hasn't been so much as a
flicker on the security feeds here."

"How do you know that?"

"I woke up, and you were gone. I checked the feeds," he said. "Then I came and found you."

He reached out and took my mug, stretching his arm to put it on the table. "Come here." He tugged me closer, and I went willingly, pressing into all that warm and solidity, breathing him in.

Had he been worried I'd somehow been spirited away while he slept? "I'm right here. You found me. You always do. And if you don't, then I'll come looking for you, okay?"

"Okay." He smiled down at me. "Deal."

Thunder boomed again, and I flinched. Damon's arms tightened around my waist. "Okay. New plan. I'm going to distract you from this storm."

"We need to sleep," I protested half-heartedly.

"Orgasms are excellent sleep aids," he said.

I laughed. "Oh, really?"

"Yeah, after a few, you'll be out like a light."

"A few? You making big promises?"

"You know I'm good at keeping promises," he said. His hands tugged at the sash holding my robe closed. He pushed it open and smiled. "You look gorgeous in the moonlight, Maggie mine."

"You don't look so—" I gasped, the words dying on my lips as his mouth settled over one of my nipples, the rasp of his tongue sending a jolt of sensation through me. "Oh, do that again."

Thunder crashed again, rattling the windows as he lifted me, carrying me over to the table. The mug crashed, too, as he cleared the surface with an impatient sweep of his arm and laid me down. I forgot about the storm as his mouth moved down over my body until he pushed my legs apart and his tongue found my clit.

Lightning heat flashed through me and above me as the storm lit up the sky and Damon drove me crazy. But the feel of his mouth, amazing as it was, wasn't enough. I pushed his head away. "I need you."

"To do what, Maggie mine?" He straightened, tugged me down closer to the edge of table, leaned forward to slide his cock over me.

"Fuck me," I said, shivering with need. Thunder rumbled around us again, the air electric as he pushed into me slowly. "*More.*"

He watched me, his blue eyes silvered by the storm light, as though considering whether to take it slow. But when the lightning flashed again, he groaned and bent to kiss me. Then he began to move, and we made our own storm, wild and free and perfect. When I came, it might as well have been a bolt from the sky, so good I nearly passed out. When I came back to myself, Damon had half collapsed over me, breath harsh in my ear.

I tried to say something, but it came out more a half-sighed mumble.

He pushed himself back up, just far enough that I could kiss him.

"Sleepy yet?" he asked, laughing down at me.

"Maybe not quite yet," I said. "But I vote for going back to bed. Nice soft mattress. More room."

"Room?" he said. "Why, Maggie Lachlan, are you going to ravish me?"

"One hundred percent," I said and laughed as he picked me up and carried me away.

The beeping of my alarm came far too soon the next morning. But when I opened my eyes, I felt far better than I had any right to feel, given how late—or early—it must have been by the time Damon and I finally fell asleep. I yawned and sat up. His arm snaked up and around my waist as I swung my legs out of bed

"Where are you going? S'early," he mumbled.

"It is. But no rest for the wicked." I glanced at him over my shoulder. Hair sticking up every which way, stubble darkening the line of his jaw, and one blue eye half open, any normal man would have looked terrible.

He looked delicious.

I turned away before he made me forget I had shit to do. "I'm going to take Yoshi to Riley for the hackathon. He was nervous last night, and I said I'd give him a lift. I cleared it with Maia. I'll go say hi to

Benji and Eli after I drop him off, then come back to the hotel later."

"But...sleep, bed. You and me," Damon said.

"I'd say you have about thirty minutes before Cat starts blowing up your datapad with all the information about whatever that was last night," I said. "You go back to sleep if you want, but I want breakfast. Coffee. Eggs. You know, food not made at a hotel." I wasn't the world's greatest cook, but after just a few days of hotel food—even the good stuff in the penthouse—I was jonesing for something boring but familiar.

Damon's housekeeper, Amy, kept his fridge stocked with everything we could possibly need, she made dinner if he asked her to and left it for us, and there were always meals in the freezer, but she was currently taking advantage of the tournament to take some well-earned vacation time.

Which might mean the fridge would be a little less stocked than usual. But at least there'd be coffee. "Eat with me or snooze, your choice."

Damon groaned but rolled over. "Feed me, woman. You wore me out."

"Hey, I was just getting up for tea. You're the one who got all enthusiastic," I said, pulling on my discarded sleep shirt and robe again.

He watched me with a smile on his face. "What can I say? Thunderstorms do it for me."

"Nice." I tossed my pillow at his head. "Just for that, you can make your own eggs."

"Just put the coffee on," he said. "I'll make your eggs."

About an hour later, full of eggs, coffee, and the couple spine-tingling kisses Damon dropped on me before I'd left, I pulled the Ventra up to the curb in front of Yoshi's apartment building. Damon had suggested Boyd could drive us, but I figured Yoshi would be nervous and might want to talk without an audience. Damon conceded the point, but I was fairly sure a Riley security car wouldn't be too far away.

Yoshi sat on the steps out front, backpack beside him, squinting down at his datapad, orange-rimmed round sunglasses shading his eyes from the morning sun.

I rolled down the window. "Hey, Yosh. Sorry, am I late?"

He looked up, shaking his head, then grabbed the pack and stood, slipping it over his right shoulder. He was still lanky and all legs and arms, but over the last few months, he'd started to fill out a little, making me wonder if he was one of those guys who was going to have another growth spurt in his early twenties. Not up in his case but out.

Whatever the reason, I liked seeing him not quite as skinny as he had been when we'd met. Hopefully it meant his life was better now.

"Morning," Yoshi said as he pulled open the passenger door. "Thanks for the lift."

"No problem," I said. I wondered if he'd already gone home by the time the power had glitched at the convention center last night. "Excited for today?"

"Yeah," he said in a tone that was more half grunt than anything.

Still a teenager, I reminded myself. Didn't matter how smart he was or how much responsibility he had taken on at a young age, he still had moments where his inner teen asserted itself. Apparently this was one of them. But I wasn't the most talkative person on the planet when I was nervous either, so I didn't worry about it.

"Today's just the briefing, right? Tomorrow you do the coding?" From what Yoshi had told me, the hackathon consisted of a three-hour presentation on the assignment today, the afternoon off to prepare, and then they all came back tomorrow to do their magical baby nerd things and see who could come up with the coolest whatever it was Riley was challenging them to do.

He nodded, then pulled out a pair of earbuds. "Going to chill a bit and think."

I amended my assessment to "really nervous."

Yoshi was normally chatty, and even though he'd been to Riley with me a few times already, he still acted as excited as a little kid heading to Disneyland every time. His current mood seemed more like a kid off to the dentist.

Maybe he was feeling the pressure. It was a big deal that he'd gotten in. The hackathons had led to job offers before. Yoshi was young, and he still had a few years of college ahead, but this was a chance to make an impression and maybe secure his future. I let him be and focused on the traffic.

The guard at the gate at Riley let me through once he'd scanned me, and I drove to the small parking lot next to the building where Damon's office was. It was kept clear, used only by him, his drivers, and a few other VIPs. There were perks to dating the boss.

"Know where you're going?" I asked as I shut the engine off. "Got your security pass?"

Yoshi nodded, not taking out the earbuds.

"Okay, good luck. Message me when you're done. I'm going to go see Benji for a coffee, maybe hang around for a bit. If I'm still here when it's over, I can take you back to the convention center if you want."

That earned me another nod, and he climbed out, closing the door with a shove of his hip.

So much for my supportive boss role.

Teenager, I reminded myself again and picked up my datapad to tell Benji I was here.

Three hours later, I was buzzing from too much coffee, and my cheeks hurt from laughing. Benji and Eli had caught me up on the latest gossip from their team and their lives. It had been nice to just relax and be normal for a few hours, and I'd lingered with them, not quite ready to go back to the tournament and hunting for demons or whatever the hell we were facing. But I couldn't play hooky forever.

I said goodbye and started back to the parking lot, sending Yoshi a message that I'd be there in about ten minutes if he wanted a ride.

I read through the few messages waiting for me as I walked. One from Damon saying he was back at the hotel. Another from Pinky saying we needed to talk that made me groan and put the datapad away. I didn't want to think about the Fae just yet.

The campus was quieter than normal, which made sense. A lot of the staff would be at the tournament, and Damon had given a few weeks extra vacation to anyone who wanted it to say thanks for getting *Serenity Falls* up and running so fast and the success of *Archangel*. Benji and Eli were already deep into working on their next project, which was why they hadn't taken time off.

It was another sunny day now that the chill of the morning was gone, and I walked slowly, enjoying the last few minutes of freedom. Mitch had let us escape for a night, but I was certain we'd be back in the penthouse tonight so he didn't have to split the security team.

In his place, I'd make the same call. And after all, walking around the grounds here, where access was strictly controlled, wasn't the same as going back out into the real world now that everyone knew I was dating Damon. The attention I'd been getting at the tournament was a taste of it, but really, most of the attendees there were more interested in the new game than Damon's new girlfriend. Though I'd gotten my share of dirty looks from both women and men old enough to know better.

I'd deliberately avoided looking at anything approaching a gossip newsfeed since the tournament had started. Plenty of time after to find out how the world was taking the news of me and Damon being a "thing."

When I got the parking lot, Yoshi was leaning against the car, sunglasses still in place.

"How did it go?" I asked. The car unlocked as I approached.

Yoshi pulled the door open. "Good, I think. Lots to think about."

"Well, that's great," I said. "Did they feed you?"

"Yeah." He drummed his fingers on the roof of the car.

Still nervous, then. Understandable if he now knew exactly what he had to pull off to win the hackathon. "Okay, well, jump in. And if you need to listen to music and chill or work on the way back, that's fine. Do you want me to take you home or to the hotel?"

"Hotel," he said. "Thanks." He pulled out his datapad and started typing.

Right. Leave the boy alone and drive.

CHAPTER NINETEEN

WITHOUT YOSHI TO DISTRACT ME, I spent most of the drive back to the hotel working myself into a state of dread about what Pinky was going to tell me when I got there.

No one else had tried to get in touch with me, so presumably this was something she was keeping between the two of us. The thought didn't thrill me. More trouble wasn't what the doctor ordered.

"What are you going to watch today?" I asked as Yoshi and I stepped out of the elevator into the lobby. He'd finally pulled his earbuds out when we'd gotten closer to the hotel, but he still hadn't said much.

"Not sure yet," he said.

"Well, don't stay too late. Save your energy for

tomorrow." Man, I sounded like his mom, not his boss. He was old enough to make his own decisions.

That earned me a grunt and nod, and he jerked his head in the direction of the convention center, one brow lifting.

"I'm going upstairs first," I said. "You go on." I wanted to find Pinky, and I didn't need Yoshi there for that particular discussion.

"Sure," he said coolly and turned on his heel, walking toward the stairs that led up to the air-bridge that crossed to the convention center.

I watched him for a few seconds, muttered, "Strange are the ways of teens," and turned to go find Pinky.

I'd only gone about thirty feet in the other direction when I spotted her standing near the concierge's desk, scanning the crowd.

Waiting for me? Just as well I hadn't taken the penthouse elevator straight up from the parking lot.

It took a few seconds for her to see me waving. When she did, she smiled in relief and made her way across to me.

"You're back. Good," she said. "Let's go somewhere and talk."

She reached for my arm as though she was going to literally drag me off if I wouldn't go, then froze. "Shit," she whispered, staring down at my hand.

I looked down. On my palm, a glyph had appeared. Not glowing as brightly as before but there.

"Maggie," Pinky said urgently. "Who were you just with?"

"A couple guys at Riley," I said. "But they haven't been anywhere near the hotel. They definitely weren't at the gala. It can't be them. And I gave Yoshi a ride back from campus. He's just going to the convention center to watch a few rounds, I think." I clenched my hand shut, hiding the glyph.

"Yoshi?" Pinky said. "Okay, we'd better find him."

My stomach twisted. It couldn't be Yoshi. Maybe I'd bumped into someone else. Though he'd been at the hackathon. Had whoever was coming for us slipped someone into that group? Being actually on the Riley campus would make hacking easier, maybe. Had someone taken that bait? I felt sick. "He was headed for the skywalk."

I turned back in the direction of the elevators. But the crowd of people swarming to the hotel had grown fast. The first heats started in about an hour, so this was peak arrival time for the spectators. I couldn't spot Yoshi's dark head anywhere.

Fuck.

I started walking. Fast. Pinky kept up. When we got to the base of the stairs that led up to the skywalk, it was clear that it was going to take at least ten minutes to make our way over to the convention center that way.

I tugged on Pinky's wrist with my non-glowing hand. "Let's go back to the elevators, take the private one up, and cross at the exec floor. It will be faster."

My stomach churned as we fought our way back through the rapidly growing crowd in the lobby. If someone tangled up with a demon had been with Yoshi at Riley—

I shoved the thought away as I collided with someone's shoulder and we both rocked back. "Sorry," I called as I dodged around them and got a glare in return. Right. I had to concentrate. It was harder than you'd think to move through a crowd with my dominant hand shoved into the pocket of my jeans. But eventually we reached the bank of elevators. I'd found using the private elevator for the penthouse weird at first, but right now, it was a godsend.

I pressed my palm on the scanner on the wall. The elevator doors opened almost immediately. I stepped through before they were fully open, Pinky hot on my heels. I hit the floor number and waited as the doors closed way too slowly.

"It can't be Yoshi," I said. "He's just a kid. God, if he's been dragged into all this...."

"It will be fine," Pinky said soothingly. "Maybe

that's only happening"—she pointed at my hand —"because I talked to Grandma."

She had? That was why she wanted to talk to me? "Did she say anything about the spell being set off again?" I asked. "She told us she'd removed it."

"Apparently she wasn't telling the whole truth," Pinky said. "I'm not exactly surprised."

"Don't take this the wrong way, but that's a shitty way to operate," I said.

"I know. Trust me, I don't like it any more than you do."

The elevator reached our destination. We headed for the skywalk, but as we rounded the corner in the corridor, Yoshi was there, moving away from the skywalk, back into the hotel. Was he meeting a friend or something? He didn't have a room here. Not one I knew about anyway.

"Yoshi!" I called.

He didn't react at first, his pace steady. Maybe he had his earbuds in again?

"Yosh!" I yelled louder. "Hold up."

This time he turned and stopped, frowning. I jogged up to him, Pinky in my wake.

"What?" he asked. "Did I leave something?" He moved a little closer.

"No," I said. "I just wanted to—"

"Maggie," Pinky said softly from behind me. "Step back."

"What?" I turned confused.

"That's not Yoshi," she said.

"What do you mean—" I glanced around, and at that point, Yoshi bolted.

"What the fuck?" I twisted back to see him sprinting away, moving like lightning.

"Go after him," Pinky yelled. "Don't let him get away."

We ran. My longer legs should have let me get ahead of Pinky, but damn, she moved fast, over-taking me quickly, then leading the way.

In a hotel, if you're running away from the eleva-tors and the skywalk and don't have a key to a room, there's not many places to go. The fire doors on the exec floor were currently coded to only open for hotel staff or anyone else with permission to be there. I hadn't added Yoshi to that list.

We caught up to him just before the next bend in the junction.

"Yosh, stop," I panted, and he turned, a strange expression on his face.

Pinky stepped forward, hand raised, and said one short phrase that sounded like the same lan-guage she'd spoken with her grandmother. Sud-denly the boy standing in front of us wasn't Yoshi anymore but a slim white guy with sandy hair prob-ably around Yoshi's age.

He looked vaguely familiar.

"What the hell?" I wanted to barf, staring at the

guy. All that time in the car and it hadn't been Yoshi? All day? I'd taken this guy to Riley and—

"Illusion," Pinky said, still breathing hard. "A good one."

My stomach rolled again, and I had to swallow hard, not sure I wasn't going to throw up. How had I not noticed? "Then where's Yoshi?"

She shook her head. "I don't know. Maggie, this isn't good."

Not-Yoshi stepped back, and Pinky spat another word. He froze again.

Not good was an understatement. So much for Zee's little lesson. I hadn't felt the vaguest hint of an illusion. If there were people roaming around the hotel wearing other people's faces and they were good enough to do that, then something bad was going to happen.

"Damon. I have to find Damon," I said, suddenly cold. "Call Mitch. Call everyone."

I turned and ran.

Panic shrieked through me as my feet pounded the carpet. Where would Damon be? He'd made a habit of stopping to eat lunch with me in the penthouse each day, and it was closing in on 1:00 p.m. Maybe he was there? I rounded the next corner in the corridor, heading back to the elevators.

Wherever Damon was, he was well guarded, I tried to tell myself. If I checked the penthouse first, by that time, Pinky would've raised the alarm with

Mitch, and everything would be locked down and fine. But the sick panic running through my veins, fueling my steps, told me I didn't believe it. Something was wrong. The glyph on my hand and Not-Yoshi proved it.

Somebody was making a move.

And I had to find Damon.

I made it to the next corner, turned right again without slowing or really looking where I was going, and crashed into Jack Miller with enough force that my teeth snapped together.

I wobbled in place, a little dazed by the impact. Jack's hands clamped over my shoulders, steadying us both.

"Maggie! What's wrong? Why are you running?" He sounded half winded, but his grip was strong. Almost too strong.

"Sorry," I babbled, stepping back. He let go. "I'm sorry, but I need to find Damon."

I went to move around him, the need to get to Damon burning just about anything else from my brain, but Jack moved, too, blocking my path.

"Calm down a moment. Tell me what's wrong." His voice was soothing, reassuring.

I blinked at him, staring into his eyes, suddenly wanting to listen to him. *Safe*, something whispered in my head. *Safe here. Nothing wrong.*

Wait, what? I shook my head, stepping back

again. The feeling eased, and fear came flooding back, making my breath hitch.

Jack blinked, then frowned. "Maggie. Talk to me."

"I have to go," I said, stepping to one side. "This is important."

"I'm sure it is," he said. "But maybe I can help?" His voice was soothing again, calming. "Let me help you, Maggie."

The words drew me in, fogging my mind again, like an unwanted breath of Sandman. I shook my head, unsure suddenly of what I'd been doing, then looked down.

The shimmer of light on my hand flashed brighter, cutting through the fog.

Damon. I had to find Damon.

"Jack, I'm sorry, but please, get out of my way. This is important."

His expression morphed from calm to annoyed. "How are you doing that?" he muttered, then, "Damn, I was hoping it wasn't going to come to this."

"What do you mean?" Panic burst through the last of the fog, triggering my instinct to get the hell away from him. I reached for my magic just as he clamped something around my wrist and the world flared white around me.

Then exploded into a flash of blinding colors

and light and sound that screeched through my brain and left me reeling from the onslaught.

It seemed to go on and on. I couldn't feel my body. Couldn't close my eyes or block my ears as the storm of noise and light crashed around me. Searing pain shot through my head, and I sucked in a breath to scream. But no sound came. Just more pain.

How long it went on, I couldn't tell, but eventually the storm of sound and light began to fade, leaving me in a void of nothing, floating and wishing for nothing more than to fall into unconsciousness and escape it all.

Slowly the pain faded, my breathing slowing from panicked rasps. The attack didn't start again, but I still couldn't feel my body. Eventually I opened my eyes. I was standing in a familiar-looking plain white room. A VR foyer.

What the actual fuck? I reached out instinctively for a kill switch, but nothing happened. Bile rose in my throat. This was definitely VR. There had to be a damned kill switch. Why the fuck wasn't it working?

I tried again, thinking the command as well as trying to move my hand. But there was no more reaction to my second attempt than there'd been to my first. I bit down on my lip hard, trying to anchor myself with a physical sensation. I felt the pressure of my teeth. That much was good. That meant my chip was working, if I was indeed in a VR. But it was also bad, because if my chip was working but I couldn't let myself out, then I was trapped.

"System override," I said desperately.

Again, nothing.

I stared around the room. The walls were blank, but they seemed to close in on me as I tried to think and not panic.

No kill switch. Okay. Was there a menu?

I snapped my fingers. "Menu."

The menu appeared. A relief for the half a second it took me to realize there was only one option on it.

One button with the words PRESS ME.

"*Press me*"? What was this, some fucked-up version of *Alice in Wonderland*? Well, I'd read the book and seen a number of movie versions of the story, and I didn't much like any of them. And nothing good happened to Alice following the instructions she was given.

I stared at the menu, running through every possible method of exiting from a game I'd ever heard of. It was a fairly short list. At least for anyone who was an active player. The systems relied all on either biomonitoring or having other people with you to hit a kill switch if you became unable to do it yourself.

Biomonitoring seemed unlikely in a system that had been designed without a kill switch. If someone was messed-up enough to want to be able to trap someone in a game, I doubted they really cared much about what was happening to that person's body in the real world or if they were having something like a seizure. And it wasn't as though I could test the theory out. I didn't even know where my body was.

I tried to remember what I'd been doing before I'd woken up. But it was vague and scrambled, as though whatever that color and light that hit me had screwed up my memory.

"Fuck!" I yelled.

The PRESS ME option started to flash on and off.

I clenched my fist, resisting the urge to tap it. It could be a trap.

Like the summoning. If the Fae could plant a spell to summon Zee and me to them, that might just mean someone could summon something into the game to be with me.

Like a demon.

The menu flashed faster, and around me, the room began to darken.

Oh hell no.

I wasn't going to be trapped in the dark. Pressing the damned thing might be a bad decision, but sealing myself in a never-ending darkness didn't seem like a great one either. Not when someone could be sending something I couldn't see to join me there.

"Fuck, fuck, fuck," I growled, then reached out and tapped the menu.

The room began to lighten almost immediately, though it didn't go back to the same bright white it had been at the beginning, hovering somewhere around twilight.

The former well-defined walls of the room were hard to see now, and I tried not to think about what might be lurking in shadowy corners. "Well, come on, then. What happens now?"

"Ah, you're with us again. Good." The voice echoed around the room.

"Who is this?" I demanded. "Let me out."

"Maggie, stay calm." The voice was odd, but there was something familiar about it.

"Why the hell should I? You've locked me in here. Calm is not the correct response to being kept prisoner." Even saying it, my heart started racing faster. I needed to get out of this damned VR. And what... what had I been doing? I couldn't bring the memory back.

"You just need to stay calm. You don't need to stay here too long. If you cooperate."

Cooperate? With what? It wasn't as though there was much I could do. No way was I going to call fire when I had no idea where my physical body was. And this was VR, not an illusion, so I had no chance of breaking out on my own. Even if it was an illusion, well, I didn't know much about those, did I? Or maybe I did?

I snarled, baring my teeth, trying to think. I knew my name. I had recognized this was a VR room. I knew how to call a menu. Why the fuck couldn't I remember what I'd been doing just before this? Or what I knew about illusions? "What do you want?"

Laughter. Reverberating around the white walls unpleasantly. "That would be a long story. And sadly, there's no time for long stories right now. But relax. It's not you we're after. Not this time."

We? Who was *we*?

Someone working with a demon? Or several humans? Or just the kind of delusional maniac movies liked to feature who talked about themselves as "we" like insane royalty? Or maybe just one person trying to make me believe they were many?

I didn't see any real options but to try and keep them talking. Maybe they'd let something slip. Maybe I'd think of something. At the back of my brain, something was prodding at me, something trying to break through the fog.

"It's hard to relax when I have no idea what's going on. Let me out of this and we can talk."

"Tempting. But no. Time is slipping away, Maggie, and there are things to do. Things you can best help by just staying here. That will make sure your Damon does as he's told."

Damon! The fog parted. I'd been looking for Damon, and I'd run into...Jack fucking Miller. "Jack? Is that you?"

No answer. For just that little bit too long. "It doesn't matter who I am. Just be a good girl and this will be over before you know it. Like I said, this time it's not about you. And you probably don't want that to change."

"Damon's not going to help you do whatever it is you think. What do you want? Some piece of his tech?" I wasn't going to mention the algorithm. If our bait had lured him in, better to play dumb, like I didn't know what they could be after.

"That's not important. And for your sake, I hope he cooperates. You don't want to be stuck in here forever."

"No," I said carefully. "But I might be more use to you in person, Jack."

"I don't need your magic," he said. "There are those who are interested in it. Fixated, perhaps. But my friends are smarter than that. They have seen the potential. Why focus on one reluctant witch when there are so many other sources to use?"

Okay, he—and I was almost certain it *was* Jack —was talking about demons. He had to be. I should have paid more attention to my initial instincts. That Damon didn't particularly like him when I first saw them together at the gala and that Jack was too charming for his own good. He'd been after something.

Rich, determined, and clearly not hampered by too many morals. Not only to deal with demons but to deal with the kind of people who'd build whatever the hell it was he'd used to lock me into this VR.

But I hadn't seen it. Though maybe I could use that to my advantage. He thought he had me fooled. Thought he was smarter than me.

"If your friends are who I think they are, then in my experience, anyone who makes friends with them comes off second best," I said.

Laughter again. "But you're still here. And don't worry about me. I'm used to dealing with the darker sides of life. Where do you think I got the means to keep you here?"

I didn't smile in case he could see me. Yeah, I'd worked that part out already. But the identity of the dark web scumbag who'd built this cage was something I'd worry about later. What mattered now was getting out of here.

Maybe that would be easier without Jack watching me. "Fine," I said. "I'll be good."

"Sensible decision. After all, if you misbehave, I can just keep you here. In my experience, with enough time alone in the dark in one of these, a person will do just about anything to get out."

The menu vanished abruptly.

"Jack? Jack Miller, you prick, let me out."

There was no reply. So, was he logged out from

whatever it was that was letting him talk to me or just testing me?

I sank down to the floor and considered my options.

One. Wait here like a good girl and hope Jack came back to let me out.

Not an option I liked.

Two. Find a way out.

That sounded *much* better. But I had no idea how to do it.

How the hell was I supposed to break out of a VR?

Clearly tech wasn't the answer. Which left me with magic. But how?

I didn't know where my body was, so it was too risky to try anything in the real world. Could I try something here? VR was a form of illusion. My brain being fooled into thinking everything around me was real. But it wasn't. Could I break the illusion for myself?

It seemed crazy to even attempt it. I knew next to nothing about illusions. And my experience with Not-Yoshi wasn't exactly a promising sign that I had any particular talent for them. I'd sat next to him in a car and not realized it wasn't Yoshi, for fuck's sake. Twice.

How could I possibly break an illusion if I couldn't even sense one? I was no Fae, able to conjure a spell that would work in-game. I was a baby witch who still barely understood how my power worked.

My pulse started to race again, fear blanking my brain. I sucked in a breath, making it slow and holding it before I breathed out again. Jack was right, panicking wouldn't help anything. So maybe I just had to take this back to first principles.

Magic was energy. Tech was energy. I could change the energy.

Right. I sat up straighter, crossing my legs. My avatar wore a stock standard black game suit. I had no idea if it even resembled me, but that didn't matter. What mattered was what I did.

See the energy, change the energy.

I breathed slowly, trying to settle my racing mind, then let my sight open to the magic. Like it had back in *Serenity Falls*, everything glowed around me, the white walls shimmering slightly as I watched them.

That was the energy. But what did I need to do with it? I couldn't just wish it away. I couldn't channel it into fire or something physical because of the whole "don't accidentally break yourself" issue. Could I feed it back into the system?

Maybe. But that system was connected to my chip. The chip sending information rocketing through my nervous system. Frying the chip or my brain didn't seem like great options.

And while I'd learned a lot about game code

working on the *Archangel* problem for Damon, I didn't understand the intricacies of how VR interacted with our brains well enough to mess with it.

Fuck. Okay, so nothing big. Maybe something little? Imagine the energy floating away as small wisps of air? If I changed enough of it, maybe the chip wouldn't be able to read it and I'd be free.

It seemed unlikely, but it was worth a try.

I sucked in another breath, stared at the shimmering walls, thought about tiny pieces of them breaking off, floating away. When I had the image clear in my head, I cautiously added some power to the thought.

Nothing.

I let some more magic trickle through, and I thought I saw the shimmer across the walls flicker faster.

Was it working? I shoved a little more magic at the walls, keeping the image in my head. I couldn't risk using too much and frying myself, but I had to push as much as I could. I stared at the walls, my eyes stinging as I tried not to blink. For a fraction of a second, I thought one of them turned a little more, giving me a glimpse of something blurry behind it. But then it snapped back, and a jolt of pain hit my head.

I let go of the magic. "Ow." I rubbed my temple even though it couldn't possibly help. Had that worked? Or had my imagination, my desire to get out of here, been playing tricks on me?

My head twinged again. Okay, so maybe a break before I tried again. I stared at the walls, counted breaths. One hundred and I'd try again...maybe use a different mental image. Find what worked.

I was almost at seventy when someone said, "Maggie!" and the walls shattered around me.

CHAPTER TWENTY

PAIN EXPLODED THROUGH MY HEAD, flickering bursts of light pinwheeling in front of my eyes.

Was I back where I'd started? In the storm of color and light that had fogged my mind? Had Jack come back?

"Maggie, can you hear me?" The voice was female. Not Jack.

"Open your eyes, Maggie." I knew that voice. Pinky.

God, had Jack caught her, too? She had a chip.

"Maggie. Shit. Open your eyes or I'm calling an ambulance."

An ambulance? That didn't sound as though she was trapped in VR with me. So where was I?

I cracked my eyes open, head still pounding. I was lying on gray concrete, cold and rough against my cheek. Not the hotel. At least not the floor of the hotel where I'd started.

"Pinky?" I managed through bone-dry lips. The sound of my voice hurt my head, and the room spun for a moment. I rolled to my knees and promptly threw up. Fortunately there wasn't that much in my stomach. I crawled backward until I bumped into something that felt like a wall and sat, propped against it.

After a few minutes, the room stopped spinning, and I risked opening my eyes again.

Pinky was kneeling beside me, looking worried. "Hey," she said. "That didn't look fun."

"No," I agreed.

She offered me a Kleenex, and I wiped my mouth. I couldn't do much about the lingering taste of vomit though. "I don't suppose you have a bottle of water as well?"

"No. There'll be something upstairs," Pinky said. "Do you think you can stand? We should get going."

The thought of moving made my stomach lurch again. Whatever she'd done to get me out of that VR nightmare, it hadn't done my body any favors. I tried to breathe through my nose, fighting the nausea, eyes closed. "I might need a minute. How did you find me?"

"Told you I was good at finding lost things."

Tanai magic, in other words. I took another

breath, my stomach feeling somewhat steadier, and opened my eyes. The room stayed relatively still.

Pinky held up a thick black leather band. It looked like a watch gone very wrong. The buckle seemed more like a fancy electronic lock than a buckle, and a weird array of wires threaded around a series of small metal discs that took up a few inches of its length. "What do you want me to do with this?"

"What is it?" I asked.

"It was around your wrist," Pinky said. She flipped it over to show me the inner side of the band. A smaller version of the kind of chip dock the game chairs used was attached, some of the wires feeding into it.

Jack's cage. I wanted to grab it and smash it so there'd be no chance of it ending up back on my wrist, but that would be dumb. It was evidence. More than that, I needed to be able to give it to Damon and get Riley to figure out how it worked. And then how to stop it from ever being used again.

"You didn't respond when I first tried to wake you up, and this was on your chip. I figured taking it off might be the fastest way to bring you back. So I did." Her eyes were wide, the green bright. "Sorry. It looked like it hurt."

"No. You did the right thing." Even though it had been risky. Gamers were told not to try and pull people out of a game other than by using a kill switch or properly shutting down a game for a reason. Too fast a disconnect could scramble someone's brain. And it was painful, as it turned out. But I wasn't going to quibble. I was free.

I swayed when I pushed to my feet, and I planted my hand on the wall, breathing fast. How long had I been locked up in that thing?

I felt weak, as though it might have been days. But Pinky was wearing the same clothes as earlier so it was probably not that long. "Keep that. We'll need it."

She nodded and stuffed the thing into the pocket of her dress. I wasn't sure whether I felt better with it out of sight or not.

"Where are we?" The room was small and badly lit. There were empty metal shelves and a few disassembled cardboard boxes against the walls.

"Storage area in the hotel basement. What do you remember?"

"I was going to find...Damon. You went after...Yoshi! Is he all right?"

"The real Yoshi, yes. They found him at his apartment. He was knocked out and tied up, but they took him to St. Isidore's."

I lurched away from the wall. "I should—"

Pinky caught my arm. "Cool your jets. He's fine. And he's not the current problem."

Was I the current problem? My head certainly felt as though it was. I rubbed my temples, the memories of what had happened before Jack grabbed me slowly coming back.

"And fake Yoshi? Do we know who he was?"

"Actually yes, a player. For the Rainbow Rexes.

"Jack's team," I muttered.

"Jack who?" Pinky said.

"Jack Miller. Yoshi and I were talking to him yesterday when you joined us. Didn't you—" No. I remembered. She hadn't met him. Jack left when he'd seen her coming. Did that mean he knew who —or what—she was? And that she might be able to sense what he was? Not that I had any idea what he was. Demon ally? Witch? "Jack Miller. He's a tech investor. Been around for years. He apparently sponsored one of the teams. He put that thing on me."

Pinky's hand went to her pocket.

"Leave it," I said. "Safer not to touch it, I think."

She grimaced. "What was it?"

"A VR with no way out." I shuddered at the memory. "Not good."

A grimace of disgust crossed her face. "Fuck. That's jagged-up."

"You're telling me."

She nodded. "Also pretty good evidence he's more than just a tech investor."

"Yep. I was sitting with him yesterday when you and Yoshi joined me. He left when he saw you coming with the snacks. That's another black mark. I think we'd better assume he knows what you are." I gritted my teeth. Yoshi. I'd let Yoshi sit next to Jack. I changed seats so he could sit closer. Was that how Jack had done whatever he'd done? I shuddered. "God. I should have seen it."

"Why would he avoid me?"

"Because it seems he's not on team good guy," I said. "Maybe he thought you'd sense it. Did fake Yoshi tell you anything?" I swallowed as my stomach suddenly turned again.

Pinky shook her head. "So far, nothing. Cassandra was talking to him when I left."

Well, if anyone could persuade someone to talk it would be Cassandra. Or maybe Radha. And then there was always Mitch. I doubted he'd have any issue doing whatever was needed to make someone talk when Damon's safety was at stake.

"Jack wants something from Damon," I said. "I don't know if he heard the rumors we planted or whether he came here to try something from the outset"—though the fact that he'd had the chip cage suggested he'd been planning something —"but I have the feeling he's the one your grandma is worried about. That thing in your pocket qualifies as dark all on its own. But he said a few things to me that make me think he's working with a demon."

"Like what?"

I held up a hand. "I don't have time to explain. What time is it?"

"Just after four. We've been looking for you for a while. Mitch was about ready to tear the building down. Whatever this is"—she pointed at her pocket —"it made the tracking in your chip unusable."

Three hours. I'd been locked away for three fucking hours. "And Damon?"

"Damon apparently called for a helicopter and left around the time we were dealing with Not-Yoshi."

"He left? To go where?"

"That part we're not so clear on. The chopper lost contact with the Riley Arts systems a few minutes later. But before you freak out, there have been no accidents reported. This city has a lot of private helipads though. Mitch thinks maybe they landed somewhere and swapped choppers. Or moved to another vehicle altogether."

Damon was missing. My hand curled into a fist.

No.

No.

No.

Not again.

I pressed the fist to my mouth, trying to stop myself from screaming.

Think. Do not freak out.

"I take it his chip isn't tracking either?"

She shook her head.

"Let me look at that thing." I reached out a hand, and Pinky dropped the wristband into it. I studied it a moment. It was clearly some sort of miniature fucked-up version of a gamedeck. But that meant I'd need some sort of interface to be able to tell more. And there was no way I was putting it on again. I tucked it into my jacket pocket and forced my brain into "work now, panic later" mode. "So we don't know where Damon is? Are we sure it was him on the chopper?"

"No," Pinky said. "And before you ask, I've been looking for him while I was looking for you. I can't get a sense of him anywhere in the hotel. My powers aren't much good beyond that range. But my best guess is he really did leave on the chopper."

"I have to find him," I said. "He's the one Jack wants. Shit. Where would he take him? Back to Riley? No. That's too well guarded. So is his house." I heard my voice get higher, aware I was babbling. "I have to go find him. He—" My knees wobbled.

Pinky caught me, shook me slightly.

"Maggie," she said sternly. "Get your shit together. It will be okay. People are already looking for him. Come upstairs. Talk to Mitch and Cassandra. They can help. You can't just run off and look for him alone. Unless you two have some sort of magic Find My Boyfriend mojo going on I don't know about."

I shook my head, trying to breathe. Damon out there somewhere alone. With someone who was clearly up to no good and, if I wasn't misunderstanding what he'd told me back in that hideous white room, working for a demon.

Which meant Pinky was right. Jack Miller was no one I should be taking on by myself.

Maia arrived to escort us back upstairs about two minutes after Pinky called to say she'd found me. She glued herself to my side and tried to apologize several times during the elevator ride.

"You have nothing to apologize for," I said. "I went out without you. And if anyone gives you grief about that, then send them to me." Mitch was very good at his job, but if someone had just snatched Damon again, he wouldn't be thinking clearly. I wouldn't let him blame Maia for my choices.

Lizzie practically tackled me to the ground in a hug when we walked into the penthouse, half knocking the breath out of me. At least it stopped Mitch from immediately pouncing on me. By the time Lizzie let go, he was already interrogating Pinky.

Across the living room, two Riley guards stood outside the second bedroom. The door was open, giving me a clear view of Cassandra sitting in a chair, Trick beside her. Interrogating Not-Yoshi, presumably.

Zee was sitting on one of the pale blue sofas, furiously typing something into his datapad. He gave me a quick relieved smile, then turned his attention back to the screen. Presumably helping with the search for Damon. Maia left me with Lizzie and went to sit on the sofa opposite him, pulling out her own device.

I snagged a bottle of water off the nearest side table and swigged it, trying to get the taste of bile out of my mouth. It helped a little. I really wanted a shower and to brush my teeth, but no time to waste.

"Has he talked yet?" I asked, tilting my head in Cassandra's direction.

Lizzie shook her head. "No. He's either very strong-willed or someone's put a spell on him to make him not spill the beans. Cassandra wants to call Ian and the others and try the demon stone."

My spine crawled a moment. "I'm not sure that's such a good idea if we want him to be able to actually talk to us." Demon stone could be fatal to anyone too far gone in thrall to a demon.

Her eyes narrowed. "You think he's been near a demon?"

"It's possible." I didn't know who Jack was dealing with. A demon. A lesserkind. A human working for one of those. It didn't make much difference in the end. The lesserkind worked for demons, doing what they wanted here in our world. They weren't as powerful as their masters, but they could travel between the demon world and ours far more easily. Though it still took considerable effort, judging by the fact that we weren't completely overrun. "I think Grandma is right, and there might be a demon involved in all this. Or a lesserkind maybe."

Mitch's head snapped toward us. "What are you talking about?"

"Jack said he was working with someone. And the way he said it made me think he didn't mean just another bad guy."

"Jack Miller?" Mitch asked, his pale brows shooting upward. Apparently Pinky hadn't gotten to that part of the tale.

"He was the one who intercepted me," I said. "Well, I guess it could have been someone else wearing his face, like Not-Yoshi in there," I said.

Lizzie snorted. "Not-Yoshi has a name."

"Right now, I don't care," I said. "Unless his name is going to help us solve this."

"Not unless he starts talking," Lizzie said. "Who's Jack Miller?"

"I met him at the gala. He's a tech investor. Well, that's what he said."

Mitch ushered Pinky over to join us. "He *is* a tech investor, but he's got an interesting rep. There have been rumors a few times that he might have fingers in some unsavory pies, but nothing has ever been proven. Or even reached the formal accusation stage."

"That would have been good to know before the gala," I said. "You know, the kind of thing that could have been in one of those security briefings you kept giving me."

Mitch's lips tightened. "Like I said, nothing's ever been proven, and he has plenty of legit businesses. And industry cred. Plus he was sponsoring a team."

"Yeah, well, I knew he was too charming to be good news."

"Trust your instincts," Lizzie muttered.

"Jack was the one who took you?" Mitch said. "And did what?"

"Is Yoshi okay?" I asked, ignoring the question and focusing on Lizzie. "Pinky said he was knocked out." I wanted to hear it from Lizzie. Pinky had found me, and I thought she was on my side, but I wanted the truth from someone who definitely was.

Lizzie nodded. "Yes. But he's fine. They took him to St. Izzie's. Meredith checked him out. They just hit him with some sort of sleeping spell. His sister is with him. They're well-guarded. Meredith will stay with them unless we need her." She peered at me. "You look pretty crappy. Do you need a healer? It wouldn't take long for Radha to get here."

I shook my head. "No. It wasn't magic. It was this." I pulled the wristband from hell out of my pocket.

"What is that?" Mitch asked, frowning.

"Some sort of fucked-up miniature gamedeck, I think. It dumped me into a tiny VR with no kill switch and no menu. Well, there was a menu, but it only let me talk to Jack—I think it was Jack. No way out. Pinky said it blocked my chip tracking as well?"

Mitch nodded grimly.

I shivered, remembering the white room and the feeling of being trapped. "Whoever made this is seriously twisted. They've probably used one on Damon, too."

Mitch swore. "We know he walked out of here to the chopper of his own volition. He and one other passenger. The pilot recorded that much. Not Jack Miller though. We haven't identified the guy. The chopper should have had a feed streaming to us with Damon onboard, but for some reason, it didn't start. But the system pinged Damon's palm scan to authorize the flight, so it had to be him."

Or someone controlling him. "I don't think you need to waste too much time trying to identify the guy. If you can't put eyes on Jack, then I'm guessing it was probably him. If they made Not-Yoshi look like Yoshi well enough to fool me, then they could've changed Jack's appearance, too.

And maybe this thing has different modes. One that would let Damon move. Jack must have used something to fool him though. Or coerce him. He told me if I behaved myself, Damon would be fine. I think I was leverage." My breath hitched.

Lizzie nudged me gently, putting an arm around my shoulder.

"It's okay, Maggie," she said softly. "We'll find him."

"We have to," I said, then turned to Mitch. "Maybe you can get someone to look at this thing. Give it to Simeon or something. See what it does. Shit, what if Jack knows I got out of it?" I hadn't thought of that before now. Jack might know. Damon would pay for my escape if he did.

"We have no way of knowing, so don't panic. We haven't had any contact, so nothing's changed." Mitch lifted the chip cage out of my hands. "I'll get someone to come and take it to Simeon. His team will figure it out."

"Isn't it evidence?" Pinky asked.

"This is a Cestis matter, not a police one," Lizzie said. "Not until we ask them." She nodded at Mitch. "Give it to Simeon."

"Okay." I clenched my hands. "We really need to find Damon."

"Trust me, we're trying," Mitch said. "We've been trying for several hours. It would help if we could find the damn chopper."

"If Jack's taken our bait, then they'll be looking for somewhere with easy access to Riley systems," I started to say, but Maia suddenly looked up from her datapad.

"Boss, there's a report on the chopper. It's been spotted at a private airfield near San Toribio. That's some small-ass town near Fairfield."

"And?" Mitch said.

"Chopper abandoned. No sign of the pilot or anybody else. The airfield is owned by a hydroglider club. It's basically a field with a short runway, some sort of prefab shed they use as a clubhouse and a hangar. Not staffed."

"Fairfield is halfway to Sacramento," I said. "You think they're going for a suborbital?" San Francisco had had a subport before the Big One. Understandably, no one had been that keen on spending the billions needed to rebuild it on a fault line afterward. So now the suborbital traffic in California went through Sacramento or San Diego.

"We've already got alerts out with the airports, train stations, and the subports," Mitch said.

"Jack's rich. He might not need commercial." Private charter suborbital was prohibitively expensive. But it existed. Damon didn't own a suborbital, but he definitely used them when he needed to be halfway across the planet in a hurry. And not always commercial. It seemed more likely than a plane—though there were plenty of private charters around

—or a train. The new solar bullet trains were fast but didn't offer many opportunities to discreetly wrangle someone who'd practically be deadweight like Damon would be if he was wearing a chip cage.

Mitch swore again. "We can't let him get taken out of state."

I didn't see how that would help Jack. Not while he still had Damon. Time was ticking now that he'd made his move. Maybe the chopper was a fake-out. If Jack wanted something from Riley Arts but didn't want to risk going to Riley, then he needed access. "Have you checked out my house?"

Mitch nodded. "Yes. We sent a team past. No sign of any activity."

"No offense, but we're potentially dealing with someone who's very good with tech and may have some magical avenues open to them. Your team might not notice." Most of the Riley security guys with magic had been pulled into the tournament monitoring anyway. All of them were very good at their jobs, but Jack had fooled me. And clearly Not-Yoshi had fooled everyone at Riley—and their security—at the hackathon. That was some high-level illusion mojo right there. "We should look again."

Damon had a link to the security system at my house. It was cutting edge, and we'd left the place warded six ways to Sunday. But as far as both the house comp and the wards were concerned, Damon was the only person besides Lizzie and me with automatic access. His schedule had been so ridiculous the last few months that it had made sense to give him unlimited access rather than me having to wait up for him on nights he decided to drive out to Berkeley after finishing work at some ungodly hour. His presence wouldn't trigger any alerts on the security system or the wards. And, once inside, he could—or Jack could force him to—disarm the alerts anyway. And he could take someone in with him.

"We don't have time to waste on a fool's errand," Mitch said.

"You don't need me to check out the subport," I argued. "I'm no use to you there. You have enough pull with the authorities. Let me go. I'll take Lizzie, Pinky, Zee, and Maia. If the five of us can't deal with anything that comes up, then we have bigger problems than splitting our focus." I looked to Lizzie. "Can Ian or Radha take over for Cassandra and Trick? Then they can go with Mitch." That would convince him maybe, if he knew he'd be taking Cassandra with him. Arguably she was more use to him in the kind of situation he'd be dealing with trying to cut through bureaucracy at the subport. The Cestis had virtually an access-all-areas, no-questions-asked level of authority when it came to magical crimes.

Lizzie nodded. "They're already in the hotel, talking with the rest of the Rexes."

Jack's team. Right. How many of them were involved? Not many, I hoped, for the sake of the tournament. Though maybe this could be spun as a simple attempt at corporate espionage after we had Damon back. Maybe Not-Yoshi had been going to try a more direct path to whatever they were after at the hackathon tomorrow. But until he talked, we wouldn't know. And right now, I didn't care whether Jack got his hands on whatever fake version of the algorithm Damon had left in the decoy. I cared about getting Damon away from him.

"Right. Then let's do that. I'll go to my place with Lizzie and the others. You chase the chopper."

Mitch looked torn.

"This is the best of both worlds," I said. "Divide and conquer or something." I hoped we'd conquer. But frankly the thought of what else Jack might have up his sleeve scared me.

"You're not my boss," Mitch pointed out.

"And you're not mine. But we both have Damon's best interests at heart. So why don't we both be good at what we do?"

CHAPTER TWENTY-ONE

I'D NEVER FLOWN in a helicopter before. It definitely made the commute from downtown to Berkeley a hell of a lot faster. Mitch had organized the choppers with one phone call after he'd agreed to us splitting up. It had taken about twenty minutes from him ending the call before one had landed on the helipad next to the penthouse.

He hustled the five of us out to the chopper and yelled last-minute instructions in my ear as the others climbed on board. They boiled down to stay in touch, call for backup if we needed it, and don't get anyone killed.

He'd spent most of the time we'd waited for the chopper repeating variations of the same to us in between barking orders at various other Riley team members who kept appearing, so I mostly ignored him. None of us wanted to do anything crazy, but if there was a demon helping Jack, then what we were flying into was stupid dangerous, and there was nothing any of us could do about it.

Even as our pilot had swooped away from the building, another chopper had been hovering on the far side of the hotel, waiting its turn to land and then take the others to Sacramento.

Their journey would take over thirty minutes. More if they couldn't get permission to land at the subport. Ours took less than ten. We'd probably be inside my house before they even landed. There was a helipad at the marina, and the rideshare we called was waiting for us. We hadn't had much time to strategize. We were still ironing out the finer details in hushed tones in the back of the minivan as we drove.

"Jack can't see you, Maggie, or he'll know the game is up," Lizzie said. "It has to be me who goes in the front."

"The game will most likely be up if he sees you, too," I pointed out. "I'm sure he knows who you are."

"Maybe. But I could just be coming home to sleep. Or to look for you. He might not think I'd bring anyone else with me. But if he spots you, he'll know we're onto him."

"She has a point," Zee said. "It might not help much, but any time we can buy is good."

Lizzie shot him an almost approving look. "See? It's the best option. And we don't have time to come up with anything complicated. You take the others and go around and into the yard from the lane. Between Zee and Pinky, you should be able to hide yourselves. You can get them through the wards."

She was right. But I still hated the idea of her going in alone. "You're only one person. Maia—"

"Don't even suggest it," Maia said. "If I leave your side, Mitch will have my ass, and I'll be looking for a new job." She flashed a grin at me. "And I like this job."

"You're insane," I muttered. But maybe you had to be to volunteer to put yourself between a bullet and your protectee. And I'd had chapter and verse on how to work with a security detail many times. I was to do what I was told and let them do their jobs. "You could take Zee," I said. "Jack might not know who he is."

Lizzie rolled her eyes in exasperation. "Look, I know I'm short and young and all, but do I have to remind you that I'm the biggest, baddest kickass witch of all of us? Cestis and all that. The rest of you kind of have to do what I say."

"Technically you're not in charge of me," Pinky said.

Lizzie gave her a look that she had clearly learned from Cassandra. "You want to be the one explaining to Grandma what went wrong if this goes south?"

"No."

"Good. Then that's settled. I'm going in the front. The rest of you will sneak in back. Which actually means we should let you out now. Message me once you're in position."

Creeping around in what was still fairly bright daylight was much easier when you had magical camouflage. Despite the fact that Mrs. Jorenson, who lived in the house directly behind mine, and her little yappy dog were both sitting on her front porch, neither of them so much as looked in our direction as we walked up her drive and into her backyard.

The ease with which we got past her kind of made my skin crawl. File that under things I'd rather not know people could do.

Aka reasons why Maggie still didn't sleep well. My next few meetings with my therapist were going to be interesting. Assuming I lived to make those appointments.

Mrs. Jorenson's yard gate was unlocked—something I'd have to remind her about—which meant we made it into the tiny alley that separated her backyard from mine even faster than I'd expected. I stopped and waited until Zee, bringing up the rear, closed the gate behind us, studying what I could see of the house. There were no obvious signs of anyone being home.

The wards hummed across the fence and around the house, shimmering to my sight. At least they were working.

Lizzie might be able to read more from the wards than me. I'd made a lot of progress these last few months, but I wasn't an expert. But I was going inside regardless of whether they told her anyone had entered.

"Stay close to me. I have to go first, or the wards will activate." I could take people through them, but they had to be reasonably close.

I moved toward the gate. The lock on it would open to my palm scan, but it would also ping the house comp that I had used it. Given time, I probably could have jimmied it, but we didn't have time. Instead, Zee boosted me over the fence after reassuring me that the illusion would hold, and then I helped Pinky—the shortest of us—down after he boosted her. He and Maia managed to climb the fence without much hassle, which made me wonder if I should've built a higher fence to begin with.

Once we were in the yard, I pinged Lizzie on my datapad and then activated the app to track her approach to the house. We'd decided that trying to hack into the house's camera feeds was too risky. If Jack was there, it was entirely possible he'd be watching them or slipped something into the system to let him know if one of us tried to access it.

My pulse hammered in my ears as the tiny red dot that represented Lizzie's datapad moved up the street, stopped for about a minute—while the driver dropped her off, presumably—then headed to the house. At that point, I didn't really need the app, as I could hear her whistling tunelessly as she walked up the drive—part of her "let's make this look normal" act.

The whistle stopped, as agreed, when she reached the front porch. I pointed at the house, and the four of us ran across the yard. The wards shimmered green as Lizzie passed through them. I waited as close to the door as I could, listening and trying to make out anything through the frosted glass of the laundry window. But as far as I could tell, the laundry door was closed, and if Jack and Damon were here, they weren't hanging out in the laundry. I bit my lip, waiting. I heard the front door click shut, then a vague thump.

Shit. I slapped my palm against the scanner next to the door.

Which zapped a shock through me that sent me back a few paces, shaking my hand and swearing.

"Allow me," Zee said. He picked up one of the

chairs that sat on the back porch even as I typed in a frantic override signal to the alarm system on my datapad. Maybe I couldn't turn it off, but the last thing we needed was the Berkeley PD arriving to investigate.

I succeeded just as Zee smashed the chair through the window. Which meant whatever Jack had managed to do to the alarm system, he hadn't completely cut off my access.

Zee wrestled the door open, and we ran into the house.

"Find Damon," I snapped at Maia.

She shook her head. "I'll find him when you do. I stay with you."

I growled, but Zee grabbed my arm and pointed upstairs. I nodded. He'd studied the layout of the house on the way over, and I figured he could hold his own. Mitch had provided him with a gun. Maia was armed, too. Lizzie and Pinky had refused a weapon. I had, too. I'd been practicing, but I didn't trust my aim well enough to shoot indoors with so many people in the house.

Zee peeled off, and I led Maia and Pinky toward the front hall at a jog.

Lizzie was struggling with Jack near the doorway, both of them facing away from us. She was tough, but his size gave him an advantage. It looked like he'd managed to wrap one arm around her throat, the other clamped around her wrist,

holding her close to him. Close enough that anything she—or the rest of us—could do magically to
try and shake him off would hit her, too.

"No point trying for her wrist, Jack," I said. "She
doesn't have a chip."

He whirled, yanking Lizzie around with him. His
mouth dropped open when he saw the three of us.
"How the hell—" He bit off the words, recovering
quickly, and pulled Lizzie closer, his arm tightening
around her throat. He'd let go of her wrist, and I
watched her hand for a moment, seeing if she was
going to try anything.

"Zee," I yelled when she didn't. "Down here."

No answer. Not good.

"If you sent someone upstairs, they're going to
be busy for a while," Jack said, recovering his com-
posure. A gun appeared in his free hand.

Maia half stepped forward, but I held up a hand.
She stopped but drew her own gun, raising it to
point at Jack, her hand rock steady.

"Where's Damon?" I snarled in reply.

"He's fine," Jack said. "You'll all be fine, too.
Just let me out of this place."

Let him out?

I didn't understand, but Lizzie's eyes widened,
and she smiled viciously.

Clearly she'd done something to the wards that
was a little more than usual after all. Jack had

gotten in, but he hadn't been able to get out. At least not without Damon. So where the hell *was* he?

Fear crawled through my gut.

Behind me, I heard Pinky step backward.

"Oh no," Jack said. Lizzie flinched as the gun pressed into her temple. "Don't move. You'll find Damon when I'm good and ready. And, just as a warning, I wouldn't suggest trying to take the deck from his chip without me. When I couldn't get out, I added some refinements to the system running his. He's just as stubborn as you, it seems. I thought he was cooperating at first. He came with me when I told him I could kill you. He let me into his system. But I figured out it was a fake before he expected. Silly boy. I was coding before he was born. And he wasn't expecting the deck. I'll let you know how to get him out safely once I'm away from here."

"Yeah, like I'm going to trust you."

"You don't have much choice. If you don't want your little friend here's brains all over your nice white walls, I suggest you let me out."

I laughed. "Jack, I knew you were dumb when you told me you were playing with the dark side. But I didn't think you were 'kill a member of the Cestis and think you'll ever be safe a moment again in your life' dumb." I was proud that my voice didn't shake. He might be exactly that dumb. Or could be made to act that dumb by a demon if he really had teamed up with one. Either way, I was terrified for Lizzie. For all of us.

"Cestis?" he said. "This girl?"

"I thought you would have researched that better before coming to San Francisco. Particularly if you've come to do a demon's bidding. That historically hasn't gone well."

"Cestis or not, she'll still die from a bullet to the brain," Jack snarled. "So will that one." He jerked his head at Pinky as though she was the next biggest threat. He had to know she was tanai, then. How? And what was he worried she could do?

"You might kill one of them, but you'll die next," I promised. "Maia won't miss."

At least I hoped not. But Jack clearly wasn't a normal human, and who knew what he was capable of? Particularly when he was backed into a corner.

"Tell me where Damon is," I said. "Once I know he's alive, we can come to an agreement."

"You don't have the authority to make a bargain with me," he said.

"How do you know? I'm Damon's girlfriend. He knows I'll do what I need to do to keep him safe. And Lizzie is one of the Cestis. She has the authority to do a lot of the things." I considered adding Pinky into the mix but decided not to. Jack was clearly wary of her, and I didn't want to make him do anything stupid.

"Tell me where he is, Jack," I repeated.

"Maggie, calm down," Damon's voice said from behind me.

I whirled. He stood there, looking slightly rumpled. Whole. Alive.

Thank God.

I stepped toward him, then froze, remembering Not-Yoshi. How did I know it was really Damon? I glanced at Jack, who was watching me, a peculiar sort of smile flashing briefly over his face.

My spine crawled. Was it Damon or just another illusion? I started to let my sight slide to magic to see if I could sense anything different. I knew what Damon's aura looked like, knew the blue blaze of it like I knew my own face.

"What the hell?" Another Damon stepped from the kitchen door.

Jack promptly shot him.

I screamed, lunging forward.

Jack laughed, and I stopped short, forcing myself to not reach for the man lying bleeding on the floor. Because he might not be Damon. Just like the first one. Who was staring down at the version of himself on the floor, looking horrified.

"Oh, the dilemma," Jack said. "Who to save. What to believe." He shoved Lizzie forward and lifted his hands, uttering a short sharp word.

Three imps appeared in front of him, and the nearest one leaped for me.

Jack spoke again, and more imps appeared. Along with another Damon or three.

Shit.

Too many illusions. Or not. The imps could well be real. And deadlier than an illusion. I reached for my magic. I couldn't take a risk on taking out any of the Damons, but I knew how to deal with imps.

A bolt of fire and the imp charging toward me stopped with a squeal, bursting into flames. Beside me, I saw Maia try the same on one approaching her. Lizzie whirled and took out a third, but another popped up behind her even as she lowered her hands.

The house became a hellhole of flickering imps, flames, and smoke.

I tried to keep sight of the others as I fought, but it was hard. At one point there were two Jacks surrounding Lizzie. I charged toward one of them but slid right through him. Lizzie flicked a hand at the other, and he dissolved in a shimmer of sparks. She grinned at me, then yelped as an imp grabbed her. It got a ball of flame to the face for its trouble, but Lizzie winced and hissed in pain as its body fell away from her.

Crap.

Maia flamed imps as quickly as they rose, but I'd lost sight of Pinky. Or she'd hidden herself away. Damn it. She of all of us should be able to see through the illusions. I shifted my sight again, sweeping my gaze across the room. All the Damons glowed bright blue. Jack, if he was the one doing these illusions, was damned good at it.

I looked for him instead. But he'd vanished, too.

I headed back to the kitchen. A Damon appeared in my path, reaching for me. "Maggie, you're here."

I steeled myself against the pleased sound of his voice and shoved my hands toward him. They went straight through his body, making my hands tingle.

Okay, well, that was one way to find out what was real.

I stepped through the illusion and scanned the room. The door to the laundry was open. Shit. Had Jack gone out that way?

But if he had, where were all the freaking imps coming from?

I took a step toward the door, but another imp flashed into sight between me and the laundry. This one was bigger, as large as the one I'd fought in Damon's garden.

I backed up as a second imp joined it.

Fuck.

I backed out of the kitchen, sending flames toward the imps. I hit the first, but the second dodged around it, coming for me.

I flung another wild bolt, then turned and ran back into the hallway, hoping to find Lizzie. I passed through another Damon illusion, skidding on the floorboards as my instincts screamed at me to go around and sent different signals to my feet than my brain. I stumbled and flung out a hand, finding the banister of the hall stairs with a smack that sent fire shooting up my arm, only just catching myself before I fell. I didn't want to go down in the chaos. I might never get back up.

I dragged myself upright, panting. My hand hurt like hell, and I shook it. The glyph blazed brightly, pulsing, and I looked up.

Zee was at the top of the stairs. He glowed like something out of a game, the glyph on his hand blazing. Mine throbbed with another surge of power and pain.

"Maggie," he shouted and reached out his hand. I threw myself into motion, clambering up the stairs, dodging illusions and sparks. We met half-way. Our hands clashed together, Zee spoke a single word that seemed to echo in my skull like thunder, and light washed through the house like the blazing beam of a lighthouse.

Every illusion blinked out.

Which took care of the Damons but still left us with quite a few imps. Only now they were pan-icked and trying to run from the light shining from our hands.

It didn't take long for the four of us to clean up. But by the time we'd finished, the rooms were thick with smoke, making my eyes stream. Throw enough fire around and even the most well-warded house would catch eventually.

Lizzie leaned on the kitchen doorway, holding her side, the fabric of her pink T-shirt stained red under her head. "We need to get out of here," she said, wincing.

Not without Damon.

"Was Damon upstairs?" I asked Zee.

"Yeah. Pinky was guarding him."

That was where she'd gone? To protect Damon?

I took back every doubting thought I'd had.

"Get Lizzie outside," I said. "Maia, you go with them. She needs some first aid." If the house was on fire, the house comp should have alerted the fire brigade. If it hadn't, then one of the neighbors had to notice sooner or later.

I grabbed a dish towel off the sink and bolted for the stairs, holding it over my mouth. I didn't know where the fire was yet, but it didn't matter. The only thing that mattered was Damon.

"Pinky," I yelled, my voice muffled by the cloth. No response. Fuck.

I lowered the cloth, getting a lungful of smoke for my trouble. "Pinky!" I yelled again, trying not to cough. "Where the hell are you?"

"In here."

Her voice sounded like it was coming from my room.

I ran down the hall. My bedroom door was open. Damon lay on the bed, looking, in the smoky air, like a bad version of a fairy tale, his skin too pale against my deep green quilt. A leather band was cinched around his right wrist, hiding his chip.

Jack's fucking cage. Shit. He'd said he'd booby-trapped it or something.

"I didn't know if I should take it off," Pinky said. "Not after what Jack said."

"No," I said. "But we have to get him out of here." Fuck, I should have brought Zee with me. Between us we could carry Damon out. But Zee was with Lizzie. And I had to make a choice if we were going to survive.

As if to emphasize my point, the sound of glass shattering sounded below us.

"Fire's getting worse," Pinky said, coughing.

"Yes. Got any good tanai magic to deal with that?"

"No," she said. "Got any witch magic for it?"

"No." I'd called lightning but wasn't going to try for rain. Rain would take too long anyway. "Pinky, you should climb out the window. Jump down onto the front porch. Zee and the others can get you from there."

"I'm not going to leave you here," Pinky said.

"You can't get him out on your own. Besides, Grandma still wants to talk to you."

"What?"

"I never got to tell you earlier. She asked for another meeting with you."

That was all I fucking needed. My house was on fire, I might be about to die, and if I survived, I had to go talk to one of the Fae again.

Fuck it. I reached down, undid the buckle, and yanked the cage from Damon's wrist. His body arched up from the bed, and for a horrifying moment, I thought I'd killed him. But then the convulsion stopped, and his eyes opened, blurry and confused but alive.

"Damon!" I reached for his hand. "Look, I know you probably feel like shit right now, but you have to get up. Pinky, help me."

Between us, we got him off the bed. The three of us staggered across to the window. I threw it open. "Pinky, you first."

Damon looked dazed as he watched her climb out. I wrapped my hand around his and sent a surge of energy into him, hoping to snap him out of the cage hangover. He straightened, eyes focusing on me. "What the hell was that?"

I shoved him at the window. "I'll explain later. Right now, we're getting the hell out of here."

He scrambled through the window, and I went after him. Zee had found a ladder, and Pinky was just about down. I'd never climbed down a ladder so fast in my life.

There were people on my lawn, hoses in hand. Not firefighters. Neighbors. I turned back to look at the house after Lizzie stopped dragging me down the drive. Flames rose from the rear of the building, clouds of smoke billowing around them.

My knees buckled. *My house.*

Damon grabbed for me, keeping me upright. "Maggie, I'm so sorry."

I clung to him, trusting him as the only real thing in the world. I'd seen another house burned to the ground just a few months earlier, hiding the evidence of imps and demons from the world. Then I'd been happy though numb.

But this. It *hurt*. Watching my house—my *grandparents'* house—all my hard work lost all over again. The sounds of sirens wailing up the hill behind me didn't ease the pain.

Too late.

We'd made it out.

We were alive. That was something.

But Jack had gotten away.

EPILOGUE

IT WAS sunny when Cassandra parked her car by the Rose Garden. It was the first time in more than a week that I'd been back to Berkeley. The last time had been to let the insurance assessor go over my house a week after the fire. The firefighters had stopped the blaze before it had completely destroyed the building, but what remained was smoke sodden and water damaged, very little salvageable.

Lizzie had retrieved some of her belongings. I hadn't yet gone after any of mine. Instead, I was living with Damon, who had pointed at my datapad and said, "Order whatever you need."

So I had a wardrobe at least, of a kind. Everything still that bit too new, not comfortable. For our visit to the Fae, I'd chosen a green sweater and a new pair of dark jeans, the amethyst pendant Cassandra had given me hanging at my throat. The boots I'd been wearing on the day Jack had taken Damon were at least familiar. Comfortable.

A reminder that eventually I might feel that way again.

Damon was doing his best. His team had torn down the devices Jack had used on us, intrigued by the size of the system. Simeon had had a gleam in his eye that suggested ideas when he'd reported to us that the core of it was just a normal VR stripped of safeguards. Nothing else they could detect. I'd searched the code myself, as had Yoshi, and neither of us had found anything else.

Jack, it seemed, hadn't left any hidden traps in the code after all. Nothing more for us to worry about. Other than the fact that he'd gotten away.

Damon had people hunting through the dark web, trying to find who might have made the cages. But the dark web was vast and deep, and it might take a long time.

Which left us with little else to do but try and get on with life. The tournament had been a roaring success, though I didn't remember much of it, functioning on autopilot after I'd slept for nearly a day after the fire.

In the end, the Diablos had come second, losing only in the final game, and the livestream of the winner's first run through the full version of *Serenity Falls* had hit something like a billion views within days of it being released. The game was selling fast, the industry media full of stories of Damon reclaiming his rightful place as king of the gaming world. The mainstream media focused more on the man and, inevitably, on me. And the tragic electrical fault that had destroyed my home.

Even if my house hadn't burned down, I wouldn't have been able to live there. Not with paparazzi staking out Damon's house and trying to do the same with the Riley campus. I was fairly certain Cassandra had used an illusion spell on her car to spirit me out through the service gates. But the Rose Garden was once again empty, as it had been the first time we'd gone to meet Grandma.

"Are we sure this is a good idea?" I asked, making no move to open the passenger door.

"You can't change your mind now," Pinky said from the back seat. "I'm not going in there and telling Grandma you've refused her invitation."

I sighed. Pinky had quite possibly saved Damon's life back at the house. She wouldn't tell me exactly what she'd done to fight off the imps, but I owed her. I'd put this visit off for several weeks, pleading the need to just get through the tournament and deal with my house, but she'd finally put her foot down, and I'd agreed. I'd talk to her damned grandmother even though I had no idea what she might want. At least Cassandra had insisted on coming with us.

"Let's get this over with."

Grandma waited for us in a room that looked like something lifted from a royal palace. Tall ceilings, gilt furniture, upholstered in pale green and pink silk embroidered with tiny flowers. The same shades that were echoed in the wallpaper and paint on the walls. She sat on a sofa in front of a table set for tea, her long silver-green dress looking more like human clothes than what she'd worn in the glade. Trying to seem more human, maybe? Though the color of her hair and the cool silver eyes made that difficult. As did the unearthly perfection of her face.

The sky outside the windows was blue and cloudless above a long stretch of lawn and garden beds full of strange flowers. No roses.

Though somehow the air smelled like them.

Which was unsettling but on the whole, this room, was better than a throne in a forest.

"Lady Cestis, Maggie, welcome." She inclined her head and gestured at the two chairs on the other side of the table. "Rosaline, come sit by me."

We all sat. Pinky, perched on the sofa about as far away from her grandmother as she could get, looked like a child who desperately wanted to be anywhere else before she schooled her expression to something neutral. I sympathized. It was hard work to keep my own desire to be anywhere else off my face.

"Tea?" Grandma asked.

Cassandra cleared her throat. "I think we're fine without, Lady."

"It is safe, Lady Cestis," Grandma said. "I promised you safe passage. I do not break my word."

"Still, Lady, we do not need tea."

"Very well, we shall get down to business. The dreamers tell me the darkness has cleared. For now. You did well, it seems."

The darkness had gone? Did that mean Jack had definitely left San Francisco? I filed that away to pass on to Mitch. Hunting for a man who could change his face was difficult. But I couldn't pretend it didn't make me happy to know he was gone for now.

"We hold our vows, Lady," Cassandra said carefully.

"Which is pleasing to know. The realm is settling with our door restored here. We would not want to interfere with that process."

"No," Cassandra agreed.

"But the darkness will come again, inevitably."

I looked down at my hands, trying to keep them from clenching. I didn't want to think of demons.

"One day we may turn the demons back forever," Cassandra said. "But not yet."

"And have you found the one who caused this trouble?"

"Some of them, Lady."

Not-Yoshi, whose real name was Blake Emerson, hadn't provided us with much information in the end. It seemed that yes, Jack had paid him to try to hack into Riley's systems during the hackathon and provided him with the illusion. A few others on the Rexes knew about the scheme. Teenagers, all of them, who'd seen it as a challenge, not a crime. They were banned from gaming leagues, and the Cestis had put the fear of...well, something into them all. But Jack and whoever his more dangerous allies were, they were gone.

"That is good. Which brings me to Maggie."

I started, looking up. "Me?"

"Yes. It seems you are of interest to our enemies."

"They were after some Riley tech, not me," I said quickly.

"This time," she said. "But there will be another. My line traditionally has stood fast against the demons. Now that we are back in San Francisco, my family here will need to learn more of what I have to teach them. Be ready if need be. Rosaline here is one of the most promising, so I will be teaching her. You are young to your powers. I thought perhaps you might like to learn, too?"

I nearly choked, glad Cassandra had refused tea for us. "I'm not fa—your kind."

"No, but our magic may work together. After all, you and Zachariah used the power I left for you to break the illusions, did you not?"

How did she know that? Because it had been her magic or because Pinky had told her?

Pinky stared at her grandmother, looking as horrified as I felt, so maybe it was the former rather than the latter.

"Yes, I suppose so."

"Good. I am offering you a gift, Maggie. You are not of the Cestis. Not yet. Therefore this is acceptable under our terms."

"*Not* yet"*? What the fuck did that mean?*

I glanced at Cassandra, who was watching the Elder with something like approval on her face. Strange. In fairy tales, gifts from the Fae were usually something to be avoided.

"You want to teach Maggie how to fight demons your way?" Cassandra asked.

"I will teach her to use her gifts. Perhaps in ways you cannot. Between the two of us, she will be stronger. Which is good for both our peoples."

"Do I get a say in this?" I asked. Demon fighter wasn't high on my list of ideal careers.

"Of course," the Elder said. "But consider that choice carefully. As I said, our enemies seem drawn to you. Wouldn't you like to be able to beat them once and for all?"

"Is that even possible?"

The Elder shrugged. "I have ideas. This would be something new."

An experiment. Awesome. But getting rid of demons...it was a tempting thing to dangle in front of me. "And what would it involve, exactly?"

"Knowledge," she said with a smile. "We will see what you can do."

"She is still learning our ways," Cassandra said.

"This will not interfere with her natural magic," Grandma said. "At least not as far as I can tell. She will be free to share with you what she learns."

Ah. Sneaky. She could teach me because I fell under some sort of loophole. Then I could teach others.

"Why me?" There must have been other, more experienced witches around.

"You are here, and you know what we are fighting," she said. "That should make you an eager student."

I wasn't sure "eager" was the right term. But I was pretty sure it was an offer I couldn't refuse. "And if I say yes?"

"Then we will begin soon. You need to deal with your house and other human concerns. Unless you would like us to rebuild it for you?"

Did I want a house magically repaired by fairies?

"Er, no. I have insurance. It will be fine. But thank you." I looked at Cassandra. "Is this something you want me to do?"

Cassandra tilted her head. "I think it is a decision only you can make. But I will say it's not the worst idea in the world."

Damn. She wanted me to do it. Magic sucking me in deeper yet again. So maybe the only smart choice was to learn how to swim like a shark. Become one of the predators in the waters. I knew who I wanted to hunt first.

I turned back to face the Elder. "Okay. I accept."

She smiled, the expression making her even more terrifyingly beautiful. "Good. In that case, child, you may call me Cerridwen."

THE END

Maggie and Damon will return in Wicked Dreams
Pre-order now!

WANT MORE TECHWITCH?

Don't worry, Maggie and Damon will be back...in Wicked Dreams. To keep up with news about them, sign up for M.J's newsletter at www.mjscott.net.

A NOTE FROM M.J.

I hope you loved reading WICKED NIGHTS. This series is a lot of fun and I can't wait to continue Maggie and Damon's adventures. WICKED DREAMS will be out in 2023.

As an indie author, it really helps me when readers get the word out about my books, so if you enjoyed the book, please consider leaving a review at the store where you purchased it and tell your friends!

If you want to stay up to date with all my news, find out about new releases and sales, then please sign up to my newsletter at www.mjscott.net.

ALSO BY M.J. SCOTT

Urban fantasy

The TechWitch series

Wicked Games

Wicked Words

Wicked Dreams

The Wild Side series

The Wolf Within

The Dark Side

Bring On The Night

The Day You Went Away (free prequel short story)

Romantic fantasy

The Four Arts series

The Shattered Court

The Forbidden Heir

The Unbound Queen

Courting The Witch (Prequel novella)

The Daughter of Ravens series

The Exile's Curse

The Traitor's Game

The Rebel's Prize

The Half-Light City series

Shadow Kin

Blood Kin

Iron Kin

Fire Kin

ACKNOWLEDGMENTS

Every book is a different journey and it takes lots of people to keep me on the track. Thanks to all the usual writing peeps who cheer me on, to Robyn and Sarah for going the extra mile, my Mum for always being there when I need and the diva kitty for kitty antics to keep me entertained!

ABOUT THE AUTHOR

M.J Scott is an unrepentant bookworm. Luckily she grew up in a family that fed her a properly varied diet of books and these days is surrounded by people who are understanding of her story addiction. When not wrestling one of her own stories to the ground, she can generally be found reading someone else's. Her other distractions include yarn, cat butlering, dark chocolate and watercolour. To keep in touch, find out about new releases and other news, sign up to her newsletter at www.mjscott.net. She also writes contemporary romance as Melanie Scott and Emma Douglas.

You can keep in touch with M.J. on:
Instagram @melwrites
Facebook AuthorMJScott
Pinterest @mel_writes
TikTok @mjscottwrites

Or email her at mel@mjscott.net

www.ingramcontent.com/pod-product-compliance
Lightning Source LLC
Chambersburg PA
CBHW020245120726
47904CB00001B/96